The Thieves of Antiquity

B J MEARS

The Dream Loft

First published in Great Britain in 2013 by The Dream Loft
www.thedreamloft.co.uk

ISBN 13: 978-0-9574124-2-2
ISBN 10: 0957412428

Dedicated to my grandfather, Major Edward Cox, *the Major*, gone but not forgotten.

Special thanks once more
to Joy for your support and for help with the blurb
to Henna for sparking an idea
to my diligent editor, Edward Field
and to all friends who have helped along the way.

Whoever saves one life, saves the world entire.

Mishnah, the Talmud

'You have enemies? Good. That means you have stood up for something, sometime in your life.'

Winston Churchill

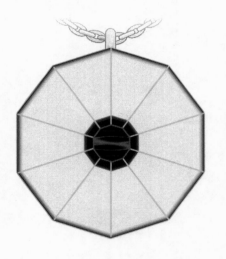

Contents

Tyler's notes on the contrap (illustration)

Chapters

1. THE LETTER
2. LÜNEBURG HEATH
3. TEMPORAL TEAR
4. THE WOODS
5. THE RAG & BONE MAN
6. A COLLECTION
7. MATRYOSHKA
8. FINGER BONES
9. THE THIEVES OF ANTIQUITY
10. SÃO PAULO INSTITUTE
11. THE MONITOR
12. INGARATA
13. DANGERS OF GHOST HAUNTING
14. C & R
15. INVALIDENFRIEDHOF
16. MEMORIA GRAVITAS
17. THE RISE OF NAZISM
18. MASSACHUSETTS GHOSTS
19. THE TEXAN
20. GRANDMA
21. THE HOUSE BY THE LAKE
22. DEAD AGAIN
23. THE BOX
24. AN INCONSTANT SMILE
25. DROP ZONE
26. DEAD ZONE
27. ROOM OF PILLARS
28. TRUST
29. THE GLIMMER
30. THE WINDOW
31. HATE & DEATH

Acknowledgments

THE CONTRAP

BACK

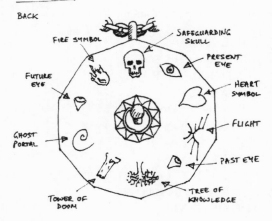

SYMBOLS

- SAFEGUARDING SKULL — SAVES FROM DEATH
- PRESENT EYE — LOOK THROUGH WALLS, ETC (TELESCOPIC).
- HEART SYMBOL — ?
- FLIGHT — MAKES YOU FLY!
- PAST EYE — LOOK INTO THE PAST!
- TREE OF KNOWLEDGE — ASK IT A QUESTION & IT ANSWERS
- TOWER OF DOOM — ACHIEVEMENT INDICATOR
- GHOST PORTAL — IT'S A GHOST PORTAL!
- FUTURE EYE — LOOK INTO THE FUTURE
- FIRE SYMBOL — ?

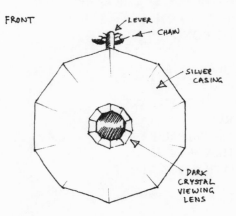

PART ONE

The Letter

Tyler May scratched a list on a perfectly folded sheet of A4.

Open letter
Post cash
Pack bags
4 p.m. @ Adolf's

She passed the living room doorway and backtracked to watch the news story through the gap.

"And now, a follow-up story on what has become known globally as *the Christmas Eve Incident*, when numerous Londoners and tourists within the capital's centre reportedly witnessed the appearance of thousands of ghosts." The TV image switched from the newsreader to a shaky, low resolution video of Westminster Square, crowded with translucent, emaciated figures. It was all too familiar to Tyler and the TV pictures were nothing compared to the vivid images in her mind. It seemed crazy to think it was over a year ago. So much had happened.

"YouTube has received a record number of hits on this, the latest in a long line of eyewitness videos. Sceptics still argue these viral videos are the work of CGI hoaxers, a claim, so far unproven, that has not slowed the continuing glut of ghost sightings reported worldwide. The question remains: Are these sightings real, or are they the workings of an infectious hysteria triggered by the prior *Incident*?"

Tyler moved on, pocketing her list and carrying the unopened letter up to her bedroom. The envelope looked harmless but Tyler had a bad feeling about it. The little voice in her head didn't like it. Birthday cards wishing her a happy sixteenth had dried up two weeks ago. She threw the envelope onto her bed, reconsidered and picked it up to study it, holding it up to the light. It clearly contained a letter of some sort, but *that* was what worried her. She wasn't expecting a letter from anyone and she didn't recognise the spiky handwriting on the front. She placed the letter on a shelf by her bed and surveyed the money.

She thumbed through a wad of bank notes, one of many that were lined up in perfectly straight rows on her duvet like a drill squad, but dropped it as soon as Pink yelled at her to 'get up and *Try*'. She had been expecting the call ever since the iPhone in her hand had arrived in the post two days ago.

"Tyler?" It was a man's voice.

"I'm here, Mr Chapman."

"How's your arm?"

"It's fine."

"Good. You'll need it. As far as the general public are concerned, you and the girls will be history students on a research field trip. You're working on an important coursework project on the history of World War Two. You'll be accompanied by your teacher, Mr Flynn, whom you have yet to meet, but in reality you'll hardly know he's there. He's just a front to help you through airports and into hotels etcetera and he's been briefed to just let you get on with things. You don't need to report to him, just to me. Now, I have some intel for you."

"*Intel*?"

"Intelligence information. There's an agent I need you to look out for. Don't worry. He's one of ours. I'm sending you an image now."

Tyler's phone beeped softly. She tapped the touchscreen and a picture of a good-looking, dark haired, sinewy, young man appeared. Tyler guessed he was about eighteen or nineteen.

"Tyler? You there?"

She put the phone to her ear.

"I'm still here."

"Okay. His name is Agent Weaver. He's not called in for a long time."

"What do you want me to do?"

"You'll be off soon. I just want you to look out for him on your travels. If you bump into him anywhere, call it in. Keep it to yourself, though."

"What makes you think I might *bump into him*?"

"That's classified."

Awkward silence.

"Okay."

"Did you receive the package?"

Tyler's gaze moved to the two black, armoured cases to one side of her bed.

"I did. Thank you."

"Good. Any other specifics you need can be sent to your field location upon request. Just call for it. Oh, and Tyler, it's codenames from here on in, okay?"

"Okay. What's *your* codename?"

"Chapman."

"Of course…"

Silly me.

*

The coffee shop they'd nicknamed Adolf's was quiet this Saturday afternoon.

"I think we have a problem," Tyler said.

"What's that?" asked Lucy.

"I was thinking about Josef Mengele's glove – you know – when he brought the contrap up out of the Thames…" It seemed an odd term, but that's what the Nazis had done: stolen live children to be merged with Nazi ghosts. The children were wearing ghosts, like gloves.

"Yes?" Melissa took another bite of chocolate fudge cake and wiped a flake from her chin.

"Well, how did he hold his breath for all that time? I mean, he seemed to walk out of the water as if he'd walked the whole way into *and* out of the river."

Melissa thought for a moment.

"Did you actually see him go in?"

"No, I've gone over and over it because it's been bothering me for ages. I'd fallen asleep. I only got to the bank in time to see him come out."

"So maybe he swam," said Lucy.

"Perhaps, but I never saw him swimming. I would have seen him on the surface, don't you think? He just walked up out of the depths. It was weird. *He* was weird."

"You think he used the ghost machine or something?" asked Melissa.

"I'm worried he might have. If he set it to the *Safeguarding Skull* he'd have been able to survive under water, according to Zebedee Lieberman."

"So how would Josef Mengele's gloved ghost know how to operate the contrap?" asked Lucy.

"That's the problem. You see, it's not the first time he's appeared to know about the contrap. When he came to me on the car park roof, I had the feeling he knew about it. Like he knew *all* about it. He wasn't concerned about it, but then I didn't have any artefacts, so it wasn't much of a threat at the time."

"Maybe he spied on you and learned a few things."

"Maybe. I just think there's something else. Something I'm missing."

"Wait a minute," said Lucy. "You say he walked out? How did he do that? I don't know about you but I float in water. Walking on the bottom would be pretty hard to achieve unless it's shallow enough…"

"Ah, but he was fully clothed, except for his hat and coat."

"So his waterlogged clothes would've dragged him down," said Melissa.

"Right," said Tyler. "I think he swam out to dive for the contrap and then used it straight away while he was still under water." She looked at her two friends who were staring back blankly. "Well? Don't you think that's odd?"

"I guess," said Lucy, studying her black painted nails.

"It *is* strange," Melissa said. "Listen, we need to talk about what we're going to do. I've done the research. Can we meet at mine? It would be easier to take you through it with the computer, somewhere private."

"Can I see the list again?"

Melissa passed the list of Nazi ghosts now gloved with the bodies of kidnapped children. Tyler examined it.

Adolf Hitler	*gloved with Kylie Marsh (deceased)*
Heinrich Himmler	*gloved with Freddy Carter (alive)*
Josef Mengele	*gloved with Steven Lewis (alive)*
Reinhard Heydrich	*gloved with Susan Ellis (alive)*
Joseph Goebbels	*gloved with Emily Stanford (alive)*
Adolf Eichmann	*gloved with Harry McGrath (alive)*

She read Kylie Marsh's name and her stomach turned. "This isn't going to be easy," stated Tyler.

*

Melissa's room had transformed since MI5 had become involved in the girls' exploits. Her boxy old computer was gone and in its place was a bank of flat screen monitors. A state-of-the-art laptop was housed on an aluminium interphase panel and locked into a larger PC. Everything had gone crazy since Chapman had recruited first Tyler and then Lucy and Melissa. Tyler recalled the conversation well. It seemed like a long time ago, now.

"I want you to help us seek them out. We'll be working together, or more accurately, you will be working for us. In return for your assistance, we shall, of course, supply you with whatever you need to accomplish the tasks, and the other matters to which you previously alluded. You, Miss Watts and Miss Denby."

"You'd help us? I mean, you want us to work for MI5?"

Chapman nodded.

"You help us and we will help you. We'll be watching you, of course. And you'll be expected to report-in from time to time as a matter of procedure, to keep us updated on progress. You'll need a budget to work from; money for travel etcetera. Cracking the NVF network will, no doubt, prove to be an international challenge."

Tyler was still suspicious, but an offer of this kind of help was such a welcome surprise that she had found herself nodding before she'd even thought about it. She thought she'd better say something.

"Alright."

"You'll need a chaperone, of course. And a decent cover story, but let me worry about that. Understand: if you do well, I'll be in a position to offer you other terms of employment when you come of age. In the meantime, I'll see to it that leave from your school will not be a problem, although you'll have to accept that any missed school work will need to be made up at some point when you can fit it in. Do we have a deal, Miss May?"

Tyler offered out her right hand.

"We do, Mr Chapman."

They shook on it.

"Alright then. If you'd like to call your father in, I think we'd best run the idea by him. You can't go running away from home every time you need to go to work..."

"Are you even listening?" asked Melissa, interrupting Tyler's recollection.

"Yes, sorry. I mean, no. What did you say?"

"I said I've narrowed it down to one artefact per glove. When I say *artefact* I'm talking about the best of what I could find. In some cases there doesn't seem to be much choice. Mr Chapman is following some leads too. So there's a chance he'll also acquire artefacts."

"Right."

"Who's first on our list?" asked Lucy.

"Himmler. He was in charge of the whole *final solution* thing, so he's probably the most evil after Hitler. I'm thinking we should go after his artefact first and take things from there."

Lucy nodded her approval.

"Ok," said Tyler. "What do we have?"

Melissa's fingers clicked away on the keyboard and a series of websites popped up on the numerous screens.

"Bloody hell," said Lucy.

"Yeah. There's a lot of info on Heinrich Himmler's grave, partly because it was all kept a secret so that no Nazis could turn it into a shrine. All the secrecy surrounding the whole thing has led to a lot of speculation and theories. Basically, he was caught hiding among other lower ranking Germans in a camp on Monday the 21st of May, 1945, when the war ended. The British questioned him and examined him. Then he bit on a cyanide capsule he'd hidden in his mouth and died before anyone could try him for war crimes."

"So there *is* a body. We can dig him up and use his remains as the summoning artefact."

"If only it were that simple," said Melissa. "That *is* what we need to do. As you know, the remains, or part of the remains, would be the best and the strongest artefact…"

"That's what Zebedee said," confirmed Tyler.

"Problem is, as I said, his burial was kept secret, which has created a lot of interest. Only four British soldiers were given the task of burying him and they were sworn to secrecy. They took the body out to a deserted place called Lüneburg Heath, dug a hole and buried him. They covered the ground with fallen leaves to hide the disturbed soil and left. There was no grave stone. No marker or sign of any sort."

"Is that the best you can come up with?" asked Lucy. "How long have you been working on this?"

Melissa scowled.

"I know it's not much but I still reckon it's our best shot. If you think *you* can do better…"

"So how do we find out exactly where the grave is?" Tyler interjected.

"Wait. I haven't finished. Eighteen months later, there came a report from British Intelligence agents saying that a cross had been put up at the site and flowers placed there. It was feared Nazis had found the grave and a cult had started: *exactly* what everyone was trying to avoid. The British ordered the whole area to be dug up but no body was found. Eventually they tracked down one of the four who'd buried Himmler, but when they dug at the place *he* claimed they'd buried Himmler, they found nothing there either. Now no one is sure if they dug in the wrong spot or if fanatical Nazis removed the body to entomb it in a secret SS shrine. I've checked the validity of all this with Mr Chapman. He's confirmed it's true as far as the records show."

"Great. That really helps." Lucy was frustrated.

"You're forgetting the contrap," said Melissa.

"You're right! It will help us locate the body. We'll go to Lüneburg Heath and search for the grave ourselves." Tyler grinned at Melissa. "It's our best bet."

"Right. So who's next?" asked Lucy, unimpressed. She unwrapped a fresh stick of gum and chewed.

Melissa's fingers danced over the keyboard. More search results filled the screens including a black and white photograph of a smiling man. Tyler felt a wave of nausea at the sight of Josef Mengele.

Melissa read out a summary.

"After the war, Josef Mengele and many other Nazi war criminals fled the country to escape punishment. Mengele himself eluded the Nazi hunters and the subsequent Nuremburg trials. He ended his years in Brazil, where he died of natural causes on the 7th of February, 1979."

"Is there a body?"

"There is. He had a stroke or a heart attack while swimming and drowned in the sea. He was buried under his false name, Wolfgang Gerhard, and later exhumed on June the 6th in 1985, for purposes of identification. A DNA test in 1992 confirmed it was Mengele. The remains were then stored at the São Paulo Institute for Forensic Medicine, Brazil. And get this: they're still there!"

"Bingo," said Tyler. "Should be a piece of cake."

"Except that Mengele's gloved ghost can sense the contrap and is following you," said Lucy. "Oh, and he seems to know everything about the contrap and probably knows where his bones are being kept too."

"Yeah. There is that," admitted Tyler.

"Next?"

"SS Lieutenant Colonel Adolf Eichmann is not so easy. After the war he was caught, tried and hanged for war crimes, for his part in organising and controlling the mass murder of the Jews and many others."

"His body?"

"Cremated and scattered at sea so that 'no nation could be his burial place' and to avoid any Nazi shrines."

"So what *do* you have for us?"

"If we'd been searching for something a few years ago we might've been in trouble, but more recently some artefacts were put on display in a museum in Tel Aviv, Israel."

"What are they?"

"Various personal belongings of Eichmann's, all recovered by the Mossad agents responsible for his arrest. Mossad is the Israeli secret service. They tracked him down in Argentina and smuggled him out of the country so they could put him on trial in Israel. The list of artefacts on display includes his house keys, a comb, a cigarette holder and a pocket knife."

"That should work. We'll plan a way to break into the museum."

"Ne…" began Lucy before Melissa cut in, glaring at her.

"*Next* on the list is Chief of Gestapo and SS General, Reinhard Heydrich. He played a major role in kicking off the whole deportation and murder of the Jews."

"His artefact?"

"There's a body but, once again, it's complicated. He died during the war from injuries after an assassination attempt and was buried with Nazi honours in Berlin's Invalidenfriedhof. That's a cemetery. The Germans planned to mark the grave with grandeur after the war but, as they lost, it never happened. The grave's been left without a marker to…"

"…prevent it becoming a Nazi shrine?" guessed Tyler.

"You got it. The exact spot is unknown but we do know the general area to look in. So once more we'll need the contrap.

"Lastly, Dr. Paul Joseph Goebbels was the Reich Minister of Propaganda in Nazi Germany. Basically, he was in charge of preaching the Nazi message to the German people and one of Hitler's closest associates. Without him, or someone like him, the masses would probably have never followed Hitler and everything he stood for.

"He killed himself when Germany's defeat became apparent. His body was cremated and the ashes scattered in the Biederitz River. There are various existing artefacts associated with Goebbels. I've narrowed it down to a handwritten speech currently on display in the Museum of World War Two, Massachusetts."

"America."

"The good old United States."

"That's gonna have some serious security," Lucy surmised.

"Look, none of this is going to be easy," said Melissa. "Nobody ever said it would be. Jeez. It's nice to be appreciated. I worked my butt off working all…"

"Okay, okay!" Lucy held up her hands. "Sor-ry. I know it's not your fault."

"Right," said Tyler. "We also need to remember the gloves seem to know about the contrap. They might know all these artefacts pose a threat to them and so they may be trying to get hold of them before we do. We need to act fast. We need to get them first. After that we can take out the gloves at our leisure."

"Listen, if I die, don't cremate me, right?" said Lucy. "I want a coffin. A good, solid coffin. No rubbish. Okay?"

*

When Tyler returned home, the envelope was still waiting for her like an unrelenting shadow in her mind. Nervously she eased a finger under the seal, tore it open and unfolded the crisp, white notepaper to reveal the same spiky handwriting as on the envelope. She read.

Dear Tyler,

You'll regret the way you treated me at our last meeting. I will have the device one way or another, you will see. I shall take it from you, along with your life, very soon. Keep an eye out for me. I'll be the one in the green coat, though you probably won't see me coming.

How would you like to die, if you had the choice? If you let me know in advance, I'll see what I can do.

I feel we're very close, you and I.

Silvia.

PS. Violet says 'Hi!'

Tyler staggered to her bed.

She pulled out a box of matches from her desk drawer ready to burn the letter. She struck one, then blew it out. Chapman would flip if she destroyed evidence. She chided herself.

Nice one, Jane Bond.

She sealed Bates' note in a forensic evidence bag and stuffed it in an envelope to send to Chapman in the morning.

She sprawled on the bed and stared at the ceiling.

Get me. Sixteen, secret agent and my very own stalker psycho freak from Hell. I've arrived!

Lüneburg Heath

Tyler stirred from a disturbing dream in which ghost after ghost told her she would live differently if *she* knew what *they* knew. Zebedee Lieberman was reminding her very seriously that 'You learn a lot of things when you die,' when he suddenly morphed into Kylie Marsh and Tyler woke with a jolt.

Her remorse was overwhelming, yet she knew there was nothing she could have done to save the girl who'd been gloved with the ghost of Hitler.

Half an hour later Tyler was walking to the post office with a brown paper package under her arm: an anonymous guilt offering of ten thousand pounds to Kylie Marsh's parents.

Not much, when you consider they'd lost a daughter.

Money was not an issue for her since the raid on South Sea House in Whitechapel. Along with Melissa and

Lucy they'd cleared the Nazi safe of seventy thousand pounds in notes. Then Chapman had entered their lives and made sure they'd want for nothing, including new identities for purposes of travelling undercover. With the forthcoming trip in mind, he'd also been good enough to send each of them an outrageous amount of cash in a variety of denominations, as well as some hefty traveller's cheques and charge cards. When Tyler had questioned him on the ridiculous sum, he'd said "You never know what you might need out there and it's better to be safe than sorry." Then he'd added "and anyway, you'd be surprised how much you'll get through once you start hopping around the globe."

*

The continuing story on Silvia Bates had been relegated to the very end of the news programme. It did nothing to ease Tyler's mind. Bates had been a crazy woman, even before the psychopathic ghost of a Tudor murderer named Violet Corpe had possessed her body.

"In Watford today, sightings of the wanted terrorist, Silvia Bates, have been reported. Police have again warned the public not to approach the woman who may be armed and suffering mental health issues. Police have released the following images perceived to be the work of Bates."

Tyler glared at the photo of Bates in the corner of the screen and read the vivid, red, spray paint graffiti.

Give it to me or you will die

It wasn't often that people spoke directly to her from the TV screen.

She finished packing her case, throwing in a pair of pink, tartan pyjamas.

Well, perhaps it's just as well I'm leaving town for a while.

*

Their fake teacher and chaperone, Mr Flynn, was a shadowy man. He appeared, on cue, to accompany the girls to the airport and see them through customs and passport control. Tyler was vaguely aware of his slim presence on the plane but he was very discreet and rarely attempted to engage conversation unless it was necessary for his role.

She found the flight tiring and spent most of it either half asleep or wishing she *was* asleep. In her semi-wakeful moments she recalled the brief but intensive training course she and her friends had endured at Chapman's insistence. It had consumed every holiday period of the last year and even a good portion of the school term time, covering some basic essentials for the modern spy: advanced scuba diving, parachuting, the use of explosives, surveillance techniques and IT, and a crash course on old and new firearms. Tyler had not wanted to do most of it. She was more eager to go after the gloves, but Chapman had insisted they train first. They were not permitted to carry guns, but the course *had* trained them to shoot. Chapman had been reluctant to supply firearms to the teenage girls, but they would be going into territories almost certainly occupied by the gloves and it was likely they would face one or more along the way. As the gloves were part ghost and part innocent child, it was deemed more appropriate to use Tasers for protection. This way, if the girls succeeded in cornering a glove, they stood a chance of holding him long enough for Tyler to use the contrap and set the child within free from the *dominant force*.

Well, that was the theory anyway.

Lucy had taken to knife-throwing, also an optional feature of this schooling, and she now carried a sheath of three throwing knives, concealed beneath her shirt when she wasn't flying. She had become expert with the specialised knives almost overnight. A natural.

"You know, you frighten me sometimes," Tyler had told her.

Melissa had undergone further training in languages and in IT as it was an area of special interest to her, and Tyler had spent several training days under the sole tuition of an agent, codenamed Locky, an ex-thief, recruited purely for his skills in lock picking.

Tyler followed their plane's progress on the inflight screen as it crossed Lower Saxony, northern Germany, and began its decent into Hamburg Airport.

"Do you think he's here on the plane somewhere?" she asked. They knew she meant Josef Mengele. He'd become her new obsession, and not in a good way.

"Probably," said Lucy.

"Have you seen him since Christmas Eve?" asked Melissa.

"No. But I get this feeling whenever I go anywhere. It's creepy. *He's* creepy." Adrenalin swelled and turned her stomach as the plane closed on the runway. She looked around at the other passengers but couldn't see the *Angel of Death* amongst them.

It was late in the chilled evening as they disembarked to wait for their baggage. Tyler shivered.

Germany. So this is where it all began more than seventy years ago...

Crowds of travellers gathered to collect luggage. Tyler scanned faces, checking for the subtle bluish glow that gave away the gloves' presence and for the tell-tale trilby Mengele was partial to wearing. Again, she saw nothing ominous. She squeezed her way through to the front of the gathering where a multitude of bags snaked their way along a baggage carousel. Then she caught herself reading baggage labels as they passed and knew she was losing her mind.

As if Mengele would use his real name...

They weren't using their real names. Tyler collected her bag labelled *Tabitha Collins*.

An hour later they were heading to Lüneburg Heath in an old, insipid beige taxi that was missing its back bumper, their baggage in the boot, while Mr Flynn went ahead of them to their hotel. Ernst, the driver, was short and thickset with grey sides to his otherwise black hair. Tyler guessed he was around forty-five. He had excessively baggy eyes and looked as though he had a port addiction. He rarely smiled but was one of Chapman's men, so the girls knew he could be trusted and he seemed harmless enough.

"Are you German?" Lucy asked Ernst as he drove.

"I am. Born and bred," he said in a clipped German accent.

"Were you around for the war?"

Ernst chuckled to himself and shook his head.

"No. I was not yet born. I'm not so old. But I do know much about what happened."

"Do you have relatives who fought in the war?" asked Lucy. Tyler and Melissa shot her looks that said 'leave it,' but Lucy wouldn't.

Ernst considered for a moment before answering.

"Yes. My grandfather was killed during the war. Listen, these days the German people are just wanting to forget about the war. They were led astray by a madman. They are not proud of what happened."

"Is it true the German people didn't even know about the death camps?" asked Melissa.

"Many knew nothing about that until after the war. For those who knew, there was little they could do. Anyone resisting the SS was shot dead, or worse. Many good men were sacrificing themselves, trying to change or stop what was going on. By the time it was found out, it was far too late to do anything. The SS were all-powerful. They were everywhere, including the law courts. There were Germans who were plotting to bring down Hitler and to assassinate him. It is our misfortune that none of them succeeded."

"Sorry about your grandfather, Ernst," said Melissa.

Ernst gave an appreciative nod and drove.

"We should go straight to the hotel. Why are we doing this again?" asked Lucy.

"I just want to see the place before we get settled in," explained Tyler for the second time.

Ernst drove with one hand for most of the way, which made it easier for him to light his thin, dark cigars and smoke out the vehicle interior. Melissa opened a window and the girls sat shivering in an icy blast, but at least they could breathe.

At night Lüneburg Heath was a desolate landscape of shadowed scrub with a sparse peppering of low trees.

Tyler swallowed hard and tried not to feel too disheartened as she took in the immensity of the place.

"We'll never find him," stated Lucy stepping from the car to join the others. "This place goes on forever. And he could be anywhere. Kind of eerie out here."

"Uh-huh," Tyler had to agree.

"Don't forget we have the contrap," Melissa countered. "Have you decided what would be the best way?"

"Not yet. I did think the *Tower of Doom* would work okay, but that was before I saw how big the heath is. We could be wandering about for years. I feel like we need to do it as quickly as possible. I'll have a rethink."

"Let's come back tomorrow and take another look." Melissa stifled a yawn. "Maybe it will be less daunting."

Tyler doubted it. She climbed back into the taxi, shuddering when moonlight caught the back of Ernst's neck briefly turning it a deathly blue.

"You know, we should be *really* happy," Lucy stated. "We're completely loaded. I always thought I'd be happy if I had a ton of money, but…"

"I guess money isn't everything," said Melissa. "I'd much rather the Nazi gloves were all gone and we were poor again."

"Ditto that." Tyler viewed stark terrain as they pulled away. She was asleep in her seat before they left the heath.

*

The next morning Tyler awoke in the Best Western Premier Castanea. It was gone eleven o'clock, local time, and she was annoyed with herself for oversleeping. She prepared for a trip to the heath and rifled through the black cases that Chapman had sent ahead.

The first contained an array of gear: an undercover surveillance communication system, three powerful Taser dart guns, and a zip-wire crossbow with cable and multiple bolts.

The second case held a set of twenty narrow, colour-coded syringes, each loaded with an almost microscopic tracer element. There was also a handheld location receiver with a small screen. With Melissa's help, Tyler worked out how to use it. When the unit was switched on, each of the tiny, coloured tracer elements corresponded to a coloured dot on the screen. Touchscreen controls allowed the user to zoom in and out of the map area represented.

Tyler lifted a section out of the case and found a set of twenty larger magnetic tracers and, below that, a set of twenty minute tracer darts, complete with a pen, which concealed a loading and firing mechanism.

"Wow, they really *do* use pens that are guns. I thought that stuff was just in films. Perfect for you, Tyler. You can shoot an enemy spy and then write his name on your list."

"Very funny. It fires tracers not bullets, Lucy. Heavy metal, almost microscopic, tracers that can penetrate flesh. They're so small they're barely noticed if they strike a person. Chapman said it's comparable to a mild mosquito bite. They're ingenious. The little dart falls away. Only the tracer head is implanted."

"Whatever. This stuff is *so* cool," said Lucy, running an eye down the crossbow's night-vision scope. When her index finger rested on the trigger a red laser dot appeared on the opposite wall.

Melissa and Tyler both looked at her. Lucy glared back at them.

"What? It *is!*"

"What is Chapman expecting us to do, exactly?" asked Melissa.

"Oh you know, save the world from a Nazi invasion from beyond the grave. Stuff like that."

"You know as much as any of us," said Tyler.

"Who does he think we are? We're just school girls…"

"We don't have to use this stuff if we don't want to," said Tyler.

Lucy was already shouldering a black leather holster for her Taser gun.

"Like the man said, you never know what you might need out there." She pulled the gun and feigned a volley of shots. "Here. We should all wear one of these if nothing else." Lucy threw them each a Taser with a holster. "Just to be safe."

A nauseating taxi ride later they were back on the heath wondering where to start. Melissa unfolded a map and pointed out the zone marked by Chapman's team as the most likely area. It was still a vast, desolate zone, no less daunting than the night before. Melissa held a brief conversation with Ernst before reporting to Tyler and Lucy.

"Ernst says the Lüneburg Heath Nature Park encompasses one thousand, one hundred and thirty square kilometres. That's four hundred and forty square miles. Ten miles away is the house where Himmler was brought in for interrogation. We passed it back there somewhere. Number 31A Uelzener Strasse." She pointed. "The four soldiers who buried his body must have collected it from there and driven out here into the heath. They probably took this old track for a while and then went off-road."

"I guess it's a start," said Lucy.

Tyler drew the contrap from her shirt and set it to the *Tower of Doom*. When the side with the symbols had rotated and the tower symbol was at the top, she peered into the crystal lens. The brooding, gothic tower crumbled slowly as huge black birds flew in lazy circles. She turned on the spot until the tower began building instead and then she set off walking, leaving the taxi and Ernst to wait for their return. Two hours later the girls could no longer see the taxi or any buildings. They were surrounded by heathland, a sprawling world of grasses, heathers, scrub and trees.

"What's the tower doing?" asked Lucy. She offered gum before folding a stick into her own mouth.

"It's building, I think, but it's so slow it's hard to tell."

"We could be here for weeks doing it this way."

"Alright," said Tyler. "Let's try something else."

"What?" asked Melissa.

"I could try the *Tree of Knowledge* but Zebedee said its answers can't really be trusted. And, since Hitler and Bagshot went in, I trust it even less."

"Good point," Lucy agreed.

"What else is there?" Melissa asked peering at the ten small symbols incised on the silver device in Tyler's hands.

"The only other symbol I think might be of some real help is the *Past Eye*. Of course there are still two symbols we don't understand but, as far as I can tell, they don't do anything. If I use the *Past Eye* I can search back through the years to the point where the four soldiers were sent out to bury the body. We can follow them and see where they dug the grave. That would lead us to the exact spot."

"But what if he's been dug up and moved since?"

"I can scan through the years and look for that too, though the whole thing could take me ages, perhaps days. I'm not sure which would be the best way."

"Look, this isn't getting us very far," said Lucy. "Try *something!*"

Tyler looked at the horizon. She had the feeling she was being watched, that they were being scrutinised.

Nothing new there.

"If we're gonna try the *Past Eye* we need to head back and drive to the house where Himmler killed himself."

Lucy shrugged and walked off.

"Why does she have to be such an evil freak all the time?" asked Tyler. "She's supposed to be helping us."

Melissa watched Lucy slope away.

"She's hormonal. Don't worry about it."

Tyler nervously set the contrap to the spiral symbol and checked the *Ghost Portal* hoping she would not bump into Hitler or Bagshot. Or Kylie Marsh. Searching the portal had become a habit when Albert had been in the contrap. Now she longed to see him and speak with him.

"Where are you, Albert?" she whispered.

"What was that?" asked Melissa.

"Oh, nothing. Just talking to myself."

"No, I mean, what was *that?*" Melissa pointed towards a bank of trees a short way off.

"What?" Tyler squinted at trees.

"I thought I saw something move. Or someone…"

Tyler studied the area.

"I can't see anything."

"Maybe it was my imagination. It *is* pretty creepy out here."

"I didn't think it was, but I *do* now. Let's get out of here."

*

31A Uelzener Strasse was a large, red brick house surrounded by newer buildings in a now deeply shadowed street. Once a British Intelligence HQ, it was presently occupied by several practices and clinics, each marked with a white enamel plate on a wall beneath a bay window. Before packing for the trip, Melissa had checked online that it was still standing and the place had seemed benign. Now it towered over them with enigmatic menace.

They climbed six stone steps to the front door and Tyler pressed one of the bell pushes. When no one answered, she pressed a few more and then all of them.

"Guess nobody's home," said Lucy, trying to see in through one of the windows.

"That's the room where Himmler committed suicide," whispered Melissa. "It's a big front room, apparently."

"See anything?" asked Tyler.

"It's too high," said Lucy. "Maybe if I stood on someone's shoulders…"

Tyler eyed Melissa knowingly.

"No!" Melissa shook her head. "No way."

"Come on. You're stronger than Lucy."

Melissa pouted sideways in resignation. Somewhere in the distance a dog barked a warning.

"Alright then."

Tyler climbed up Melissa with some difficulty, assisted by Lucy, to stand on Melissa's shoulders and peer into the dark room beyond the glass while leaning against the sill. Melissa groaned.

"There's a gap in the curtains. It's just enough to see through."

Lucy cleared her throat to draw their attention.

"Er, guys, we've been noticed. We better come back later."

Tyler turned and saw an elderly couple watching her suspiciously from the pavement outside the house. She jumped down.

"Evenin'."

"Thank God," said Melissa.

"We'll wait in the cab until it's really late," said Tyler. "Then nobody will be about."

The cab was comparatively warm and Tyler dozed uncomfortably for several hours. When it was gone midnight they went back to work. She drew out the contrap, set it to the *Past Eye* and looked into its little, polished lens. When she pulled the lever clockwise, it was as though she was watching a movie in reverse. The further she drew the lever around the contrap's edge, the faster time travelled backwards in the crystal. Ten shoulder-breaking minutes later Melissa was complaining.

"I can't stand here forever with you perched on my shoulders. You weigh a ton! My spine can't take much more."

"Just a bit longer. I've never tried to look back this far before. I don't know how long it's going to take but I must be quite a few years back already. The people I can see look kind of old fashioned. You know, flares and chunky jumpers. The wallpaper's kind of garish."

"Sounds like you're in the sixties, maybe the seventies. Then again, that sounds like my uncle's place... Keep going," said Lucy.

"Can you go any faster? I think my back's about to snap."

Tyler had the contrap's little lever pulled round to its limit. From its starting position at twelve o'clock she'd moved it clockwise all the way to one minute to twelve. Years were flicking past and she could only make any sense of what she was seeing by periodically drawing the lever back to around one o'clock, which was slow enough for her to see people moving around at high speed.

"Jeez, we could have bought a ladder with us," said Melissa. "Why don't we come back later with one?"

"Just another few minutes! The clothes look really old now."

"How will you know when you've reached the right date?" whispered Lucy, pacing to keep warm.

"Well, I'm just looking out for the right kind of uniforms. Then I can slow down and look for Himmler."

"Slow down as soon as you see British World War Two uniforms. It can't have been long before the British left that Himmler was captured and brought here," Melissa explained.

Lucy kept watch as Tyler searched the visual history of the front room. Then, just after Melissa announced that she was going to collapse if Tyler didn't get off her right now, Tyler found what she'd been looking for.

"This is it! I just saw Himmler bite on a cyanide capsule and die. It was horrible."

Temporal Tear

Tyler climbed down from Melissa's shoulders.

"Next time it's your turn," Melissa said to Lucy.

"Quickly!" said Tyler. "They've collected the body. He's wrapped in two grey blankets. They must be going out the back way." She set off round the side of the building and then slowed to position the contrap and peer into the lens again. "I see them! There's an army truck on the road." She watched as four British soldiers in green loaded Himmler's body into the back of the truck and climbed in. "Get in the car. They're leaving!"

The girls hurried into the cab, Tyler taking the front passenger seat. She told Ernst to turn the car and head for the heath, and she concentrated on tracking the army truck through the contrap. It was already some way ahead of them.

"Faster! They're not hanging around."

"It was all done in secrecy. They'd have been ordered to be quick," Melissa explained.

"If we lose them I'll have to start all over again. Put your foot down, Ernst!" Through the lens Tyler watched the camo-green truck speeding away in front.

"Is there a number plate?" asked Melissa, grabbing the door handle to steady herself.

Tyler read out the licence number and Melissa jotted it down. They followed the truck for miles and eventually hit the heathland. When the cab met the rough, old track, Ernst swore.

"Scheiße!"

The car bumped and lurched.

"Do you still have them?" shouted Melissa over the engine's roar and the metallic creeks and groans of the suspension.

"Yes. Don't worry, Ernst. Just drive. Right! They're going right. Just there." Tyler pointed up ahead to a low gutter at the track's edge.

"What? They're going off-road?"

"We're screwed." Lucy drew a skull smiley on her fogged window with a fingertip.

A moment later they plunged into the haphazard grasslands with a jolt that nearly threw Tyler through the windscreen. She raced to reposition the contrap and locate the truck.

"Scheiße!"

"You can say that again," said Lucy.

"Got it!" Tyler cried. "Can you go any faster?"

Ernst looked terrified, his face a deep shade of beetroot.

"This would be easier if I can be seeing what I am chasing," he complained.

"Can't you slow that thing down?" asked Lucy, hugging the headrest in front of her.

"I'll try, though it's risky," Tyler explained. "At this speed if I slow down time too much the truck will start to go backwards. It will shoot right through us and I'll quickly lose them." She focused on the contrap momentarily. "Yep. Lost them. Wait." She moved the contrap about searching for the truck. "They're back. Left, Ernst! They're over there!" again she pointed. "They're getting away from us. Faster!"

Ernst gritted his teeth and sped the car through heathers and tall grasses. They climbed a small hill for the next few minutes as Tyler screamed directions, but all the time the army truck pulled away from them and they lagged further and further behind. They hit what looked like a small ridge and the cab suddenly left the ground.

"Aaagh!" cried Ernst.

It returned with a heavy crunch of metal and they came to rest at an ominous angle, Ernst accelerating, back wheels spinning hopelessly.

"Scheiße!" Ernst bashed the wheel with both hands. "Scheiße, scheiße, scheiße! We are very much bottomed out."

Tyler continued her attempt to trace the truck as they each recovered from the impact.

"What now?" asked Lucy, looking at blood on her fingers that she'd wiped from her forehead after colliding with the doorframe.

Tyler kicked her door open and clambered out.

"If I can find them I'll follow on foot as far as I can." Then she was away, stumbling over dark heath, searching with the contrap and feeling small in the vast, dark expanse.

"Come on," shouted Melissa. "We've got to stick together!"

Lucy and Melissa followed.

"I can still see the truck," Tyler shouted as she ran. "Just." She had a choice. She was going to lose the truck soon either way, unless it stopped, but she could try to keep her eye on it through the contrap and move more slowly while it grew ever more distant, or she could sprint in the direction it was travelling and then search for it again. If she could hold the contrap's tiny lever in exactly the same position, she figured the latter might work. She took a gamble and sprinted. The truck was heading for a gap between two stretches of woodland. She lowered the contrap and ran as fast as she could towards the breach, doing her best to stabilise the lever. When she had covered two hundred metres or so she stopped, breathlessly, to take a bearing. She searched again with the contrap as Lucy and Melissa caught up.

"I lost them. It's gone."

No one spoke for a moment. Tyler peered into the distance.

"Never mind," said Melissa.

"What do you mean 'never mind'?" spat Lucy. "Never mind, we can't find Himmler's grave so he's going to roam free forever, doing just whatever the hell his Nazi ass wants? Is that what you mean?"

"Sor-ry... I didn't know what else to say. Jeez-louise."

"It's alright," said Tyler, truly frustrated. "We'll find a way. Damn! We were *so* close!"

"Alright, alright. I'm sorry," said Lucy while looking around at the moonlit scrub. Cloud drifted across the

moon and the world darkened further. "Do you think we
are close? Do you think they were about to stop?"

"Well, either way, we're closer than we were before,"
said Tyler. She took a pack of tracer darts from her inside
coat pocket and inserted them into the firing pen.

"What are you doing?" asked Melissa.

"I'm leaving a tracer. We can come back tomorrow
and carry on. With the tracer we can find this exact spot
again."

"Shouldn't we carry on now?" asked Lucy, though
she looked like she wanted to go home.

"We don't have a car. It's late. It's cold. We're tired
and we've lost the truck. I think we should go back, get
some sleep. Maybe I can find the truck tomorrow and we
can follow it the rest of the way." Tyler clicked the pen
and the small dart disappeared into the darkness towards
the treeless gap.

They returned to find Ernst enveloped in a smoke-
filled car. A narrow, hazy smoke stream issued from a
small point in his side window. Melissa opened the
passenger door and peered inside coughing through the
cloud as it escaped.

"Jeez-Louise. Ernst, your cigars *really* ming…" She
turned to Tyler and Lucy as they drew level, her face
draining of colour.

With the car now almost clear of smoke, Tyler saw
the bullet hole in the fractured glass of Ernst's window and
then the entrance wound in his left temple. Ernst was
upright and staring blankly out of the open passenger
door, a smouldering cigar still wedged between unfeeling
fingers.

"Oh," said Lucy, suddenly understanding.

Melissa looked at her horrified.

"We've got to get out of here!" said Tyler. "The shot must have come from somewhere over there." She pointed to the short ridge of trees some distance away on the side with the shot window.

"A sniper," stated Lucy.

"Yep. And that means he's most likely still there and we're in…"

A bullet tore past Melissa's head. A second shot shattered the windscreen with a spectacular explosion of fragments.

"Help me get him out of the car!" screamed Tyler. Lucy followed her around the nose of the cab to help drag Ernst's body free.

"Who's driving?" asked Lucy.

"I don't know, but it won't be Ernst. What about you?"

"I've driven my Dad's rally car off-road."

"Great! You're driving," Tyler confirmed, dropping Ernst's body on the ground. Lucy stole his cigar and took a drag while Melissa stared at the scene in shock.

They gathered at the rear, Tyler dragging Melissa by the arm.

"What do we do if we can't get it free?" asked Melissa, wide eyed.

"Die!" shouted Lucy.

"One, two, three, NOW!"

They pushed and the car lurched but remained stuck. A bullet zipped overhead. Another plinked into the car door.

"Push harder!" screamed Melissa. She backed away from the boot to take a run-up. "One, two, three…" She launched herself at the car bellowing a wordless noise.

"Auwaughhhhhhhh!"

34

"PUSH!" Tyler shouted. This time the car broke loose from the rock with a groan.

"Get in, Mel!" Tyler yelled as Lucy rushed to the driver's seat. "We did it!"

"Goodbye, Ernst," called Lucy, slamming her door. "Nice knowing you." Glass rained about her as shots peppered the car.

"DRIVE!" screamed Tyler. The engine kicked into life.

Lucy drove, over-revving badly.

The cab bumped over the heath, wheels spinning, lunging and listing. When they hit the old track Lucy raced the engine and soon they were heading out of Lüneburg Heath.

*

Room service had finished hours ago and so they sat around in their hotel room, hungry and traumatised, trying to come to terms with what had just happened. Tyler took out her mobile and hit a speed-dial number using FaceTime.

"Agent Ghost?"

"We have a problem, Mr Chapman."

"Yes?"

Tyler explained what had happened.

"Don't worry. Leave the keys in the car. It's fine in the hotel car park. I'll have a team sort it out within the hour. Were you followed home?"

"I don't think so. And Ernst?"

"I'll sort him too. It's a shame. He was a good agent." There was a pause as Chapman did something beyond Tyler's view. "I see you left a tracer out there.

That was smart. Just look after yourselves and get some rest. Stick together. You're going back tomorrow?"

"We must."

"Your new driver is called Klaus. I'll have him pick you up around – it's late – let's say ten a.m.?"

"Okay. Thanks."

"I'll be watching your progress via satellite and I'll have someone on hand. Even so, be careful and don't hang around if you feel threatened. If this sniper makes another appearance there'll be little I can do immediately, so you're on your own, so to speak."

"That's comforting. I feel a lot better."

"That's field work for you."

"I guess."

"Ghost…"

"Yes?"

"Chin up and good luck." Chapman hung up.

*

Breakfast was a lifesaver. They loaded their plates from the vast array of food on offer and sat around a small table away from other guests.

"So what's the plan, exactly?" asked Lucy.

"I can't believe you stole his cigar and smoked it," muttered Melissa in disgust.

"Sorry, *Mother*. Hey, you only live once, as proved by Ernst."

"We'll go back out there." Tyler spoke between mouthfuls. "Find the tracer and then I can use the contrap again. Damn. I should have asked Chapman for a four by four."

A slight hotel waiter with a bony face and a hooked nose approached their table.

"Er, excuse me, ladies. May I see your room cards?"

They each gave him their door key cards and he examined them briefly before returning them.

"Ah, yes there has been a small mistake. If you would be so kind; your table is this one over here." The waiter smiled apologetically and motioned for them to move to a table near the huge hotel windows.

The girls shrugged and settled around the new table.

"What difference does it make?" asked Lucy, scowling after the waiter.

"Who knows?" said Melissa.

They resumed eating and Lucy went for more juice.

"She's so bitchy," said Melissa in her absence. "I'm not sure I can work with her for long. She drives me nuts."

"Me too. Look, don't worry about it. We'll get these gloves sorted and then we don't need to ever see her again."

"Except at school."

"Except at school."

Lucy returned. Melissa eyed her.

"What?" asked Lucy.

"Nothing," Melissa shrugged and focused on her bacon roll.

"What's this?" asked Tyler suddenly. She reached into the small pot of flowers on the table and pulled out a suspicious looking plastic tulip.

Melissa looked sideways at her.

"Errrr, it's a plastic…"

Tyler put her finger to her lips. The others looked at her, bemused.

"Um, I'm going to get a croissant. You want one?" she asked nobody in particular while motioning for them to follow her away from the table. When they reached the buffet bar she whispered to them.

"It's a bug. Someone's listening in!"

The others' eyes widened.

"Cool! This is just like James Bond or something," said Lucy.

"It's not cool. It's not cool at all!" said Melissa.

"Right. From now on watch what you say while we're in the hotel. If they're bugging our breakfast table, they must be bugging our room too."

"The sneaky, little…"

"Okay. Back to the table, but no talk about anything important…"

The girls finished breakfast and returned to their room to get ready before heading out to meet Klaus. Tyler paused outside the door to search for bugs with the contrap, switching it to the *Present Eye* and scanning through the solid door and walls. She found a bug on the ceiling light, another beneath a coffee table and a third on a picture frame. She informed Melissa and Lucy before entering.

"Watch what you say. We'll leave them for now. They might come in useful."

Tyler went into the bathroom and quickly checked for bugs there too. She'd not been able to find any before with the contrap and her naked eye revealed nothing obvious either. She ran the shower for some background noise, just in case, before setting the contrap to the *Ghost Portal*. Her stomach did a summersault.

"Albert? Albert, are you in there?" She peered into the lens but saw only shifting shadows within the swirling mist. A shape formed and drew nearer. Tyler was suddenly unnerved, though she didn't know why. She considered switching back to the *Safeguarding Skull* but stopped at the last moment. The face was growing clearer and it wasn't Hitler. That was now obvious. Nor was it Albert. Tyler had an uncanny feeling she knew the translucent girl.

"Who are you?"

The ghost girl, wearing jeans and a purple anorak, stood there looking back at Tyler.

"Who are you?" Tyler repeated.

"My name's Kylie Marsh. Who are *you*? What's happened to me?"

Tyler flicked the switch before anxiety blossomed into a fully-fledged panic attack. With the contrap safely set back to the *Safeguarding Skull* she no longer had to face the ghost of Hitler's latest victim. A sudden pang of regret and guilt made her switch back to the portal but Kylie had gone. Tyler breathed a sigh of relief and wished again that Albert was there. She was still mystified as to what had become of him since she'd set him free of the contrap. At least, that's what she thought she'd done. But where was he now?

She noticed something else in the drifting fog: a vertical streak of hot colour off to the left. Bringing the lens closer to her eye, she focused on the intense flash of orange-red. It seemed to shimmer and glow as though it boiled. It was not like anything she'd ever seen in the *Ghost Portal* before. A smoky mist-like essence issued from it. As she studied it she realised it looked like a tear, a rip in the edge of the world into which she peered.

"What *is* that?" she heard herself say.

A sudden banging on the bathroom door startled her from her thoughts.

"Sorry, but I really gotta go," said Lucy from the other side.

"It's all yours." Tyler tucked the contrap back into her shirt and left the bathroom. She found Melissa sweeping a hand held device over the hotel furniture and walls. The machine beeped.

"What's that?"

"Oh, just something Mr Chapman sent through along with all the IT gear. It communicates wirelessly with the laptop."

"I mean what does it do? What are you doing?"

"Scanning for fingerprints. Mr Chapman said it might be a good idea to check who's been in our room."

"Well, we *are* being spied on."

"And this little guy might tell us who's spying on us."

"Do you have anything yet?"

"So far only hotel staff, reassuringly. Oh, and us of course. But I've just sent through another whole batch of scans. Give me a minute." Melissa put the scanner down and settled on her bed with her laptop. She hit a key and the screen divided into a multitude of small windows, each showing a white print on a black background. Some were clean and recognisable as fingerprints. Others were little more than smudges while some were partial handprints.

"That's odd," stated Melissa as she studied the results. "Look, there are some that have this greenish blue kind of tint."

Tyler studied the prints.

"I've not seen that before," Melissa admitted. "Also, they're not being recognised by the database."

"What does that mean?"

"It means the person, or people, who made those prints aren't in the system for some reason."

"So what do we do?"

"I can send them on to Mr Chapman. He might be able to track them down. He's probably got access to a much larger database."

"Good idea. Do it. Wait. Look at that one. It's an entire handprint."

Melissa squinted at the screen.

"It almost looks like it was made on purpose."

"Can you zoom in?" Tyler asked.

Melissa touched the screen with her fingertip and the handprint suddenly filled the screen. Lucy emerged from the bathroom.

"Hey, Lucy, you've got to see this."

Lucy joined them and they all stared at the handprint. Beyond the ridges of the skin surface something else had been picked up by the scanner. The hand's articulated finger bones could be seen clearly in a bluish green hue.

The Woods

Wind ravaged heathers and ragged low trees. Shrieking bird calls heralded the girls' return to the site of Ernst's murder and Tyler stared at the rock that had waylaid the cab, scrape marks vivid in daylight. No sign of Ernst, though. Not even a spot of blood on the grass. Chapman's clean-up team were proficient.

She scanned Lüneburg's horizon and found the familiar breach between woodlands where she'd last seen the army truck heading off.

"This way." She put the tracer monitor away and strode on.

The tension between Melissa and Lucy had not waned. Melissa had frowned ever since they'd discovered the bug at the breakfast table and Lucy stalked about in her black leather jacket and big boots like a trapped panther, arms perpetually folded.

"Eyes peeled," said Tyler, unimpressed with her friends. "If there's a sniper in those woods I want you to spot him before he spots us."

"Some chance," growled Lucy.

"Just try and help will you?" shouted Tyler. She stopped to draw the contrap from her shirt when she was directly between the two forests. Setting it to the *Past Eye*, she used it to search for the truck that had passed through there in May, 1945.

Klaus watched the girls work from the comfort of his seat. Chapman had been thoughtful enough to send a combat-green Land Rover kitted out with bullet-proof glass. Klaus started the engine and crawled behind the girls. He did not smoke and was some twenty years younger than Ernst, with blond hair swept back from his face, a square jaw and a dimpled chin. When he smiled, which was often, Tyler couldn't help but smile back.

He's cute.

She considered him a vast improvement.

An hour later she was frustrated, still trying to locate the army truck carrying Himmler's corpse. It was harder work than finding the time period through the window of the house in Uelzener Strasse as this wilderness had few visitors to use as fashion references. The heath simply morphed through seasons and so it had taken only minutes for her to feel utterly disorientated in time. Now she no longer knew if she was fifty years into the past or five hundred. Either way the heath looked the same. Another half hour passed and the girls grew restless. Tyler considered suggesting they repeat last night's task of following the truck from Uelzener Strasse, but she knew how that would go down.

"Any sign of the truck?" asked Melissa.

"Nothing yet. I'm lost. I lost count of the passing years ages ago. Guess I might need to start…"

Lucy came over, interrupting and looking concerned.

"Guys, I think I saw something over there in the trees. I'm going to check it out."

"Okay." Tyler didn't take her eye from the contrap, glad to be rid of Lucy's sulky persona for a while.

When twenty minutes had passed with no sign of Lucy's return, Melissa approached Tyler, who was still glued to the *Past Eye*.

"Do you think she's alright?"

Tyler was wandering hopelessly through years and on the verge of giving up. The disturbance was a further irritation.

"Who?"

"*Emo*. She's been gone ages."

Tyler looked into the contrap's lens again, watched its power dwindle and die. The ghosts were exhausted for the meantime. She accepted defeat and put it away.

"Right. Of course. We'd best go after her. I'm getting nowhere anyway."

They told Klaus to wait for them before they set off towards the woods.

"Got your Taser?"

Melissa took out her Taser gun, holding it at the ready.

"Yep."

They walked on spongy moor that soon gave way to forest. The wind had died and the place was silent as they stood peering into ominously shadowed trees.

"She went in here?"

"Yeah. I watched her while you were busy with the contrap."

They headed deeper into the woods, crunching pine needles, fallen twigs and leaf litter.

"I don't like this," said Melissa.

"Come on." Tyler slipped out her Taser gun and led the way. Further in, the trees grew more densely and less light penetrated.

"Do you think we should call her?" whispered Melissa.

"I don't know. Do you mean her mobile? What if someone else is in here somewhere? What if they have Lucy already?" They searched around nervously while Tyler dialled Lucy's number and then put her phone away. "No signal. I guess we should do *something*."

"I wish we could speak to Mr Chapman. He'd know what to do."

"Try your phone. Try Lucy if you get a signal."

Melissa took out her mobile but shook her head when she saw the screen.

"Luuu-cy?" Tyler called and then listened to silence when her tree-dulled echo died. She shouted again and Melissa took up the call. They went further into the woods, finding no indication that Lucy had even passed that way.

Melissa turned.

"Wait. Where did we come in?"

"Back that way..." Tyler looked back before turning full circle. "Oh no. I think we're lost."

Melissa froze, listening.

"Shuuush. Do you hear that? Someone's moving."

"I hear it. Where is *that* coming from?"

"Over there." They ran ahead, chasing the sound before pausing to listen. Again they heard movement and followed. Several times they ran and paused to listen before stopping and calling Lucy's name. Suddenly Lucy's face peered back at them from behind a tree.

"Hi, I'm here." She beckoned for them to join her. "Did you hear that?"

"What?" asked Melissa.

"Someone's moving."

"We heard someone moving but I think it might have just been you."

"I heard something. I've been tracking it for ages. Last time it came from over there." Lucy pointed.

"Let's get out of here," said Melissa. "This place is freaking me out. How do we find our way back?"

"Do you still have the tracer monitor?" Lucy asked Tyler.

"Of course! It will lead us right back to the gap in the trees. I'm with Mel. I think it's time we got out of the woods."

"How are you doing with the army truck?" asked Lucy.

"Not so good. It doesn't matter though, 'cause I've had a better idea. We need to get back to the hotel asap."

*

The girls ordered a late lunch via room service and sat around eating pizza and garlic bread. Tyler finished eating and took the others out into the corridor to whisper.

"We'll need to get well prepared if this is going to work; food, warm clothes, a couple of sets of binoculars would be handy. Basically anything you think we might need on a long stakeout. Once we've let the information slip, we'll need to get back out to the heath pretty quickly and set watch. We follow any vehicle that goes anywhere near that gap in the trees. If it works, they'll not only lead us to the grave, but they'll dig it up for us too. Only problem is, we don't know how long the whole process might take."

"That's if it works at all," said Lucy.

"I think it's good," countered Melissa.

"Okay, it's worth a shot," Lucy said. "But if they do dig him up, they'll also take him away."

"And we follow them. Watch where they hide him and then break in when it gets dark. Take what we need. Drop Chapman the address. Everyone's happy."

"It could work."

"It *will* work. It *has* to."

They gathered the gear they needed and packed bags with warm clothes and extra layers. Tyler slipped away to the bathroom. She turned the shower on, as before, and set the contrap to the *Ghost Portal*. The ghosts had recuperated.

"Albert?" she called softly. "Zebedee? Is anyone there?"

A pair of grey-looking, malnourished twin girls in tattered clothes drifted into view and gazed back at Tyler quizzically.

"Hello," said the twin on Tyler's right in a strong Polish accent.

"Who are you?" asked the other.

"I'm Tyler. Is Zebedee there? Do you know Zebedee Lieberman? Or a boy called Albert?"

"Do you mean *Mr Lieberman*?" asked the right twin, quietly.

"Yes. Yes! Zebedee Lieberman? You *do* know him then? Is he there? Can you fetch him for me?"

The twins nodded slowly in duel motion before drifting away out of view. Tyler waited.

Kylie Marsh appeared suddenly and screwed her face up at Tyler, making her jump.

"I know you," Kylie said.

Tyler swallowed hard.

"*How* do I know you?"

"My name's Tyler. I go... We used to go to the same school."

"Tyler..." Kylie watched her suspiciously for a moment. "Do you know what happened to me?"

Tyler rubbed her face wearily.

This is all I need.

Her head hurt.

"Yes. I can tell you what happened, but it's complicated and you're going to think I'm talking rubbish, or that I'm just plain mad. You were used... Your body was taken over by the ghost of Adolf Hitler." She waited for this sink in. It sounded ridiculous even to Tyler. "You were gloved with Hitler. Some really bad men did it. There are more still out there."

"Gloved?"

"Like I said, it's complicated. The people who gloved you are Nazis. You were not the only one. Five other kids were also taken and used to bring Nazi ghosts back to life."

"Where am I?"

"You're in a ghost machine. *My* ghost machine. It's called a *contrap*. I didn't know you were in there until I saw you this morning. You must've been sucked in along with all the others after Hitler exploded." This last statement Tyler said to herself as much as to Kylie.

"Hitler exploded?"

"Like I said…"

"…it's complicated."

"Right. Listen, I was trying to save you when the bomb went off. I'm sorry. I failed. And you were killed."

"And now I'm in your ghost machine?"

"Yeah." Tyler realised something. "But that means the contrap is unbalanced, so I can let you out! I mean, I think I can let you out. If you want."

"I don't know what I want. I don't know what's going on. I'm scared. It's lonely in here but there are thousands of others. I know I'm not making sense."

"Believe it or not, I think I understand. I'd better talk to Zebedee about this. I have some questions…"

"Will I see you again?"

"Yes. I'll be right here. Don't worry. I have some friends in there. They'll look after you." As soon as she'd said this Tyler remembered that Hitler and Bagshot were also in the contrap somewhere and she felt even worse.

Tyler could hear the tapping of a cane. Kylie became nervous and quickly vanished. Zebedee strode into view waving his top hat merrily as though he might burst into a verse of *Zip-a-Dee-Doo-Dah* at any minute.

Tyler didn't think it *was* a 'wonderful day'.

"My dear girl, how the devil are you?"

"I'm fine, Zebedee. A lot has happened since I last saw you though. I need your help again."

"Zebedee Lieberman at your service, ma'am. How may I assist you?"

"Firstly, I was wondering if you'd seen Albert lately. I thought I'd set him free from the ghost machine but he seems to have disappeared altogether."

Zebedee thought about this for a moment before shaking his head.

"No, like I said last time you asked, I haven't seen him at all lately. I suppose you must have released him."

"Okay. Secondly, I saw something very strange in there, in the *Ghost Portal*. It was like a tear in the portal's edge. Like a rip in a piece of cloth. I could see right through into something else, or *somewhere* else. I don't know. It was weird. Do you know what it was?"

Zebedee looked unsettled, his brows knitting in concern. He was silent for a while.

"No. I don't know what it was that you saw. Can you be more descriptive?"

"It was as though the edge of the *Ghost Portal* was torn and I was peering through into another place. A hot place. It looked like fire."

Zebedee shook his head again.

"Makes no sense to me. Very strange. I'll see what I can find out, though. Anything else?"

"Yes. It's about Kylie Marsh, the girl who died when Hitler's bomb exploded. I found her in the ghost machine this morning. Guess she got drawn inside with all the other ghosts, but you said the ghost machine should be kept balanced. I mean, if a ghost goes in, another needs to come out."

Zebedee nodded.

"That's right, in theory."

"Well, what happens if it stays unbalanced? She must have been in there for a while now and I didn't notice anything different, except for the tear of course."

"I see. Yes, good question. In short, the ghost machine will be unstable if it's unbalanced. It could get dangerous if it becomes too unbalanced. I doubt one ghost alone could unbalance it to that degree, but the problem is we don't really know how unbalanced the thing was when you found it. Do you see?"

"Do you think that's what caused the tear?"

"My dear child, I really don't know. It *is* odd that an extra ghost has entered the device and has had no apparent affect." Zebedee muttered to himself. "But then, this *tear*... Oh dear, I wonder what is going on."

"Do you think the old woman would know?"

"You mean Izabella? She might. I'll try to find her."

"I was also wondering about Hitler. Have you seen him in there? If so, what's he doing? Did the Polish ghosts do something to him?"

"My dear girl, so many questions! I simply do not know what has become of Hitler, but I shall endeavour to learn all I can. Seek me out again soon and I might have some answers."

"Thanks, Zebedee."

"You're most welcome, my dear. Oh, and Tyler," he added. *"Do not* forget the warnings I have given you. It can be very boring in here at the best of times and we ghosts like a little mischief. You'll need to think carefully before taking too much advice from the contrap."

"I will, Zebedee. I promise."

Tyler left the bathroom and scribbled out a shopping list of extra things she thought they might need.

Winter sleeping bags x4
Crisps
Snacks
Sandwiches?
Bottled drinks

"Who wants to get this lot?" she waved the paper in the air.

"I'll go," said Lucy, snatching it from Tyler's hand.

"Get anything else you think might be useful."

"Will do."

"Alright for cash?"

"Loaded."

When Lucy was gone, Tyler switched on the TV and gazed at the closed door.

"What's bugging you?" asked Melissa, peering over the top of her computer.

"Oh, it's probably nothing."

"It's Lucy, right?"

Tyler nodded.

"Do you think she's even on our side?"

"I sometimes wonder," Melissa confessed.

"I mean, what happened out there today? She was gone for ages. What was she doing all that time?"

"You're thinking someone was spying on us and she met up with them."

"Wouldn't that explain a lot?"

"I guess it would. So what do we do about it? You really think Lucy's a ..."

They locked eyes.

"...a *double agent*," said Tyler. "I think that's the correct term. And to answer your question, I haven't a clue."

The laptop chimed. Melissa studied the screen.

"Chapman got a hit on the handprint and some latents."

Tyler joined her on the bed to view the results. One name peppered the multiple print displays including the remarkably complete handprint: Josef Rudolf Mengele.

"You're joking! The *Angel of Death*."

"Uh-uh. No joke. Mengele's gloved ghost has been poking around in our bedroom."

"Well, I suppose it's good to know I'm not paranoid," said Tyler. "Can you tell when he was here?"

"Not really. Best guess? This morning while we were out chasing shadows."

Tyler dialled a number on her mobile.

"Ghost, you received the forensics report?"

"Yes, Mr Chapman. We did."

"Sorry it's not better news."

"It doesn't matter. He's been following me since before Westminster Square. I have another issue I thought you might be able to help with. Did you say you'd be watching us?"

"I did and I am, whenever possible."

"So *you* had our hotel room bugged?"

"No. That must've been another *interested party*. Most likely your Nazi friends."

"And out on the heath?"

"I've been keeping an eye on you via SHSS. Sorry, that's the *Satellite Heat Signature System*."

"You watched us today?"

"After last night's events - yes - every moment. I must say I was left a little confused."

"Because..."

"Because one of your party apparently left the group for no reason and, by the way, against my direct orders, to wander around aimlessly in a patch of woodland for a while. I don't really understand why. I'm guessing the heat signature in the Land Rover was Klaus."

"So you didn't see a foreign heat signature near us somewhere? We thought someone was spying on us from the woods. Lucy went to investigate."

"I see. No. You were completely alone out there. Only four signatures at any one time. All above board and accounted for."

Tyler considered this momentarily.

"Right."

"How are agents Pointer and Cog?"

"Fine. Well, Pointer is Pointer, but I'm keeping an eye on her."

"Anything else I can help you with?"

"No. Thank you." Tyler ended the call.

"You sure you saw something in the woods?" she asked Melissa.

"I saw what *you* saw. We followed something or someone. I don't know if it was just Lucy or not."

"Chapman says we were alone out there. If there was a presence watching us from the woods, it wasn't human. It didn't have a heat signature."

"You're thinking it was a glove spying on us? And that they are cold, like dead people?"

"If that is true, and if Lucy did meet up with another agent, the agent was a ghost or a glove."

The Rag & Bone Man

By the time Lucy returned, staggering with shopping bags, Tyler and Melissa had drafted a brief script revealing the necessary information for the prying ears around their room. Lucy dumped four bulging bags on the carpeted floor and peered over Melissa's shoulder, nodding approval.

"All set?" she asked.

"Ready when you are," said Tyler.

"Are you sure they'll have enough time to get organised?" whispered Mellissa.

"Not really, but leave it too long and they'll wonder what we're waiting for. We need to panic them into action."

"Okay. Wait, won't they wonder how we found out?" Melissa asked.

"Let them wonder," said Lucy.

"Right." Melissa was edgy. "Of course."

"You okay?" asked Tyler.

"I guess."

"Let's do it."

Tyler turned the TV off and Melissa began dramatizing the script.

"So now we have the exact location of Himmler's burial, when're we going to excavate the body?"

Tyler scanned the page and swallowed. Drama was not her thing.

"I just got the message. It's gonna take them two days to get a digger over here." Tyler checked the date on her watch. "We can't dig him up until Thursday morning."

Lucy read her line.

"Can't they get the gear any quicker? Don't they know we're in a hurry?"

"I know, I know. We're going to have to just sit tight and wait," Tyler concluded.

"Oh well," said Lucy going off-script. "I guess there's no rush. Those dumb, Nazi scumbags haven't a clue we know."

Tyler shot her a warning glance which Lucy shrugged off, mouthing *What?*

They made hot drinks and prepared for the vigil while making small talk as naturally as they could. Lucy had bought four camouflaged, thermal sleeping bags which they packed along with the supplies and warm clothes. Tyler made a quick call to check Klaus was ready and they left the hotel via a service entrance at the back, climbing swiftly into the green Land Rover before Klaus sped them away. Tyler checked her Taser gun and looked over their gear in the back.

"You got the spades and the tarps?" she asked Klaus.

"Four spades, a pick and two tarpaulins."

"Great."

"What do we need all that for? I thought *they* were going to dig him up for us," said Lucy.

"It's just in case."

They drove out to the heath and soon found a sheltered patch of scrub tucked between wooded outcrops where they spent half an hour camouflaging the Land Rover further with bits of tree and bush. When they'd finished, Tyler stood back to admire their work. Even from twenty metres away it was difficult to spot. If someone was to pass by at fifty metres or so, it would be thoroughly hidden.

She climbed back into the vehicle and made herself comfortable. Through tiny gaps in the camouflage she could easily spy on the woodland breach where she'd last seen the truck carrying Himmler's corpse.

Klaus was the only one who didn't seem affected by the sleep-inducing tedium of the wait. When Tyler caught herself falling asleep some two hours later, she jolted upright and took a long, reviving swig from her water bottle. She saw Melissa had dozed off and Lucy looked set to follow. Klaus was brightly awake in the front seat next to her. He flashed her a smile and Tyler wished she'd checked her makeup before setting out. She wiped condensation from the narrow windscreen to scan the wilderness beyond. The bright, chilly afternoon was ebbing into ominous shades of grey and, beyond the tree line, the sky blazed with tones of fire, as though Hell itself was opening.

"You awake, Lucy?"

Lucy stirred and fought to sit up.

"I am now."

"I nearly fell asleep, too. We'd best take turns to stay awake and keep watch or we might miss them."

"Right."

"I can watch, if you wish," said Klaus.

Tyler studied him briefly, wondering how far he could be trusted.

"I won't fall asleep. I can promise you that. I have been trained in surveillance. I will sleep when the mission is successfully completed. I will wake you, of course, if anybody comes."

"Right. Thanks. All the same, I think I'd feel safer if at least two of us were awake at any one time. Lucy, you can sleep now. Klaus and I will take a shift. Then I'll swap with you or Melissa."

Lucy shrugged and flashed an insincere smile.

"You woke me up to tell me I could sleep? Thanks." She turned over and huddled against her sleeping bag.

"We brought you a sleeping bag too, by the way," Tyler informed Klaus.

"Thank you. That was thoughtful. I may be glad of it when the temperatures fall later on."

Tyler noted the bulge in his jacket.

"You armed?"

"Chapman's orders," Klaus confirmed, patting his gun through the fabric.

Tyler checked the tree line again. The heath was still. She listened at the cracked window for an engine but heard only a solitary, haunting bird call. She imagined Ernst's lonely soul wandering the heath, seeking a home, and she shivered. When she could stand it no more she climbed out to get some fresh air and stretch her legs, checking her mobile. The signal was weak, almost non-existent and, as she watched, it died altogether.

Sod's law.

At ten p.m. she woke Melissa and swapped places. Tyler settled down in her sleeping bag in the back, fighting to stay warm and was soon asleep.

*

A vibration in her pocket startled her awake. Beyond the steamed windows the night was fully dark. She scrabbled to pull the phone out and gazed blearily at the small screen, shivering at the cold.

Missed call: Chapman

Great.

Tyler checked the signal. Zip. She pocketed the phone.

"Alright back there?" asked Melissa from the front seat.

"Fine. Just a missed call from Chapman. What time is it?"

"Two thirty…" Melissa stopped talking and cocked her head to one side. Tyler heard it too: the low rumble of a large engine some way off, but growing louder.

"They're coming!" Tyler shook Lucy awake and fought her way out of her sleeping bag.

"Chapman called to warn us," Melissa concluded.

"He tried."

"What's up?" asked Lucy.

"It's happening. They're here. You need to wake up." Tyler saw lights growing closer through the foggy windows and brush camouflage.

"Do we drive? Walk? How do we follow them?" asked Melissa.

"If we drive they'll see the lights," said Lucy.

"Don't worry," said Klaus. "I'll drive without the lights. I'm trained in night combat driving and I've been sitting in the dark for hours. I can see very well."

"You speak very good English, Klaus," Tyler stated and then caught herself. She wasn't here to flirt.

"Thank you, Miss May. I studied at Oxford University."

Lucy rolled her eyes at Melissa.

"They're heading for the gap."

Tyler glimpsed a dark coloured truck as it passed by and caught sight of a large search light mounted above the cab. Klaus waited until it was well beyond their position before starting the Land Rover engine and slowly pulling away to follow the shrinking red tail lights.

"It worked," said Melissa.

"I know!" said Tyler. She'd not meant to sound so surprised.

The truck rambled on like a lost cyclops for less than a quarter mile before slowing.

Klaus stopped the Land Rover a good distance away and waited, watching to see what the truck ahead would do. It crawled the last few metres, its monstrous, glowing eye sweeping about the ground as it drew to a halt and Tyler saw its other lights blink out and dark shapes leave the cab. Torch lights dappled the rolling heath and Tyler discerned hints of voices. The new arrivals were searching for the exact spot where Heinrich Himmler had been buried in 1945.

So the body has yet to be moved. It is *still here!*

A call went up and torches closed in. Men fetched spades from the back of the truck as Tyler switched the contrap to the *Present Eye* and focused-in closely on the diggers. As she watched, a team of three men struck into the ground and began piling up a spoil heap to one side. Two others stood opposite looking on.

"How long does it take to dig a grave?" she asked nobody in particular.

"It depends how deep you need to go and what the ground is like," offered Klaus. "But a grave six feet deep usually takes two men a good four or five hours."

Tyler didn't like to think about why Klaus might know this.

"So we could be in for a long wait. Better make yourselves comfortable, girls."

*

Tyler didn't want to wear out the contrap again so she kept tabs on the diggers' progress sporadically. She watched the pile of soil grow over the next three hours as Melissa and Lucy slept. She realised dawn would soon be approaching and the Land Rover would be easily seen. She also realised that if they started the engine now, the diggers would certainly hear it and come searching for them. She cursed, kicking herself for not foreseeing this. Close by was a clump of trees at the edge of a low outcrop of rock, so Tyler woke the others and with some effort and much help from Klaus, they pushed the Land Rover behind this cover and continued to spy on the excavation.

"We'd best get the tracer in place while it's still good and dark," Tyler said to Lucy.

"I'll go now," Lucy replied. She peeled off her black gloves and opened a small tin of black greasepaint which she smeared over her face. She was already wearing all black and with her gloves back on she appeared little more than a shadow.

Tyler fished about in the black cases from Chapman while Lucy made the finishing touches to her new night-ops look. Tyler handed her two magnetic tracers.

"Here, use these. If one falls off for any reason we'll still have the other to track."

Lucy took the tracers and jogged away into the gloom towards the truck and the diggers.

"You sure we can trust her?" asked Melissa when Lucy had been gone for a minute or so.

"No," said Tyler. "I'm not sure at all. That's why I'm going to watch every move she makes." She focused the contrap.

Ten minutes later Lucy was back, a fleeting tone among shades of black.

"They're both on the undercarriage of the truck," she said. "No problem. The men are all very focused on the dig. They didn't notice me at all."

Tyler checked the site through the contrap again. Two figures stood over the hole while three others dug. She used the contrap lever to close in on these two supervisors. She wondered who they were and briefly thought she recognised one of them. She tried to shake off the notion, but a while later was studying them again through the lens and wishing she was closer. With the contrap's lever she could zoom as close as she wanted but, from her current position, the angle was all wrong and faces were hidden. An idea hit her.

"Wait here," she said to the others. "I'm going for a closer look." Tyler set the contrap's switch to *Flight* and gently brought the lever down clockwise, leaving the ground and heading up into the brightening sky. It was still dark enough to give her adequate cover, though she didn't want to risk getting too close. She angled the contrap forwards and felt it carry her effortlessly over the heath towards the diggers, some fifty metres above the heath, before closing on them and dropping lower. Her view was still not great. The problem of distance had been replaced by a problem of perspective. She looked down at the tops of heads.

A sudden movement from below startled her. A face turned upwards and peered directly in her direction. Tyler recoiled, tugging on the lever so hard that she shot up at a blinding rate. She'd recognised the face with the soft, eerie, blue glow. It was Himmler's glove and he'd clearly sensed the contrap. She returned to the Land Rover, shaken by the thought that Himmler was overseeing the exhumation of his own remains. The gloves knew exactly what the girls were doing and now Himmler probably knew she was close by.

Had he seen her before she'd bolted into the night? She could not be sure.

The diggers seemed to be in a hurry now and there was an obvious buzz about them. Tyler imagined Himmler's glove barking orders to speed things up.

Klaus peered through night-vision field glasses.

"They have found the body. They are taking it out, bit by bit," he said.

Tyler grabbed the binoculars and looked for herself.

"Take it easy, Fräulein," said Klaus. "There are more in the back."

Tyler focused and watched figures passing out bones and small bundles from the grave pit. She could not see faces from this distance but the view was close enough for her to see the rag and bone man being assembled on a bier at the graveside. They had found what was left of the Nazi war criminal, Heinrich Himmler.

A Collection

The diggers did not wait around to refill the grave. They wrapped the remains, loaded them into the back of the truck and hastily drove away.

Tyler figured that even if Himmler's glove had not seen her, he still knew she was close by because he'd sensed the contrap, so it made sense that he'd want to escape quickly. He would need the new resting place of his bones to be kept secret.

The next phase of Tyler's plan was the most worrying. She couldn't follow right behind the truck because that would be too obvious, so, solely reliant upon the planted tracers that they could track from a distance, she took out the tracer monitor from her bag and switched it on. The small screen flashed into life, displaying a geographical map of Lüneburg Heath and she used the touchscreen to close in on a moving red dot ringed with a blue circle.

"That's the truck," said Melissa. "The red tracer and the blue tracer. When they're within four metres of each other they appear as rings of colour on one mark."

"Right." Tyler watched tail lights disappear behind a tree line. "It should be safe now. Let's go, Klaus."

Klaus started the Land Rover and they pulled away, tracking the tagged vehicle.

Forty-five minutes later they pulled up against the curb in a backwater street, searching for the truck. Tyler studied the tracer monitor and pointed to a house set back from the road ahead.

"It has to be over there somewhere."

Klaus inched the Land Rover forward along the road and the rear of a black truck came into view at the top of the house's driveway. As they watched, two men emerged from the house and opened the rear doors of the truck, collected the remains, still folded in a blanket, and carried them inside.

Melissa scribbled down the address in her notebook.

"Mr Chapman's gonna love this."

"What now?" asked Lucy.

"We wait and watch." Tyler took out the contrap, set it to the *Present Eye* and focused on the activity within the house. She followed the body bearers as they wound their way through corridors to a doorway, on to a stairway and then down into a cavernous chamber. She noticed immediately that the room was no normal basement. It was far more interesting than that and Tyler once again felt that frustration of peering through a single small viewing glass. She longed to be in the room, to be able to survey it for real.

"They've taken him to the basement. It's some kind of shrine. Like a tomb. There's a stone plinth already waiting. They're putting the remains on it now." She continued her commentary as the body bearers stood around the plinth formally and she realised they were performing a ceremony of sorts. A chalice was procured from a nearby niche and passed around in an un-holy communion. "They're some kind of brotherhood."

"Like a cult?" asked Lucy.

"The Aryan Knights," said Melissa. "It's a Nazi shrine. This is exactly what they were trying to avoid when they took him out into the heath and buried him in secret."

"I think it's finished," explained Tyler, blinking weary eyes. "They're locking up and leaving."

A few minutes later the three diggers and Himmler's glove came out of the house and drove away in the van.

"That leaves one man still in the house," said Lucy.

"I expect it's his house. Maybe he lives there. He must be guarding the shrine."

*

The house was four storeys high and seemed taller in the darkness. The roof's apex appeared to melt into the stormy sky that brooded over the street. Tyler shivered and checked her watch: 1.30 a.m.

The man was soundly asleep in the master bedroom on the second floor. She gave the others a nod and they quietly left the Land Rover. Klaus stayed in the cab at Tyler's request although he had offered to accompany them, but Tyler wanted him ready at the wheel in case they needed a quick escape.

"I'll keep a lookout and I'll be on comms," he said. "Keep your earpieces in. Stay in touch."

She didn't need the contrap to pick the side door lock. It was nothing special. She made short work of it and they slipped silently into a long, dark, oak-panelled hall. She grimaced at the old-school décor in the shadows as they listened. There were a multitude of tiny sounds: The house creaked, the wind rattled trees beyond a high stained-glass window at the end of the passage, and dubious pipework glugged softly as an antiquated heating system strained, but no footsteps sounded from the upper floors.

The girls looked at each other. Melissa was so nervous she shook.

"I really think I'd best go wait with Klaus," she whispered. "You don't need me for this."

"You're coming with us," whispered Tyler. "There's something very odd in the basement and I want you both to see it. This way." She led the others down the passage and round a corner. Here the corridor entered a tall antechamber that met with the front porch and doorway. More stained-glass and old pipework. An antique, veneered sideboard housed a sizable, black, Bakelite phone and a bronze statue of Pan playing his pipes, cast shadows over a worn, tiled floor and intricate rug. To their right, stairs ascended to the realm of the sleeper.

Tyler took a left and they threaded another panelled passage which ended at two closed doors. Tyler paused, sensing something wasn't right.

"There should be another doorway." She recalled the journey she'd witnessed the body bearers make. "Where's the cellar door?"

"Maybe we passed it," whispered Melissa.

Lucy looked around, hands on hips.

"We better try these doors," she said. "Maybe it's one of these." Lucy opened the door closest to her and quietly closed it again. "Living room."

Tyler tried the other.

"Kitchen. Backtrack. Check we didn't miss a door."

A short way down the hallway she drew the contrap from her shirt and searched.

"Over there. The basement steps are just the other side of these panels." She began pushing panels, testing seasoned joint-work. The others did the same and a moment later a panel swung open onto the stairwell with a loud groan. They froze, listening.

The old house creaked, pipes glugged. A late night driver passed the house, dashing lamplight across the antechamber at the end of the hall.

"Let's go," whispered Tyler and she crept down steep stairs into the cold tomb of Heinrich Himmler. As the others followed behind, she saw a vaulted, stone chamber open up before her. Four large candles, left burning at each corner of the plinth, offered a meagre, wavering light. The girls took out Maglites and looked around.

Himmler's remains had been carefully arranged and rearticulated, as far as had been possible, so that it appeared a man built of soiled rags and mouldering bones lay on a stone plinth. On the wall behind his skull a vast black swastika in a white circle dominated a red painted arch and beneath this was mounted an engraved brass plaque. Melissa read it aloud.

"Albeit Macht Frei." She translated it. *"Work sets you free."*

"That's weird," said Lucy.

"That's what was written over the gates of Auschwitz. It was part of the Nazi ploy to make the Jews think they were entering a work camp when really they were going to their deaths. Tyler, can we go now? This place is evil."

On the walls, either side of the ragged bones, shelves bore many items that reminded Tyler of a museum display. There were Greek urns and pots, Celtic brooches and figurines, pieces of ancient-looking stonework with Indian decoration, Roman brooches and archaic coins in shimmering glass cases.

"Not yet. We haven't done what we came to do." Tyler crossed to the plinth and, setting the contrap to the *Ghost Portal*, placed it on Himmler's soil-stained skull.

"What are you doing?" asked Lucy.

"I'm going to use his remains to draw him here. His entire skeleton will make the most powerful artefact. You know that. Then I'll put his ghost into the contrap. Wasn't that the plan?"

They looked at each other.

"Yeah," whispered Lucy. "But if you use it right now won't Himmler's glove just hit the wall outside and stay there, pinned by the force of the summoning? And anyway, doesn't the glove need to be close by? I mean, close enough for the draw to take effect. We don't even know where Himmler's glove *is* right now."

Tyler lifted the contrap.

"You're right. This isn't going to work. Not right now."

"Why don't we take him with us?" asked Melissa. "We can pick our time and place to use the remains."

"What? All of him?" hissed Lucy.

"We don't need all of him. All we need is one bone." Tyler reached out to claim a finger bone from the skeleton.

"We'll each take a small bone. Just in case. Maybe they won't even notice they're gone."

Lucy took a distal phalanx and Melissa, pulling a disdainful face, did the same.

"Great. Can we go now, Tyler?" Melissa tucked the mouldering bone into a compartment of her backpack.

"Yes." They headed for the stairs where she eyed the vast array of objects on display and stopped.

"Wait."

"What now?"

"Look at all this stuff. Why's it here?"

They shone torch beams over the collection of ancient objects.

"That's what I was thinking." Lucy seemed happy to hang around there all night.

"It all looks pretty old to me," said Melissa, her fear giving way to intrigue. "Look here. This pot has a swastika on it."

"What?"

"And this one," added Melissa.

"These too," said Lucy, running her Maglite down a length of shelving. "If you look closely, each object has a swastika somewhere, even the coins."

"Take them," said Tyler.

"You're joking," said Melissa.

"We'll take the lot." Tyler began filling her bag with the objects. Where they were small and numerous, she swept an arm across the shelf to scoop them in.

"Right."

"Come on, Mel," Lucy urged. "The sooner we get it all, the sooner we leave."

Reluctantly, Melissa bagged items.

Klaus' voice alerted each of them via their earpieces.

"Girls, a car is pulling up outside the house and one of the men inside is glowing blue."

The girls bolted up the stairs to head back through the groaning house. They reached the side door, where they'd entered, as a shadow swept across the small window accompanied by muffled voices. Someone knocked loudly on the door.

"Too late!" whispered Tyler. They doubled back sprinting down the corridor.

"Wait, if it's Himmler we can put him into the contrap now!" said Melissa, though the idea clearly terrified her.

"She's right," said Lucy.

"But what if it isn't him?" whispered Tyler. "We need to know! If it's one of the other gloves, they'll kill us."

As they reached the antechamber, footfalls thudded on the stairs above them. The sleeper had awoken.

They darted down the passage, past the secret door, and stole into the kitchen, closing the door swiftly, but quietly, behind them. Tyler switched the contrap to the *Present Eye* and viewed the gathering of figures back in the antechamber. She immediately recognised one of the three men as Josef Mengele.

"It's not Himmler. We're in danger. We need to go."

Lucy tested the back door and found it led out into a scullery and on to another door, this one locked. She signalled for them to turn back and, mounting the kitchen work surface, unlatched a window and offered Melissa her hand.

"You coming?"

Melissa clambered up and Lucy jumped from the sill into the back garden with Tyler close behind. They fled down the side of the house to the Land Rover and Klaus sped them away before Tyler could slam her door.

"Thanks for the heads-up." She looked back towards the house and saw two dark figures and a faintly glowing man run into the street after them.

"Goodnight, Josef."

Matryoshka

Tyler ate breakfast while penning a new list.

Artefacts Acquired

Heinrich Himmler
Josef Mengele
Adolf Eichmann
Reinhard Heydrich
Joseph Goebbels

She put a tick next to Himmler's name and wrote:
Finger bones.

One down, four to go.

She took another mouthful of muesli and thought
again about the hoard of ancient objects they'd purloined
from the shrine.   Someone was going to be livid with

74

them. Still, only one more night in the Best Western Premier Castanea and then they'd be leaving for Brazil.

What could possibly go wrong?

"Let's go shopping!" suggested Melissa. There was an air of triumph over the girls after the success of the last night's raid and all animosity had seemingly dissipated. Even Lucy appeared happy, which Tyler found quite odd. She considered Melissa's suggestion and it appealed.

"Okay with me. Give me ten and I'll be ready. Klaus can drive us."

Lüneburg's history was apparent from the traditional red brick and timber framed houses and shops around the town and the waterfront, a picturesque place: tall elegant buildings with grand frontages and waterside cafés and restaurants. They bought supplies for a little celebration later that evening in their hotel room and found souvenirs from gift shops.

Tyler perused *Finkel Spielzeug,* a quaint, old toy store with a broad stairway leading up to an open galley on the second floor. The shop was mostly populated with gaudy wooden creations but amongst them was a rack of Russian Matryoshka dolls that caught her eye. She paid the huge-bearded, and rather grouchy, shopkeeper for a doll before re-joining the others and returning wearily to the hotel where she made hot chocolate and collapsed on her bed for a while. When she stirred an hour or so later, it was to remove a used micro-tracer syringe she'd been laying on uncomfortably.

She took out the Matryoshka, opening layer after layer until she removed the little solid doll from the centre. In its place she put the finger bone she'd taken from Himmler's remains, before encapsulating it with layers of painted dolls. She tucked the Matryoshka doll into her suitcase and forgot about it for the rest of the afternoon.

They searched unfamiliar TV for a music channel but failed. In the end Lucy plugged her iPod into the TV system and turned it up loud. Delain's *Are You Done with Me?* filled the room with dark sound. She poured drinks and passed them round. Tyler sipped.

"What's this?"

"Fruit juice," said Melissa. "We found it in this weird, little store. We couldn't read the label but Lucy thought it looked good." She took a gulp. "Wow! It *is* good!"

Lucy drained her cup and refilled it.

"It's okay," agreed Tyler.

The track finished and she realised someone had been knocking at their door unheard. She opened it to find Klaus grinning and presenting her with a bottle and a box of biscuits.

"Good evening, Fräulein May. May I join the party?"

"Er…"

"Klaus is here!" beamed Melissa from across the room.

"Come in, Klaus!" Lucy poured another glass of juice and took it to him, adoringly. Tyler hadn't realised Lucy also liked him, but it was obvious enough now.

"Who invited Klaus?" Tyler asked Melissa while Lucy occupied him.

"We did."

"Right. I thought it was just going to be us." She would have put makeup on if she'd known.

"Chill. Loosen up. We're supposed to be celebrating. We can't have a party with just the three of us."

But Tyler didn't feel like celebrating. She escaped to the bathroom and grudgingly sorted out her face wishing she'd done her nails. Too late for that now. She didn't understand why she wasn't pleased to see Klaus. After all, she *really* liked him. Fancied him even. When she came out, the others were dancing and two of Klaus's friends had turned up.

"The music's too loud," she told Melissa.

"No one's complained yet. Stop being such a damp rag," countered Lucy. She took a bottle and slopped the contents into every glass.

"Raise them, girls. And Klaus," she giggled. "To us, to fun and to killing Nazi ghosts. Again!"

*

Tyler turned in her sleep. She was listening to a familiar voice she couldn't quite name.

"Wake up!" the voice whispered urgently. "Missy, you gotta wake up!"

Tyler turned over again and tried to shut the voice off.

Am I dreaming?

She knew deep down somehow that she had the power to shut the dream down and get some proper rest.

"Tyler May! Wake up! 'E's 'ere!"

"Albert? Is that you?" She thought it was odd to be dreaming about Albert but then again, she missed him, so perhaps it also made perfect sense.

"Wake up, Miss Tyler! You ain't a'dreamin'!"

Tyler opened her eyes. She *was* awake now. Fully awake. Albert's translucent, grubby face was inches from hers, and he was drawing a finger to his lips.

"Albert?" she whispered. "What's going on? Why..." She had not seen the ghost of Albert Goodwin since releasing him from the contrap. She was momentarily confused.

"Shush." Albert shifted his finger to point across the bedroom. Tyler followed it and saw a shape moving in the darkness. She squinted, trying to make out some detail before catching a glimpse of a pale blue glow.

"Himmler?" she whispered.

Albert nodded. Himmler knew they'd stolen three phalanges and he had come to reclaim them.

Tyler thought desperately. Her hand found the contrap on her chest but the finger bone she needed as the summoning artefact was in her case. The case that was across the room where the stooping figure searched. She reached instead for the Taser gun beneath her pillow. The movement alerted Himmler and he dashed to the door and fled as Tyler aimed.

"Dammit!"

She tore out of bed and hit the light switch. She shook Melissa.

"Wake up! Himmler was here!"

Melissa mumbled but refused to wake.

She tried Lucy, noticed she'd gone to sleep with gum in her mouth. Neither of the girls would stir. She picked up the empty juice bottle from Lucy's bedside table and examined the label, read the fifteen percent marker. Alcohol.

Oh great. They're drunk!

Even if she could wake them they'd be useless and Himmler was getting away.

"Sorry I couldn't wake you sooner, Missy. I only just got 'ere."

"That's alright, Albert. Where've you been? Never mind. Tell me later. It's good to see you." She turned to look at him but Albert had vanished. Tyler searched her suitcase. The only thing missing was the Russian doll. Albert reappeared next to her case.

"He's taken the artefact and I don't know where Lucy and Mel put theirs." Tyler threw on clothes and ran after Himmler, hoping she might still find a chance to put him into the contrap. She didn't worry about which direction he'd taken until outside. She used the *Past Eye* to watch him leave and she gave chase, crossing the hotel car park in time to see a dark saloon pulling away, a blue glow behind its tinted glass. No time to call Klaus. She hailed a hotel cab and instructed the driver to follow the dark car, wondering if Himmler knew she was following.

She tailed the saloon into Lüneburg where it pulled up alongside a curb opposite the river.

"Stop. Right here."

The cab driver pulled over and Tyler stuffed a fist full of notes into his hand. Concealing herself behind the corner of a red brick restaurant and a narrow walkway overlooking the Llmenau's rippling surface, she watched Himmler leave the saloon and walk briskly down the road and around a corner.

Tyler followed from the shadows, wondering where Albert had gone. Several turns later she recognised the street Himmler had joined and watched him break into Finkel Spielzeug, the smashing of a pane of glass the only sound in the night.

What are you up to?

She waited a few moments before focusing in on the shop interior with the *Present Eye*. Himmler was casually strolling about the shop like tourist. Every so often he picked up a wooden toy and examined it before gently replacing it on the shelf. She lost sight of him and searched around with the lens trying to locate him again.

Dammit. Where are you?

She crossed the street, sneaked in and closed the door, glass remnants tinkling to the floor. Behind her the shop bell jingled merrily and she jumped.

"I've been waiting for you, Fräulein. What took you so long?"

Tyler scanned about but could not find him. Marionettes hung motionless. Clowns and dolls smiled from corners as wooden trains travelled nowhere.

"I found your Russian doll, Fräulein. I do not think you should have it. I did not think it fair. But then, I decided I should, perhaps, give you a chance to reclaim your little *memento*. And so I brought you here to the place where you purchased it."

From what she could tell, Himmler was somewhere above her. She viewed the second level, but still could not see him. He was hiding somewhere, teasing her.

"All you need do is find it and it is yours. I will not intervene a second time. I have reunited the doll with her family, Fräulein May."

The little voice in Tyler's head stated Himmler was lying but she couldn't help herself. If she could get the bone back, she'd be able to use the contrap now. She could put Himmler's ghost straight into the *Ghost Portal* and set Freddy Carter free. She would be able to cross Himmler off the list for good. The prize made the risks worthwhile.

She crept around a central display counter heaped with marionettes and doll's houses and tried to find the rack of Matryoshka dolls. She found it near the back of the shop and quickly opened layer after layer of glossy painted wood. There were rows and rows of identical dolls and any one could be concealing the bone. She scanned the small army of figurines and tried to work faster as opened dolls spilled onto the ground. Sweat trickled from her temple. She heard the ceiling creak as Himmler shifted and sensed he was up to something somewhere above her on the next floor.

Albert materialised beside her and she stifled a shriek.

"Jeez, don't do that!" she whispered.

"Look out, Missy! 'E's got a gun," whispered Albert, ignoring the complaint. "I don't fink the doll is 'ere."

"How do you know that? It might be here."

"He just wants you 'ere so 'e can…"

A shot passed through Albert's head narrowly missing Tyler's left ear before shattering a glass shelf. Tyler ducked behind the central counter with Albert as further shots trashed the shop.

"Guess you were right. I'm a sitting duck." She took out her Taser gun and held it ready. If she could take him down with a Taser dart she figured she might be able to put him into the contrap.

Albert nodded.

"So you think he still has the doll?" she asked, peering over the counter and its mound of toys.

"The fing what he took from your suitcase? Aye. In 'is pocket, I'll wager."

"Can you get it for me? Presumably he also has the bones Mel and Lucy took."

"I don't know about that. A ghost 'as to be real strong to shift somefin' in the real world, but I can try. Wouldn't be the first time I picked a pocket. Wait here."

Tyler looked about as if to say *I can hardly go anywhere*, but Albert had already dissipated. More shots rained down from the upper level.

"Really, Fräulein, you *must* try harder," Himmler goaded, over-articulating in his German accent. "How will you ever find your prize, if you do not firstly try to seek it out?"

"You're a lying Nazi and I'm not listening to you," she countered. Shots ploughed into the counter inches from her head. She hunkered down and shivered, wondering what the Lüneburg police were doing.

Eating donuts with coffee?

She imagined a heaving beer hall of lederhosen-clad policemen swigging from tankards and dancing on long tables. The splintering of wood from another bullet sobered her.

Something small bobbed its way down the central stairway of the shop and then Albert appeared carrying it. He brought the wooden doll to her and she discarded its layers feverishly.

"You did it! Albert, thank you!" She tore open the final doll and swore: empty! "He still has it."

"Sorry, Missy. 'E must'a taken it out before I got there."

"It doesn't matter, Albert. Thanks for trying."

"I can go back."

"Wait a minute."

The gunfire had subsided and after a few seconds of silence, Tyler wondered if Himmler was still there.

"I'll go see what's 'appenin'." Albert vanished again.

Tyler risked a peek up the stairs. All was quiet. Then she heard distant police sirens.

"Albert?" she called.

"It's alright, Missy. Himmler's scarpered," Albert called down from the gallery.

She climbed stairs to join him. Too late again. A tall open window wobbled in its frame, opened in a hurry. Beyond it, a silhouetted figure disappeared among Lüneburg's rooftops.

Finger Bones

Lucy sat up and gingerly put a hand to her head. She pulled stale gum from her mouth, binned it and rubbed her eyes. When she looked up, Tyler was staring at her, reproach in her eyes.

"You got everyone drunk."

"Morning," mumbled Lucy. She scratched her head and squinted back at Tyler, clearly in pain. "Can someone *please* close the curtains? It's *way* too bright in here. Could you turn the TV off?"

"We need some background noise. The TV stays on. Last night you got everybody drunk. Except me, that is." Tyler confronted Lucy with the empty juice bottle. "Read."

Lucy screwed up her face, trying to focus on the label and then looked away.

"It's just fruit juice. Isn't it?" She took the bottle and tipped it upside down. "Wasn't it?"

"It was alcoholic," stated Tyler.

"Really? Sorry, *Mother*." Lucy fought her way out of bed and stumbled across the hotel bedroom to shut the curtains. She flopped back onto her covers and hid her face with her hands. "Good night though."

"It might have been a good night for you, but while you were out, comatose, Himmler's glove broke into our room and stole back his bones. I don't know what else he's taken."

Lucy sat up again. Across the room Melissa struggled out of bed, roused by the conversation.

"Himmler was here?"

"I think he came for the contrap but he went looking for his bones first. I disturbed him while he was going through my stuff. He ran. I followed."

"Why didn't you wake us?" asked Melissa, joining them and pulling a bath robe over pyjamas.

"I tried. You were both out cold."

"But…"

"That juice was fifteen percent alcohol." Tyler passed her the bottle. "Exactly how much of the stuff did you drink?"

"I don't know. Think we bought five bottles." Melissa groaned and dug around inside her robe. She relaxed when she found what she was looking for.

"He didn't take my bone. It's still in my pyjama pocket."

Tyler looked distastefully at Melissa.

"You *slept* with Himmler?"

"Gross," said Lucy.

"Don't say that. Eweh! He *was* in a plastic bag. I thought it was the safest place. Anyway, it wasn't *him*. It was just his finger bone."

Lucy laughed aloud until she felt a sharp pain in the shoulder.

"Ow! What you hit me for?"

Melissa stared her out.

"You slept with him too…" Melissa pointed to a steel money capsule strung on a chain around Lucy's neck. Lucy had scratched Himmler's name down the side with the tip of her throwing knife.

"Hmmmm. It was the safest place…" said Lucy.

"Wow. You are *so* annoying," said Melissa.

Tyler smiled for the first time that day.

"Well it's a good job you did what you did. Otherwise we'd have lost all three bones. At least we still have two left.

"Oh! Someone else visited during the night too," she added. "You can come out now, Albert."

Albert materialised, to Lucy's and Melissa's amazement. They had seen ghosts before, but not beyond the contrap's portal, not except for the gloves. Albert doffed his cap. He stood there with them, a Dickensian ghost boy in a tattered waistcoat and knee-length shorts, grubby from head to foot, as transparent as a jellyfish and Tyler's equal in height.

"Wotcha."

"Albert? Is that really you?" asked Melissa. She reached out and passed her hand through Albert with no resistance.

"Hey, watch it!"

"Sorry, Albert."

"Hi, Albert," said Lucy, staring at him open-mouthed.

"That's not all," explained Tyler. "Albert, here, can move things. He can vanish and reappear as he wishes. And he can move stuff. It's pretty cool."

"Oh yeah. Only small fings, though. Nuffin' big, like."

"Go on, Albert. Show them."

Albert drifted over to the bedside table where an empty juice bottle now stood and tried to grab the bottle. His hand passed through the glass but he managed to knock it over. It clunked onto the carpet and rolled to a halt.

"Oh. Guess that were just too big. See what I means?"

"Don't worry, Albert. You're doing fine," said Tyler. "Do you know what gives you the power to be able to move things?"

"Can all ghosts do that?" asked Lucy.

"I dunno. I finks they can, but some probably never even tried. It feels like – I dunno – like if ya really feel strong about somefin', you can shift it. Like if I were real angry, I could do somefin', make somefin' in your world move."

"So the stronger your emotional state, the more powerful you become?" suggested Melissa.

"Yeah, maybe. Somefin' like that I s'pose. I don't really know 'ow it works."

"Can everyone see you, or is it just us?" Lucy had picked up the bottle and was looking dubiously at the label again. "I think I may still be under the influence."

"He's here, Lucy," Tyler confirmed. "It's not the drink."

"I need a coffee," said Lucy, replacing the bottle. She went to the corner where there was a tray for hot drinks, checked the water level in the kettle and switched it on.

Tyler had some catching up to do.

"So, Albert, where've you been since you left the contrap? I thought you'd appear in my bedroom but you just vanished." She tried to sound matter-of-fact about this but could not conceal her frustration. She realised she was angry with him for abandoning her and she wanted answers.

"I, er, I been busy, Missy. I been searchin', ya see."

"What for?"

"Well, I kind'a been searching for old Adolf."

"What?"

"What?"

"*WHAT?*" asked Tyler.

Albert raised his hands defensively.

"I been lookin' for Adolf Hitler. Alright?"

"Why, exactly? We know where he is. He's in the contrap. I put him there."

"Beggin' ya pardon, Missy, I ain't so sure. After he were sucked in wiv all them other ghosts, them Jews put him in this room. Like a sort of prison, it were. That were all well an' good. Problem is, 'e didn't seem t' stay there for too long." Albert shook his head sadly and absently brushed ghostly soot from the corner of his waistcoat.

Tyler's pulse quickened. She was sure bad news was coming and she didn't want to hear it. Albert became more timid. *He* didn't seem happy either.

"What? Why? Where did he go?"

"That's the problem, Missy. Nobody knows. I searched everywhere for him after that. I mean everywhere in the *Ghost Portal*. 'E were imprisoned in

88

there, but I searched his prison. Couldn't find hide nor hair. 'E'd gone."

"So why didn't you tell me?" asked Tyler. "You never said anything about it."

"I were gonna tell you, honest I were! But then you started talkin' about setting me free from the portal an', anyway, I didn't like to worry ya. I thought you 'ad enough on ya plate what with all them other gloves an' all."

Tyler sat down on her bed, head in hands.

"Anyway, when you set me free from that contraption, I fought I'd better broaden the search."

"*Broaden the search*?" said Melissa.

"Aye. I fought 'e might be 'angin' round 'is grave. You know… Tha's what ghosts like to do, in general. We kind o' get this pull. We end up 'angin' round places we used to know. Houses we lived. Places we worked. Don't ask me why. We don't mean t' do it. It just 'appens. The ones who suffer it the worst are called *reveries*. Reveries just 'ang around like they're in a trance. They don't do nufin' else."

"Are they dangerous?" asked Melissa.

"Oh no," said Albert matter-of-factly. "Reveries is 'armless really. It's like they're looking for somefin' – some lingerin' sign of life – some kind of human feelin' or 'motion. You don't want to get caught up wiv too many of 'em, though. They can latch on to your 'motions. They'll leave you real dead inside."

"Don't you mean *emotions*?" asked Lucy.

"That's what I said, ain't it? It's like they'll drain all the 'motions right out of ya. And without 'motions you ain't human no more, and you don't have no reasons to do nufink no more. You just sit there like – well – a reverie.

Stay there too long an' they'll suck the very life from ya bones. Then you'll be one of 'em. You end up forgetting every good reason you ever had to live. Then you just wants to ends it all. Most folks kills 'emselves. Come to fink of it, they ain't 'armless at all. Them reveries is deadly!"

"So you thought if Hitler had escaped the contrap, he might've returned to the place he died, or to the place he was buried," said Melissa.

"Was he there? Has he become a reverie?" asked Lucy, perching on her bed and cradling a cup of coffee.

"No," said Albert with concern. "I couldn't find 'im anywhere. It's like 'e's just gone."

"Well, he *is* only a ghost now," Melissa pointed out. "He can do that, can't he?"

"Ghosts can hide 'emselves from the livin' but they can't hide from the dead. I been seeking 'im ever since I left that contraption."

"You mean, you can see other ghosts and we can't?" asked Lucy.

"I can. Thousands of 'em. And millions. Everywhere I go."

"So are there ghosts here? Right now? Ghosts other than you?"

"Oh yeah. Of course." Albert doffed his cap to an area of thin air over by the door, nodded his head in greeting before turning back to the girls. "But don't worry. They're alright. Well, most of 'em." He grinned.

"So how did you find Tyler?"

"We ghosts can sense that contraption. We can feel its power. It weren't 'ard to find Missy."

"Of course," said Lucy.

"And you should know; them gloves feels it too."

90

Tyler took out her list, drew a line under the last name and wrote.

Find out what has become of Adolf Hitler

*

With everything that had happened in the last two days, Tyler wanted an end to Himmler sooner rather than later. They had planned to collect as many summoning artefacts as they could before attempting to trap the gloves, but Himmler was still around Lüneburg somewhere. The small voice in her head told her so. She relived a conversation as they waited in the Land Rover a short way down the darkened street from the house concealing Himmler's shrine.

"We must go back," she'd said, sitting on the edge of her bed.

"Way too dangerous," said Melissa.

"I agree," said Lucy.

"With who?"

"With Tyler. We go back. Break in again. We still have two finger bones to use. If Himmler's there, Tyler can trap him."

Again, it all sounded so simple, but in Tyler's experience nothing ever worked out that way. She tried not to dwell on it for fear anxiety would send her into a panic attack. She wiped condensation from the Land Rover window and peered down the road at the old house.

"This is suicide," said Melissa. "We must be certifiably nuts."

It was two in the morning and Tyler was as prepared as she could be. She checked the contrap. The bone Melissa had taken from the shrine was clamped to the device with a rubber band. She didn't want to lose the artefact during any struggle and the elastic worked fine. The other remaining finger bone was safely in Lucy's money capsule, suspended around her neck. Tyler checked the house interior again with the *Present Eye*. All quiet. No sign of any human activity anywhere. It was odd. Where was the sleeper? He should be in bed on the second floor. The place looked different.

"Something's wrong. Let's go in."

They found the driveway empty and Tyler picked the lock as before. The house was cold inside and she quickly noticed the antique sideboard was gone, along with its phone and bronze. Further probing revealed all the furniture had been removed and they hurried to the basement, hoping to find some evidence of what they'd previously discovered, but this also had been cleared. The shrine was empty except for the huge stone plinth that had held Himmler's fragile remains.

"Guess we spooked them," said Lucy.

Tyler swept her torch around hoping to find something but even the swastika and its surrounding paintwork had been scrubbed away. She sat resignedly on the edge of the cold plinth.

"They've cleaned up and moved out, bones and all."

"What now?" asked Melissa.

Tyler couldn't talk. She was too busy *kicking* herself. She'd been so close to Himmler but had let him slip away.

"I guess we call it in. Tell Chapman. Move on," said Lucy. "Maybe he can track down the truck with the tracers. That might lead somewhere…"

Tyler remembered something then. It had been a precaution at the time and she'd since put it out of her mind, not even sharing it with Melissa. She smiled to herself.

"There is one thing."

"What's that?" asked Melissa.

"When we got back from here the other night, I injected one of those micro tracers into the bone I took. I forgot I'd even done it 'til just now."

"You mean…"

"Himmler took a tracer without knowing," Tyler confirmed.

"And as long as he keeps the bone with him we'll know exactly where he is," said Lucy.

"Exactly." Tyler took out the tracer monitor from her bag and switched it on. A map of their location appeared on the screen, devoid of any markers. She widened the area until a marker consisting of numerous, coloured concentric rings showed itself.

"That's our hotel room," explained Melissa. "That's the case of tracers."

Lucy stared at the screen.

"So where's Himmler?"

The Thieves of Antiquity

Himmler had fled. They found him on the tracer monitor, a green dot, halfway over the North Atlantic.

"Looks like he's on a flight bound for South America," said Melissa.

"Forget him," said Lucy.

"For now," said Tyler. "At least we know we can track him down when we're ready. We've more important business. Each of the remaining gloves will be trying to secure artefacts to make sure we don't get them first. They now know what we're doing. I say we get on with it. It'll make things easier later when we're ready to trap them. Maybe we can get them all in the same place. Get it over with. Trap them all at once and get on with our lives."

"And Hitler?" asked Melissa.

"Hmmm. I guess we keep a lookout for him. Until we know where he is, I'm not going to worry too much.

He could still be in the contrap. What if he hid himself away in there? Albert could have missed him."

"Maybe I did, Missy," said Albert, appearing beside Tyler and making her lurch. "Suppose it's possible."

"Albert, don't *do* that!"

"Sorry."

"We'll call this place in to Chapman. Let him know the address and that something dodgy was going down here. He'll be able to trace the house owner and have them investigated."

"Something's been bothering me," said Lucy. "How did Himmler know where to find the finger bone you took? You said you hid it in a Babushka doll, right?"

"Their proper name is Matryoshka dolls."

"Whatever. It doesn't change the question."

"I don't know how he knew it was there. Maybe he guessed."

"Spies," said Albert.

"Could be, I suppose," said Melissa. "They do have our room bugged."

"I checked all the bugs," said Tyler. "There were only audio bugs. No visual. They had no way of looking into our room."

"Wrong," said Albert.

"How then?"

"Them gloves are ghosts, right?"

"Ghosts and children. Yes," Melissa confirmed.

"So them gloved ghosts can see other ghosts."

"Ghost spies…" concluded Tyler. "You mean they've already enlisted ghost spies into their little club."

"I expect," said Albert. "What would you do if you was them?"

The girls exchanged horrified glances.

"Of course, them gloves can probably sense their own bones too."

"We're going to need you, Albert. You'll have to be our lookout. We can't even see them."

"I will, Missy. I swear. I'll watch over you. I fink tha's what I'm 'ere for."

*

The girls prepared to leave for Brazil, their previous celebratory mood dispelled by a crawling apprehension and the knowledge that Himmler had apparently gone ahead of them. Tyler wondered if Josef Mengele was travelling with him.

Chapman was fairly philosophical when he'd heard the news, seemingly pleased with the leads their trip had provided so far. He arranged for their newly acquired archaeological collection to be delivered independently to their hotel in São Paulo, Brazil, along with the black cases.

Tyler, relieved to be free of the bugged hotel, sought an empty washroom in the airport lounge, shut herself inside a vacant cubicle and switched the contrap to the spiral.

"Zebedee? If you can hear me, I need to see you. Zebedee Lieberman?"

She waited only a few moments before Zebedee appeared in the contrap's crystal, puffing on his long-stemmed pipe.

"Hello, Miss May. How are you this fine day?" he asked with a subtle nod.

"Hi, Zebedee. I've been better," said Tyler. "I was wondering if you managed to find out anything else about the tear?"

"The what?" Zebedee waved his pipe.

"The tear. The gap I saw in the *Ghost Portal*."

"Oh, yes!" Eyes flashed with recollection. "The tear... No. Sorry. Not a sausage. I really don't know anything about that." He puffed enthusiastically on his pipe until he was enveloped by a small cloud of tobacco smoke.

Tyler studied him as best she could through the haze. All he seemed to want to do today was smoke and she sensed something was wrong, but didn't know what.

"So you *did* look for Izabella? To ask her about the tear?"

"Oh, yes! Izabella! You know, that completely slipped my mind. Tell you what, I'll go right now and see if I can find her."

"I thought she might..." began Tyler, but Zebedee had already turned and was tapping his cane and humming to himself as he walked away.

"Zebedee?" Tyler called after him. "Wait! Mr Lieberman..."

Zebedee's spidery form dwindled into the portal's mist until she could see him no more.

That was strange.

It was unlike Zebedee to be so inattentive. Tyler began to turn the contrap, meaning to switch it to the *Safeguarding Skull*, when she stopped. Someone else was coming out of the fog in the crystal. Two figures drew near and she recognised the Polish twin girls.

"Dzien Dobry," they said in unison, adding short bows to their greetings.

"Hi," replied Tyler, wondering if they wanted something. She waited a moment as they watched her. When neither spoke, she asked them, "Can I help you?"

The twins glanced at each other and then back at Tyler.

"It is *we* who wish to help you," stated the one on Tyler's left.

"Okay."

"Yes," said the other twin. "We want to help. We've heard about you. We want to help you fight the prześladowca."

"The *oppressor*, she means."

"Great," said Tyler. "I could use all the help I can get. Thanks, but how do you think you can help me fight?"

The twins looked uncertainly at each other.

"We don't know yet, but we want to help. The bad men took us and locked us away. They took us away from our family and experimented on us."

"Then we became sick and died," continued the other twin. "We want to help because we cannot bear the thought of it all happening again, but that is what will happen if *he* is not stopped."

"We don't want it to happen to other people, to other boys and girls, to other families."

"Who are you? Where are you from?"

"I'm Danuta and my sister is Kinga," said the left twin.

"Our parents were Hungarian gypsies who travelled into Poland before we were born. We don't know what happened to them. They are not with us. The Nazis took us. They rounded up our whole community, took our horses and burned our wagons. They put us all into work camps. They lied to us."

Tyler recalled the slogan from the gates of Auschwitz that had been used in Himmler's shrine.

98

Work sets you free.

"The oppressor is coming," said Kinga. "He is moving and planning. He is getting ready."

"Who's the oppressor?" asked Tyler.

"He is the spirit of intolerance. He is false. He sits in judgement where he has no right to judge," explained Kinga.

"The oppressor will kill innocent people. He wants to kill many," said Danuta.

"As many as he can gather," added Kinga. "He is the spirit of the Nazi and he opposes the righteous. He brings false hope to those he misleads and war follows in his wake. And suffering and death."

"And the Underworld," added Danuta.

Tyler was unnerved. She wanted to end the conversation.

"When the oppressor took our families, he did many cruel things…" said Danuta.

"I'm sure you can help me somehow," said Tyler, secretly wanting to go. She didn't wish to hear details of the twins' slow torture and death in what was, undoubtedly, Hell on Earth. She couldn't bear it. She hated everything the Nazis stood for and the more she learned, the deeper her loathing grew. "Listen for me. I'll call for you if I think you can help with anything."

She said goodbye and slipped the switch to the skull before returning to Melissa and Lucy, looking pale and feeling giddy. She told the girls what she'd learned from the contrap and they sipped drinks at a coffee bar as they waited uneasily for their boarding announcement, in desperate need of distraction. Melissa bought a newspaper and read it while an iPod piped gothic rock into Lucy's ears. Tyler sat watching people walk by, looking for Josef

Mengele or Silvia Bates, and mulled over Zebedee's strange behaviour and the twins' portentous words. She wanted to talk to Albert about it all, but he didn't seem to be around.

A moment later, Melissa lowered the paper, looking shocked and spoke in a hushed tone.

"Hey guys, I think we made the headlines."

The other two looked at her. Lucy removed her earphones.

"What?" asked Tyler. "What headlines?"

Melissa turned the paper to show them the front page where a bold title read *Die Diebe der Antike*.

"It says, *The Thieves of Antiquity*. And I think it's about us."

Lucy and Tyler shuffled their chairs closer to lean in.

"Read it," said Tyler, nerves jangling.

" 'A recent burglary on a privately owned house on the outskirts of Lüneburg has today been condemned by the victims as *an unforgivable act of extreme national injury*. Among numerous other irreplaceable archaeological artefacts stolen were priceless Greek urns, ancient Celtic broaches and a coin collection of considerable worth. The private collection was of great value to the owners, and to German antiquity itself.' "

"Oh no!" said Tyler, feeling her heart jolt. "They're turning this into a political attack."

Melissa continued.

" '*These thieves of our antiquity should be tracked down and held to account*, said the collection's owner today, who has requested anonymity. *They are not only stealing other people's property, but also eradicating important evidence of our nation's past.*

" 'Police are today dubbing the culprits the *Thieves of Antiquity* and are busily seeking connections with other possibly associated archaeological crimes, with a view to furthering investigations. An anonymous source has suggested the theft is the work of foreign spies who do not blanch at personal profiteering through damage to the German nation.' "

"That's not good," sang Lucy.

"I think we made a mistake taking all that stuff," said Melissa, panic elevating her voice.

"Good job we didn't try to bring it with us," said Tyler, suddenly tensing. She felt a wave of nausea and the start of a panic attack. Melissa was quickly there with an arm around her shoulder, speaking the words Tyler needed to hear.

"It will be alright. It will be alright, Tyler."

The attack subsided and Tyler revisited the washroom to splash cold water over her face and the back of her neck. She looked at herself in the mirror.

What are you doing? You're sixteen years old! You should be at home with your parents. You should be playing Xbox games in your bedroom, flirting with boys, or working on your athletics form, not chasing Nazi ghosts around the world on some mad quest to save it from 'the oppressor'...

She straightened her clothes and her makeup before re-joining the girls and ordering a fresh hot chocolate. She felt a tangible need for sugar.

"They seem terribly upset about losing a few old pots and coins," said Melissa when Tyler had sat down and composed herself. "Do you think we took something important?"

"More important than a collection of priceless antiques?" asked Lucy. She folded a fresh stick of gum into her mouth.

"Yeah. That's exactly what I mean. All that stuff must've been there for a reason. Maybe we missed something. Maybe there was something among the pieces they *really* didn't want to lose."

PART TWO

São Paulo Institute

1.45 a.m.: São Paulo airport, Brazil.

A humid heat hit Tyler as she descended from the Boeing 767, among a multitude of travel weary passengers. Airport lights fought back the night. It was summer in Brazil, but a monsoon had pummelled the area as they'd landed and it rained still as the girls made for passport control in the shadow of Mr Flynn.

Tyler knew that somewhere in this city the bones of Mengele rested uneasily. She shivered and it wasn't because of the rain.

When they reached their pre-booked hotel, the Parque Balneario, they were astonished by Chapman's choice of venue. The hotel was luxurious, set in a stunning position within a picturesque, sweeping cove. From their shared bedroom suite, they stepped out onto a veranda overlooking beaches and the shimmering sea. It was beautiful even at night, moonlit with accents of electric lighting, warm yellows and neon blues.

"Not bad," said Lucy, who had barely spoken for the last two hours but had played *Pandora's Tower* on her Nintendo nonstop, bloodshot eyes a testimony.

"It don't get much better than this," said Albert, joining them once their porters had left.

Tyler wished she was here for a different reason. It would be fantastic to hit the beach and holiday, relax, read, suntan and play beach volleyball. Another time. In the morning they were to stakeout the São Paulo Institute for Forensic Medicine and plan a way in. Still, she hoped she could squeeze in at least an hour on the beach to recuperate from the flight before they went to work.

The hotel phone rang and Melissa went back inside to answer it.

"The cases arrived ahead of us," she said when she returned. "Reception asked if we wanted them sent right up to the room so I said yes. They should be here any minute."

"Thanks."

Tyler yawned and went inside to unpack, though she hoped it would be a short stay. She couldn't resist taking out her list and checking it. Himmler's name was already ticked. Below that was Mengele, soon to be ticked off, and then only three Nazis remained. She was exhausted but was tempted, even so, to head out to the Institute right away. She thought she might sleep well if she could just tick off one more name.

She gave up on her unpacking when Chapman's delivery arrived at the door, hauled by a thin, moustached porter. Between them, the girls dragged the cases to a space in the middle of the room and carefully opened them. Everything was there, packed carefully, just as they had left it. They stacked the two black cases containing equipment at the end of Lucy's bed and turned their attention to the hoard of stolen goods. Lucy took out the first object and passed it to Melissa, who unwrapped it for them all to examine: an ancient terracotta bowl with a single incised swastika on one side.

"Looks Celtic to me," she said, setting it down and accepting the next object. "Before the Nazis hijacked it, this symbol simply meant good luck, or well-being. It was a symbol common to many civilizations." In this way they studied each of the artefacts in the cases and confirmed that they all bore one or more swastikas, though some of the symbols were clockwise facing and some were anticlockwise.

They stopped, with a third of the objects still in their packaging, when Melissa unwrapped a small, worn, lead box. This too, would have been placed alongside the growing collection, but it was different from the rest as it bore no markings at all, only the patina and distress of time. It was ten centimetres square and five deep, with a hinged lid. With trepidation, Melissa carefully prised it open and peered inside.

"Empty," she said, showing the others.

"Wonder what was in there." said Albert.

"Whatever it was, it's gone now," said Lucy.

"Do you think someone tampered with our stuff?"

"Who knows?" said Tyler.

Melissa passed the box to Tyler. It was heavy for its size. She set it to one side and they examined the remaining items, but there was nothing else strange or out of place as each piece carried a swastika, even the Indian artefacts and coins.

"Odd that this is the only item in the collection without a swastika," said Tyler.

"Very," agreed Lucy.

"I'm not seeing anything that stands out as being more valuable than the rest," said Melissa. "But I'm not sure. I'd say the lead box is probably worth considerably less than the other pieces. I don't think it's that ancient. I'll photograph and catalogue everything in the morning, run each artefact through the British Museum database, see what comes up. I'll see if Chapman has any contacts who'll help us out."

*

The sky was a faultless, celestial blue as they approached the São Paulo Institute for Forensic Medicine in the taxi, passing high-reaching palms and lush shrubbery. Skyscrapers dominated the sprawling city of São Paulo. A sticky heat forced them to drive with windows fully down as the high midday sun glanced across windscreens with blinding flashes.

Their driver, one of Chapman's operatives, named Fabio Costa, was tall and dark, clean shaven and excessively polite. His taxi looked like it belonged in a museum and was devoid of air conditioning, but he insisted on wearing a garishly new chauffeur's hat and big, sixties-style, mirrored shades. He proudly showed the girls photos of his wife and seven children from his wallet while driving, and laughed when he almost sideswiped another car. Horns blared. Traffic weaved chaotically on vast, multiple-lane roads. Fabio dropped them off near the Institute and drove away with the promise to return upon one call to his mobile phone.

The girls watched the old taxi join an eternal stream of traffic and turned their attention to the stately building of the Institute and its pleasant, landscaped grounds. The Institute itself was an impressive, three storey, pale-stone building. Its imposing front was grand, with two sets of steps leading up to an arched entrance, sided by Romanesque columns. Other magnificent university buildings stood close by, across the broad lanes of Rua Teodoro Sampaio.

The girls sheltered from the sun beneath a huge, purple-flowered tree.

"Where do we start?" asked Lucy, looking around and shrugging.

Tyler passed around camouflaged, miniature, remote access CCTV cameras; three each.

"We take a stroll around the grounds and plant these wherever we see a good view of the entrances. Use anything to hand as an anchor point. Hide them if you can, or put them where no one will notice."

"If we split up we'll do it faster," suggested Melissa.

"Good idea. Meet back here when you're done. If anyone questions you, stick to the cover story. Try to look like you know where you're going," Tyler added. "We'll draw less attention that way and with any luck we'll be taken for students. Like Chapman said, we'll give it twenty-four hours and see what the Micro Sat Cams pick up. Then we'll have a pretty good idea what we're up against."

Tyler knew she could have used the contrap to spy on the Institute and its visitors, but this way was less conspicuous and it also meant the other girls could do their fair share of trolling through hours of footage.

Less than twenty minutes later they met up again beneath the same purple tree.

"All done?" asked Tyler as Lucy arrived.

"Yep."

"All done."

"Great." Tyler took out her phone and dialled Fabio's number. "Let's hit the beach."

*

The beach was unsettlingly relaxing. Tyler wanted to forget all about their mission for a while but she found that almost impossible. Images of Mengele and Himmler kept finding their way into her mind and she heard the twins telling her over and over that 'the *oppressor* is coming.'

All the same, the sun on her skin felt like it was doing her good and she watched holidaymakers enjoying themselves for several hours.

Lucy caught a cab back into town, ignoring Melissa's objections. Melissa returned to her towel on the beach.

"You think she's meeting up with a Nazi spy?" she asked, passing Tyler a chilled Coke. Tyler cracked the ring-pull and took a swig.

"I don't know. What do you think?"

"I just don't trust her. Even after everything we've been through."

"Yeah, I know what you mean. And wouldn't you expect everyone to want the beach? Oh no, not Lucy. She has to go into town. What's she say she's doing, anyway?"

"I think she said shopping. I don't know."

"Right. Well, she loves spending money alright. Maybe she's afraid the sun will tan her pasty, gothic skin."

"You think we should follow her? Find out what she's up to?"

"For sure. We should."

"Are we going to?"

"Not today," said Tyler. She sipped her Coke and turned over to get some sun on her back.

*

Twenty-four hours passed quickly and Tyler awoke late the next morning having slept more deeply than she had in a month. She checked her watch and groaned.

11.00 a.m.

The Micro Sat Cams needed to be collected and the footage examined.

Melissa scanned the walls of their room and then furniture, door handles and light switches.

"Anything?" asked Tyler, when Melissa had fed the data to her laptop.

"Nothing of note. Hotel staff. And us, of course. No gloves."

"Good."

Several hours later, the three girls had collected the MSCs and were back in their hotel room, trawling through a tedious amount of footage that had been recorded each time the motion-sensing cameras were triggered into action. Even with this limitation, nine cameras secluded around a busy university institute still generated a remarkable amount of footage. The prospect of examining all this felt mind-numbing to Tyler.

Ahh! Chances are I'll die of boredom long before the gloves get me.

They ordered pizza from room service and sat for hours, barely speaking and trying to stay focused. Melissa used her laptop to view footage and she'd rigged the hotel TV to receive an image from another source for Lucy. Tyler was lumbered with the tracer monitor and she could feel eye strain steadily mounting, the longer she squinted at the small screen. She watched students coming and going, professors carrying armfuls of folders and, once, a lab technician pushed a shrouded cart past the secluded camera. Later on when the daylight had gone, the same camera showed her short segments of a patrolling security guard's movements.

At five minutes past six, Melissa gave a shout.

"Ha! I think I've found something! Come see this."

The others paused their footage, grateful for the interruption and went to peer over Melissa's shoulder. Melissa rewound the digital video, clicked 'stop' and then 'play' within the software control panel. On the laptop screen a grainy, dark image of a figure waited by a side entrance of the institute, in shadow. Tyler watched for a few seconds, wondering who it was, until the figure absently took a few steps forward and looked around the doorway, down the path leading away into the darkened grounds. She caught a flash of moonlight from the peak of an official cap.

"What was that?"

"It's just a security guard," stated Lucy.

"Uh huh," said Melissa. "But watch this next bit. It gets more interesting."

As they eagerly watched, a second man entered the screen. He stopped to talk with the guard before passing something to him. The new figure took something small from his pocket and also passed this to the guard. Then he nodded and made a mock salute before leaving the same way he'd come.

"Can you close in on that a little?" asked Tyler.

"Sure. The resolution will get worse, but I'll try it." Melissa rewound and played the clip again, now with a close-up of the meeting point.

"It caught my attention because of this guy's trilby," she said, pointing to the visitor.

Tyler's stomach lurched.

"I'll bet money that's Mengele."

"What's he doing?" wondered Lucy.

Melissa rewound the video, closed in again and slowed the play rate. They watched Mengele talk with the guard and tip his hat in slow motion. He then reached into his inside coat pocket and passed something wrapped in a brown paper bag, to the guard. Before leaving, he took a small indiscernible object from another pocket and passed that also. The guard accepted each of these offerings with a curt nod.

"Bribing the security guard," said Lucy.

"You think he passed him money?" asked Melissa.

"Yeah. Think about it."

"And the second thing he passed over was his phone number," said Tyler.

"He's primed the guard to call him if he sees us turn up," Melissa concluded. "That's a shame."

"At least we know about it," said Tyler. "We'll go in tonight. If he's bought one, he's probably bribed them all. We also now know they only have one, maybe two, security guards there at night. Forget the rest of the recordings. We found what we we're after."

*

Fabio dropped them off outside the institute's closed car park and drove away. The girls, dressed completely in black, checked about to be sure no one was looking before clambering over the wall and the tall fencing, helping Melissa as she struggled clumsily. They gathered behind a taller patch of wall where trees grew closely together. Lucy rubbed her arm where she'd snagged it and swore under breath. Here they were hidden from the road and the institute building.

Tyler squinted into the crystal. The contrap was set to the *Present Eye* and she made a visual inspection of the institute. In a far corner of the building, she found a room with a row of TV monitors behind a desk, each one showing a different external part of the building. She passed the contrap's focus through laboratories, meeting rooms and storage chambers where row upon row of narrow drawers carried small labels. In one of these drawers she hoped to find Mengele's bones.

Most areas were unlit and unoccupied until she alighted upon a security guard pacing a corridor. She followed his movements until his patrol of the building and grounds ended at the room with the monitors, where he made himself a coffee, sat with his feet up and opened a magazine.

She lowered the contrap and turned to Lucy and Melissa.

"I know the route the guard takes now. Next time he leaves the security room to make his patrol, we'll go in. He'll be away from the monitors for fifteen to twenty minutes. That should give us a chance to find the bones."

Melissa's gaze flicked nervously from Lucy to Tyler.

"That's not very long," said Melissa. "That place is massive!"

"It's the best we can do. Unless anyone has a better idea?"

Lucy shrugged.

You're so helpful.

"So what happens if the guard sees us?" asked Melissa.

Lucy drew her Taser gun and feigned a shot.

"We take him down."

"Ready?" asked Tyler. Now her friends were giving her the jitters.

The others nodded. The girls pulled black balaclavas down to cover their faces.

"Comms check," Tyler said. The others checked their earpieces and microphones were working.

"Check."

"Check."

"Good. Let's get this over with."

The Monitor

Tyler led the way but the mission felt wrong from the start. Her nerves were shot and when Melissa tapped her on the shoulder to tell her Albert had joined them, she jumped a mile and almost shrieked. The little voice in her head was whispering something over and over. She tried to hear it more clearly over a cacophony of other thoughts and fears.

He's watching you. He's watching you. You know he's watching you...

Tyler sent Albert ahead to check for enemy ghosts.

She glimpsed movement in the bushes ahead of her and made everyone wait in silence for what seemed an age, until a black cat noticed them and darted away.

"I don't like it," Tyler whispered as they took brief respite. "I think we're being watched."

"By who?" asked Melissa.

"Mengele. He's here somewhere."

"You don't know that," said Lucy. "It's just your imagination. No one's watching us. Come on." Lucy took the lead and they continued under trees and shrubs, skirting the open ground of the car park. Albert returned to them.

"All clear," he reported. "Just a few reveries 'anging around their old bones. I didn't see Mengele anywhere."

They found the side entrance unguarded as they'd hoped.

"You're up, Moriarty," said Lucy, nodding to the locked door.

Tyler scanned the lock mechanism briefly with the *Present Eye* to see how best to pick it. She set to work, but her hands were shaking and the feeling of pressure to do it quickly actually made it harder. She faltered and withdrew the lock-pick, wiping sweat from her eyes.

"Come on!" harried Lucy with a sharp whisper. "We haven't got all day!"

Tyler met her gaze and offered her the tool.

"You think you can do better? Be my guest."

"Okay, okay. I'm sorry! Just get back to it. We've lost five minutes already because of that flaming cat and we only have about ten minutes left."

Tyler went back to work and was surprised when the door lock sprung open a moment later. She tested the handle and the door gave way. Melissa closed it gently after them, trapping them in the deeper darkness. They switched on their Maglites and viewed their surroundings. A corridor led to a flight of stairs and other passageways. The girls whispered.

"Right, ten minutes to search this place. We'll split up. Use the comms. Keep in touch. If you find anything, tell the others. If you..."

Lucy interrupted.

"Tyler, we know what to do."

"Okay. Right. Sorry."

"Good luck," said Melissa.

"Wait. Are you sure this is a good idea? I just…"

"Tyler, get a grip!"

"Right. Okay. Let's go."

They separated, Lucy heading upstairs while Tyler continued straight on and Melissa took a left turn into an adjoining corridor. Albert kept pace with Tyler, gliding.

"You alright, Missy?" he whispered. "You seems a bit out of sorts, like."

"I'll be okay, Albert. I guess it's what the twins told me that's got me so freaked out. But I'm glad you're here with me. I missed you." She didn't talk about Mengele. Didn't want to mention his name in case that somehow summoned him into her presence.

Albert grinned affectionately.

"I missed you too, Missy."

Tyler soon came to a room with floor-to-ceiling drawers. She began working her way from the bottom up on one side, reading each of the drawer labels. She quickly realised all the drawers in this room only contained single bones, or collections of bones, but all of the same type. There were no actual skeletons or collections that represented individuals, so she abandoned that room and moved on. She found the next few rooms devoid of any bones, or any other storage and figured they were lecture rooms or something similar. She entered another passageway and caught a glimpse of a torch beam sweeping about.

Albert materialised next to her.

"It's the guard. 'E's coming this way. Hide!" he warned before disappearing.

Tyler slipped back into the room she'd just exited and ducked beneath a large desk at the end of the room. She watched the light around her grow as the guard approached but it soon dimmed and left the room altogether.

"'E's gone," whispered Albert appearing again.

"The guard's just passed me on the ground floor," she informed the other girls via comms. "He's heading for the door we came in through."

Tyler eyed Albert.

"Could you follow him and let me know which way he's going? Don't let him see you."

"Right you are, Missy." Albert vanished.

Tyler crept back out into the corridor and headed deeper into the Institute. She was searching the next room when Albert reappeared.

"I ain't sure why, but that guard's left the 'ouse. 'E's gone," Albert reported.

"What? He's gone?"

"Yeah. He went the same way you came in, didn't 'e?"

"He's gone outside?"

"Last I saw of 'im, 'e were 'eading down the road," Albert confirmed.

"Why would he do that?"

"I dunno."

"Girls, you hearing this?"

"Yes," said Melissa through Tyler's earpiece.

"Roger that," said Lucy.

"What's going on?" asked Melissa.

Silence.

"I'll let you know when I find out," said Tyler. She searched the rest of the drawers in the room and found several disarticulated, yet complete, skeletons, but none of them were labelled as Josef Mengele. Several rooms later she stumbled upon the security room with the monitors and, thinking time was not so much an issue since the guard had gone, she decided to take a look around, wondering what she might learn. She took in the various views from the black and white CCTV cameras and thought, since the opportunity had arisen, that it would be a good idea to disable the recording device and erase any recordings it had made of her and the team. She was busily attempting this when Albert alerted her again.

"'Ere, Missy, there's another room in there. I just 'ad a look. There's one of them boxes with a man inside it." Albert was standing by and pointing to a door which, until now, Tyler had not noticed. Tyler saw the substantial padlock clamping a bolt on the door securely closed and her curiosity was aroused.

"You mean there's a TV in there showing a man on the screen?"

"That's what I said, ain't it?" said Albert.

Tyler searched about for something with which to prise off the lock and bolt. She found a toolbox under a bench and was soon jostling a crowbar in behind the bolt. She tugged and even hung from the bar, but the bolt didn't budge. She considered picking the lock.

"I've come to a stairway," she heard Melissa say. "I'm going up."

"Okay," said Tyler.

"Right," Lucy responded.

Tyler fetched a hammer from the toolbox and slammed it onto the end of the crowbar. The bar sunk a centimetre or so. She hit it again. And again. The fourth strike ripped the bolt's housing away from the wood and another smack sent it scudding across the floor. She opened the door and went in. A single PC monitor lit the small room. She sat on the only chair and watched the lone figure with interest. The screen showed a wiry, young man of about nineteen years old, Tyler estimated, chained and isolated in a dim cell. It was a prison. She hadn't expected this. The video image was an unwelcome distraction. She was looking for bones and resented this sudden complication.

"Give me a break," she muttered to herself. Then eyeing the prisoner, she said, "Who the heck are *you?*" She found the PC keyboard and used software, already up and running, to remotely close in on his face. She took out her phone and swore as she compared the image Chapman had sent to her phone before she'd left England. The prisoner was Weaver, Chapman's missing agent.

"Er, Cog? A little help down here," she said into her headset mic.

A moment later, Melissa responded.

"I'm heading down. Where are you?"

"Security. Far end of the building, just off a main corridor."

"I'll find you," said Melissa.

"Pointer, you got anything?" asked Tyler.

"Three plastic skeletons and some jars with weird stuff floating inside. I guess most of the storage must be on ground level."

Tyler left the PC monitor and went back into security to wait, but one glance at the bank of monitors chilled her. Mengele was approaching the building on the far right screen. He had soon left the image area which, Tyler judged, meant he was about to enter the Institute. She swore.

"Girls! We have a problem. I just saw Mengele heading this way."

"Huh?"

"What?"

Lucy said, "It's funny, but it sounded like Ghost just said *Mengele is heading this way*."

"I did. He is."

"That's not good," said Lucy.

"Pointer, get down here asap!"

"Roger that."

Melissa arrived and stood staring at Tyler, trying to catch breath.

"You said you needed help," she gabbled. "I mean, before Mengele showed up."

"In there," Tyler told her, urgently. "I need to know where they're holding the man on the screen prisoner. And I need to know fast. Presumably it's not here. We still haven't found the bones and now *he's* here. Can you trace the address somehow? There must be a signal coming from that camera, wherever it is."

Melissa peered past Tyler through the open doorway at the prisoner on the screen.

"Okay. I'm on it. It might be possible to track the IP address of the system. If we had the IP address we might be able to track the actual location. Maybe with Chapman's help we can…"

"Do it. Whatever it takes. We'll handle Mengele. Buy you some time."

Tyler dashed out into the hallway in time to glimpse Mengele passing the end of a passageway some distance away. He stopped and looked at her, smiled and raised his hat in greeting before disappearing around a corner. The classical tune he whistled echoed down the passage.

Well, if you think I'm going to follow you, think again.

"Albert, see what Menegele's up to, will you?"

"Will do, Missy." Albert darted away.

Tyler plunged into another room and searched drawer labels again. This room had complete, or nearly complete, skeletons in storage, but the drawer labels told her nothing except reference numbers from a cataloguing system. She froze when she heard the pounding of feet and peered out of the room to see Lucy running towards her.

"Lucy! In here!" Tyler beckoned urgently.

Lucy arrived and they both searched frantically.

"We need to find a logbook or a reference sheet or something. Something that tells us what's in each drawer," said Tyler.

"Where's Menegele's glove?" asked Lucy, going through files on a desk in the corner of the room. "Here. Think I found it."

"I'm not sure. He's up to something. He saw me. He knows we're here." Tyler looked over Lucy's shoulder at the open file she'd found. There was a list of names on a page, each with an accompanying reference number.

"That's it," said Tyler, going to the door again and checking down the corridor for Mengele. "Is he on the list?"

A sudden ringing startled them. Somewhere, someone or something had activated an alarm. It echoed deafeningly throughout the building.

"Have we triggered a security alarm?" bellowed Lucy.

"Sounds more like a fire alarm to me," shouted Tyler. "Keep looking."

"There's pages of this stuff," Lucy complained.

Tyler went to Lucy's side to help check down columns of names. Lucy let out a cry of frustration.

"He's not here!"

Albert materialised, drifting into the room and bringing a waft of air from the corridor. Tyler smelled smoke.

"'E's gone an' set alight to the place. It's on fire," Albert informed Tyler. "And 'e's 'eadin' back to the room where Mel's workin'."

"Oh no!" said Tyler. "Lucy, keep searching. I'll go help Mel." She headed back towards security at a sprint, slowing when Mengele emerged from a stairway some twenty metres from her. She stopped, drew her Taser.

"Give it up, little girl!" Mengele called to her, smiling smugly. "You cannot win."

"We've heard that line before, Josef," she called back and took aim. Mengele let something fall from his hand as he turned for the stairs. Tyler fired but missed him. She watched the small object he had dropped roll across the floor, smoking, and she ran as it exploded in a cloud of flame behind her. She felt the blast but managed to stay on her feet, stumbling into the security room where Melissa was hard at work.

"Hurry, Mel!"

"Ten seconds." Melissa's fingers rattled on the PC keypad. She scribbled notes on a piece of paper and crammed it into her jacket pocket. "All done. I think."

"Good. Mengele's still here somewhere, but he's set the place alight. We still don't have the bones and the police are gonna be here any second now. We have to get going, bones or not."

They left security and found the hallway amassed with smoke. The fire was spreading rapidly and they saw flames at either end of the building.

"Lucy?" called Tyler, trying to get her bearings. "Lucy, where are you?"

A man's voice replied. Mengele was eerily close by, hidden in the smoke.

"You will not find what you seek. You should leave before you are overcome by the fumes." He sounded pleased, almost happy, but then he spoke again and Tyler wondered if it was still Mengele speaking.

"You will get what is coming to you! You are nothing but a stupid, ignorant beast."

Tyler thought she saw a shape in the haze and fired another Taser dart. She felt the wire slacken and knew she'd missed again. She coughed uncontrollably and buried her lower face in the neck of her jacket, trying to filter the air she breathed. Her lungs burned.

Albert was instantly there, an inch from her face.

"This way, Missy! I can't see Mengele anymore. I think 'e's gone."

They followed Albert through a mass of smoke and came out into a small, windowless room where Lucy was still at work.

"It has to be in this room somewhere," she shouted. "I checked every drawer in the others. This is the last one." She pulled open drawer after drawer, not bothering to close any.

"I'm not sure," Tyler shouted back. "Mengele just said we wouldn't find them here. Sounded like he'd already moved them. Guess he's been watching the place the whole time."

Tyler examined the drawers as best she could through the haze and saw why Lucy had abandoned the labels. None of the drawers she could see were labelled at all.

Man, how do they ever find anything in this place?

Tyler felt sick from fumes and deaf from the fire alarm's maddening din. All she wanted to do was get out. She heard part of the building above them collapse and wondered how long it would be before it fell on them.

Then Lucy screamed.

"Lucy, we gotta get out now or we're gonna burn to death!"

"There's a safe. His bones have to be in the safe!"

Igarata

Lucy focused the *Present Eye* on the safe's locking mechanism and painstakingly cracked it, click by click. She opened the door to reveal a set of darkly-stained human bones, stored in numerous plastic bags, complete with a skull showing damage to the left brow ridge and some post mortem reconstruction of the upper jaw. She grabbed a bag and read Mengele's name on the label.

"That's it!" shouted Mel as Tyler opened the bag to lift out the skull. "I recognise the skull from a picture on the internet. It's all still here."

"Try the *Ghost Portal*, Tyler!" Lucy urged. "He can't be far away."

Tyler took the contrap from around her neck, set the switch to the spiral symbol and placed it on Mengele's skull to summon him.

"Grab the other bones! Albert can you locate Mengele? And we need fire extinguishers!" she barked.

Albert vanished, returning only a moment later to lead them to the next room where he pointed out of a small window.

"'E's right there, Missy!"

Tyler squinted into the darkness beyond the glass and saw a lone figure standing, watching them. Again Mengele tipped his trilby to the girls.

"It's not working," said Tyler. "It's like he's taunting us."

"What's wrong with it?" asked Melissa.

Outside, Mengele turned and walked away.

"No idea," said Tyler. The fire alarm died as, somewhere in the building, the system melted in the heat. Tyler snatched a thigh bone from a bag and pummelled the window until she had a clear shot, but Mengele was already out of range for her Taser, so instead, she fired a tracer dart at the retreating figure and had no idea if she hit her target or not. She grabbed three yellowed phalanges from another bag and pocketed them.

"Leave the rest. Come on. We're leaving."

Smoke was thick and choking in the corridor, blinding them.

Albert directed them to an extinguisher at the bottom of a smoking staircase and another at the end of a hall and they fought a path through burning debris to an exit, dowsing flames as they went with great blasts from the extinguishers.

They left the grounds, running. Mengele was gone and Tyler wondered why the contrap and the artefacts had not dragged him into the *Ghost Portal* as they should have done. The girls pulled off their balaclavas and slowed when they were a safe distance from the burning Institute.

Smoke spewed into the night sky, funnelling high over other buildings and trees.

The three girls looked at each other, breathless and stunned by the contrap's failure.

"If he knew the artefact wouldn't work on him, why was he even here?" asked Melissa.

"Yeah, if he knew *that*, why'd he bother watching the place an' everything?" agreed Lucy. "Jeez, I can't believe we went through all that for nothing."

"I guess he came for the contrap," said Tyler. "He wants it but he's also scared of it, doesn't want to get trapped in it. *You see?* He knows all about it! I think he hoped we'd all die in the fire and he could just collect it afterwards. I don't think fire would damage it."

Sirens wailed and flashing lights passed on the road as emergency vehicles closed in.

"Well, one thing's for sure; this mission just got a whole lot weirder," said Tyler. She took out her list and penned a tick next to Mengele's name. Then she fished around in her backpack for the tracer monitor and switched it on. An amber dot showed the tracer dart's position.

"It's moving," said Lucy as they gathered around the small screen.

"You only hit him," stated Melissa. "Bloody good shot!"

Tyler was amazed. She'd not dared hope the tiny tracer dart would find its mark, but it clearly had and, what's more, it seemed Mengele was unaware that it was lodged in the fabric of his coat or hat, or had penetrated his gloved body. Tyler smiled. For some reason that she did not understand, the artefact and the contrap had failed to summon him to the *Ghost Portal*, but at least she'd tagged him and, for the time being, she could locate him at will.

*

Tyler paced the hotel room, torn. The OCD part of her wanted very much to pack up and move on to the next target, but there was a problem.

Agent Weaver.

She wrestled mentally for an hour while Lucy and Melissa each took a shower and dressed. She tried to watch TV for a while but, although she craved a diversion, it was somehow too distracting. She switched it off and took out her list. Beneath the last item, she added a new one.

Rescue Agent Weaver

She hated herself for it but, ultimately, she couldn't leave him imprisoned, not knowing he was *one of theirs*. She picked up her mobile and hit speed dial.

"Good morning, Ghost."

"I think I found Weaver."

"Oh? Where?"

"Not sure yet. He's in a prison of some kind. We saw him on a CCTV monitor. Can you trace an address from the camera IP?"

"Are you sure it's him?"

"Certain."

"A CCTV camera won't have its own IP address but the system it's hitched to will."

Tyler read out the information Melissa had scribbled down the night before, in the Institute.

"Well done, Ghost. Are the girls okay?"

"Fine."

"Good. Stay put until you hear from me. Weaver is most likely in São Paulo or somewhere close by. I'll be in touch." Chapman ended the call, leaving Tyler frustrated, but she was not waiting long. When her phone rang five minutes later she snatched it up.

"Yes?"

"Are you up for another jaunt tonight? We've established an address."

"Of course."

"Good. I'm texting it to you now. Get Weaver out. And, Ghost, try not to leave a mess behind. As far as the authorities are concerned, Weaver is not even in the country. I don't know what state he's in, but we can't afford to have him unearthed. He could be tried as a foreign spy."

"We'll do what we can."

"Get him out. Keep him safe. You can trust Fabio with your life. He doesn't look much but he's one of the best MI6 have in the field."

"I thought you were MI5."

"I am but I frequently work alongside MI6. I'm what they call a *bridger*. Good luck."

Chapman ended the call.

Tyler collapsed onto her bed and breathed a heavy sigh. It was going to be another long day.

*

Palms fluttered in a temperate wind and the surface of dark water rippled as the girls cruised. The grounds of the big house up ahead had a tropical ambiance, beautifully landscaped with patios, walkways, arbours, planted beds and verandas overlooking the lake where a stylish motorboat gently bobbed at the lake's edge. A nearby pool was edged with shimmering white tiles and floodlit a neon blue, though in this exclusive neighbourhood it was just another grand villa.

Chapman had informed Tyler of the owner's name and occupation: Senhor Barros, an international trader of outboard motors. The CCTV system in the locked room of the Institute led here and so it seemed Weaver was being held captive at this address in Igarata, a village, clustered around a hill-pitched lake, a little over twenty miles to the north east of São Paulo.

The girls viewed the house from Fabio's boat as he killed the engine and let the craft idle near the adjacent bank. Two hundred metres away, pool lights reflected on the lake.

"This is as close as I go," explained Fabio. "You can walk from here. I'll wait for you." He finished mooring the boat to a post on the bank and poked a Cuban cigar into his mouth.

The girls thanked him and clambered awkwardly ashore. Tyler checked her watch: 10.50 p.m.

"Why would a man who sells outboard motors have a guy held prisoner in his house?" asked Lucy. "It doesn't make sense."

"He's obviously involved in some *extra curricula* activities," said Melissa.

Tyler surveyed the property through the *Present Eye* and focused upon something on the kitchen floor.

"Any sign of Barros?" Lucy asked.

"Not yet, but I think he has a dog. I can see its bowl."

"Great."

Tyler rotated the contrap's gear and made her way visually into other rooms of the house. She passed through a lavish, but empty, bedroom and an exquisite bathroom before settling her view on a figure reclined on a couch with a dog curled up at one end.

"I found Barros. And his dog, though it looks pretty docile to me. Barros too, for that matter. I can't see any prisoner. No cellar. Nothing like a prison, or a cell." Tyler switched the contrap to *Flight*.

"Wait here," she said. She eased the lever round and gently left the ground. She flew high over the house and, after checking that nobody was around to witness her appearance, descended outside the front door. She tested the handle. Unlocked!

Phew! This is going to be easier than I thought.

She had an idea and flew over the house to the back where the pool and grounds edged the lake. She lowered herself until Barros and his dog came into view through large, glass doors. Barros was a big man, overweight, but still well-muscled, wearing a grubby, white vest and massive shorts that ended around his broad knees. He kept a long, oiled moustache as though this might compensate for his retreating hairline. Ogling a boxing match on a widescreen TV and systematically stuffing corn chips into his wide mouth, he was oblivious to her presence.

Tyler pocketed a handful of stones from a gravelled plant bed and flew back up over the house to settle gently on the roof, leaning on the apex with her forearms. From here she had a good view of the back end and the pool area. She whispered to the girls through her headset.

"He's pretty relaxed. His front door's unlocked. You two make your way round the front. I'll cause a distraction at the back. His lounge exits onto the pool area so he'll probably just use the patio doors. Search the house while I keep him busy outside. See if you can find anything. A secret door or something I've missed. Be quick."

"Right."

"If you say so."

Tyler aimed a stone at a huge planter that housed a stocky palm and ducked behind the roof's apex when the pot shattered with a loud smash. She heard the dog inside barking and was surprised when other dogs joined in the clamour.

"That should do it. Go!"

"We're going in," said Lucy.

Tyler used the *Present Eye* to follow Barros as he left the couch to peer out of the back doors. Three more dogs had entered the lounge and were heckling to get outside. Barros slid the doors open and stepped out by the pool as the dogs streamed out around him, snuffling at the ground and baying at the scented air.

"Did you say he has *a* dog?" Lucy asked. "It sounds like more than one."

"Er, yes. He has a dog. And three others," explained Tyler. "I must've missed them somehow. But it's alright. They're all out the back around the pool. I'll do what I can to keep them here while you search. But hurry!"

Tyler launched a second stone high into the air and it came down on white tiles with a sharp crack. The stone skittered away into the lake as a keen hound made after it, skidding at the water's edge.

Another stone landed in the pool with a plop and sank while a crazed dog leapt in after it.

Barros shouted something in Portuguese and peered into blue, chlorinated water. He seemed not to notice the small missile settling on tiles at the bottom of the pool. He caught hold of the struggling dog and helped it out of the water, hauling it by the scruff. The dog shook, to Barros' displeasure.

"Are you about done in the house?" Tyler whispered to Lucy and Melissa.

"Can you buy us a little longer?"

"I dunno. I think you'd best leave. He's not gonna stay out here all night." Tyler was aiming another stone when she noticed a large, heavy-looking trapdoor out beyond one edge of the pool. It was bolted shut and fastened with a heavy padlock.

Hello...

Tyler let another two stones fly, but decided she shouldn't push her luck when Barros peered up into the night sky. He was catching on to her game and *that* was dangerous. He bellowed a command in Portuguese to the dogs and headed for the lounge.

"Get out! He's going back in!" warned Tyler. "With the dogs..." She heard the girls swearing through her headset as she left the roof. Knowing Barros would be back in the lounge by now, she closed on the patio doors and hovered close enough to gently kick the glass, twice, before propelling herself back over the roof to look for the others. She joined the girls as they bolted from the house. They were ahead of the dogs and Barros, thanks to Tyler's last minute distraction, and were able to shut the door so that when Barros arrived in his porch, hounds wild with the scent of intruders, he had no reason to think anyone had just left.

The girls hid around the side of the house and heard, rather than saw, Barros open the door to check outside, restraining the snarling dogs. Again he shouted commands.

They heard the door close, much to their relief.

"What sort of dogs are they?" asked Lucy.

"Big ones," said Tyler. "Come on. I think I know where Weaver is." She led Melissa and Lucy back round to the pool and on to the trapdoor where she kept an eye on the lounge through its glass doors. Inside the house the din of frenzied hounds continued as they were driven mad by the trespassers' presence.

"Quick, while he's checking the house!" Tyler tried the trapdoor as Lucy dug about in her backpack. A moment later Lucy was prising a crowbar under the bolt and levering the lock clean off. She tried to lift the door but it remained shut under its own weight until Melissa and Tyler helped. Finally it came up and over, and they let it down quickly to rest on the ground the other side of a set of steps that descended into darkness.

Suddenly the noise from the dogs broadened and they knew Barros had released them. Hounds came tearing around the house with incredible speed and were at the girls, only slowing to consider who to attack first.

"Oh my God! We're gonna die!"

"What *are* they?" asked Lucy.

"Doberman Pinschers," Melissa stammered. "Guard dogs. Very good ones."

"Tasers out!" shouted Lucy, drawing her stun gun and shooting at the huge dog that was shouldering its way towards her. The dog reeled to the ground, whining, as electricity coursed.

"Yeah, that dog's *really* docile," said Lucy, levelling eyes at Tyler accusingly.

Melissa screamed as a dog launched itself at her, its black jowls foaming. She closed her eyes and turned away as she squeezed the trigger and shocked the animal with a Taser dart. She screamed again. The dog fell to the ground, where it remained, quivering. Tyler shot the third dog with her Taser and wondered how she might deal with the fourth as it stalked forward bearing long, yellowed teeth. She smelt its animal breath. Three Tasers. Four dogs. The maths wasn't hard. She fumbled with her Taser and the contrap but managed to leave the ground with Taser wires dangling, before the fourth dog reached her. She hovered beyond reach of the snarling, leaping creature, all the time shocking the other dog.

Lucy expelled the cartridge from her gun, reloaded and levelled it again at the cowering dog before her but, now released from the current, it recovered and fled, yelping into the night. She tasered the dog leaping at Tyler's feet instead, and Tyler dropped to the ground as Barros arrived at the pool brandishing a shotgun.

"Well, well, well. What have we here? Three little girls?" His Portuguese accent was strong but Barros was able to speak English well when he chose to. He pointed his gun at them. "You will release my dogs now, I think."

The girls did so. The dogs ran. Tyler heard a distant, soft snap and a small, green flower suddenly blossomed on Barros' thick neck, beneath his chin. A moment of unease passed before he dropped the gun and slumped to the ground. When Tyler investigated she saw that the green blossom was the tail of a tranquiliser dart. She turned to peer out over the lake towards Fabio's small boat and caught a glimpse of him waving back at her. Barros was unconscious and, she guessed, would be for some time. She removed the dart and cast it into the lake.

"Thanks, Fabio," said Lucy. "Nice shot!"

Tyler headed down the unlit stairway into the prison chamber below. She flashed a Maglite around stone walls and illuminated a filthy, battered figure, hunched in the gloom.

"Weaver, we're taking you out of here," she said, crouching beside him.

"Who are you?" asked Weaver, wincing at the sudden intrusion of pool light.

"I'm Tyler May."

Lucy skipped down steps and looked at the man's dirty, bruised face. She cocked her head to one side.

"William? William Blake?" she questioned.

Tyler shot Lucy a quizzical look.

Weaver said nothing but rose painfully to his feet with Tyler's aid.

Lucy spoke urgently.

"Mel's signalling to Fabio. We need to vacate the premises."

Weaver struggled to walk. Tyler threw a supporting arm around him.

"Hey, easy, tiger," he managed to rasp with a half-smile. Lucy rolled her eyes and added her arm to his other side.

As they left the cell, Fabio brought the boat in and pulled Agent Weaver aboard with the girls' help. The girls boarded quickly and Fabio sped them away across the lake under the neighbours' scrutiny, accompanied by the distant baying of hounds.

"What was in the dart?" asked Tyler, enjoying the wind in her face.

"Nothing too serious," said Fabio. "Horse tranquilliser. Barros will wake up in twelve hours and wonder why the world won't stop spinning. He'll not remember much, I think."

She smiled at this and looked across the boat at Lucy and Weaver.

William Blake? What the heck has poetry got to do with MI5 and Nazi ghosts?

Dangers of Ghost Haunting

Weaver slept in the boat. He was cold and shivering, despite the warmth of the night. Fabio dug out an old blanket and tossed it over to the girls, who wrapped it about Weaver's shoulders.

By the time they reached the hotel room, he had revived a little and was able to talk.

"Thanks for getting me out."

"You're welcome," said Tyler. "Take a hot shower. We'll find you some clean clothes that aren't too girly. Then we'll head out to eat. You look like you could use a decent meal. Did they torture you? Are you hurt? I mean, apart from the bruises."

Weaver shook his head.

"Nothing broken, at least, I think not. They threw me around a little. Mostly I'm hungry."

Lucy tossed him a pair of black jeans, which he caught and examined briefly, assessing the size.

"You can have these until we buy you something more suitable in the morning. Mel's sorting out a shirt for you."

"Thanks, Lucy."

"Let me get this straight," said Tyler. "You two know each other, right?"

Weaver and Lucy nodded.

"He told me his name was William Blake," said Lucy.

"I remember!" said Melissa, bringing a white shirt and handing it to Weaver. "He's the guy you teamed up with to get the book – to break in and steal the book by Zebedee Lieberman."

"Ghost Haunting," said Tyler.

"Only, when you went to the meeting point after you got the book, you said William Blake never showed," said Melissa.

"That's right," Lucy confirmed.

"Wait, wait a minute," interrupted Tyler. "Let him get cleaned up. We can talk about this later. Right now he needs a shower and some food. We'll go to a safe house; one on Chapman's list."

*

The lavish restaurant was exquisite with decorative bamboo furniture and cascades of green suede drapery falling to rose and white marble floors. The girls' corner was well away from other customers and Chapman had confirmed it was a safe place where they could talk without fear of being bugged. An establishment run by *friends*. Weaver, looking much refreshed and passable in borrowed

141

clothes, ate freshly baked, buttered rolls ravenously while they waited for their orders to arrive. A waitress brought drinks and Weaver sipped a chilled beer gratefully.

"So what happened?" asked Lucy. "Why'd you stand me up, William Blake?"

"Sorry, but I had a good reason and it was nothing to do with you." Weaver seemed reluctant to explain more. He scanned his surroundings, nervously, every so often his eyes settling upon Tyler. Tyler became aware of his attention and felt heat rise to her cheeks. She couldn't help but offer a subtle smile the next time she caught him looking. She tried to weigh her attraction to him, but her head was overloaded with thoughts of her mission and she reached no clear conclusion. He was surprisingly well spoken.

In another lifetime, maybe...

"We know you're with MI5," she said. "Chapman told me you're one of us. Were you on a mission?"

Weaver nodded.

"Yes. Can I borrow a phone? I really should give Mr Chapman a call."

Tyler eyed him suspiciously but took out her mobile and called Chapman, who greeted her as always.

"Agent Weaver for you, Sir." She passed Weaver the phone. He took it and listened for a moment.

"Bridgewater," he replied. He listened again before saying "Yes, Sir. It's all clear. The girls tell me we're on safe ground. Putting you on speakerphone right now." He touched the phone's screen and they heard a thin rendition of Chapman's voice through miniature speakers.

"Can you hear me, girls? Weaver?"

"We hear you."

"Yes, Sir."

"Loud and clear."

"Good. I can confirm that this is Agent Weaver, as Ghost suspected. I want him to tag along for a while. He can help you out. We need to get him out of the county pretty quickly, so he might as well travel with you to your next target.

"Weaver?"

"Yes, Sir?"

"Do what you can to aid the girls. You'll need to brief them on your original mission, but that's okay. There's a clear connection and they'll, equally, need to fill you in on a few things. In short, I want you to learn from each other and crack on with things, okay?"

"Right," said Tyler, speaking for everyone.

Chapman wished them well and ended the call.

"Want to tell us what you know, Agent Weaver? William Blake. Whatever your name is," asked Tyler.

Weaver measured each of the girls in turn with his gaze.

"If Mr Chapman trusts you, I trust you. I don't know how much Lucy explained about what I was doing when we first met, but I was on a mission, a fool's mission, as far as I was concerned. I'm one of the youngest on the MI5 team. At least, I was, until Mr Chapman enlisted you three. As a new guy, inexperienced and supposedly naive to the ways of the world, you take some flack. And you take the rubbish work nobody else wants. That's what I thought my mission was. Some crack-pot woman brought in a lead she said we should follow up and, when she'd gone, our entire crew was in hysterics, including Chapman."

Their food arrived and Weaver paused until the waiters had left. He bolted a few mouthfuls of lamb shank and brown rice, and almost swooned at the taste before continuing.

"Anyway, I thought it was a joke, a complete waste of time. Then I started looking into the lead, as I'd been tasked to do. It got more interesting. My original brief was to check out the claim that a mysteriously powerful, ancient artefact or device had come to light in Dover. The information was sketchy at best. And it sounded like a prank to me, or maybe a hoax, but the more I learned the less sure I was.

"The trail led me to Watford, where I tracked my lead back to a man named Leopold Bagshot Mcguire, the head of some scientific research business and I became convinced he knew about the device. I figured, at least, that he knew where it was and I suspected he might even have it. Then I discovered the book and I happened to meet Lucy around the same time."

"The book was *Ghost Haunting*," said Tyler.

"Yeah. I was poking around in Bagshot's house when I stumbled upon the small, dark red, leather-bound book. It seemed pertinent to my investigation, so I took it. The problem was Bagshot somehow knew I'd taken it. I still don't know how, but he knew. He must've followed me, or perhaps he had one of his men do it. He stole back the book before I had much of a chance to study it. That's when I brought Lucy in to help me. I wanted to get some evidence together to report in with, enough to prove the whole thing was not a dud mission, enough to get Chapman taking it seriously, and I guess I wanted to do it without bringing anyone else in from the agency. They wouldn't have taken it seriously anyway. Sorry, Lucy. When I asked for your help to get the book, I got you involved. I shouldn't have roped you in. But I did."

Weaver stuffed another forkful of meat into his mouth, washed it down with beer.

"So how did you end up in a one man prison in Brazil?" asked Tyler.

"Well, that's why I couldn't meet Lucy when we'd planned. I spied on some of Bagshot's people and overheard them talking about the missing pages."

"You mean the chapter torn from the book? *The Dangers of Ghost Haunting,*" asked Tyler.

"Yes. They were talking about it and something they said caught my interest. I was trying to get closer, to see and hear better those talking, when I was knocked unconscious. They must have drugged me, too, because when I came round I was in a cell and had a hellish headache."

Tyler's head was buzzing. News on the missing pages...

"What did they say about the missing chapter?" she asked quickly.

"They seemed to think it contained some secret information about the device. Some hidden magic, maybe encoded in the text. Whatever it was, they seemed to think it was important."

"There's definitely something different about the missing chapter, or else why would anyone rip it out?" said Lucy.

"Exactly," agreed Weaver. "Anyway, I lost the book and I never did get my hands on the device, whatever it was."

"The contrap," said Tyler.

"What?"

"It's called a contrap. As in 'contraption' and 'con trap'." Tyler lifted the contrap over her head and placed it on the table between her and Weaver, who studied it with interest as she continued. "It's a ghost machine. It uses power from the ghosts trapped inside it. It can do some amazing things and Zebedee's book, *Ghost Haunting*, talked about it..."

The girls went on to explain all that had happened, about the contrap and about Bagshot, the GAUNT machine and the Nazi ghosts, gloved and at large, and their thwarted attempt to blow up Westminster Abbey thereby assassinating the prime minister, about Zebedee Lieberman and finally about Albert's recent appearance.

Weaver listened, amazed, as he ate but his stomach had shrunk so much since his imprisonment that he soon gave up on his lamb shank. He pushed the plate away to nurse his beer instead.

*

Weaver slept soundly. Alone and locked securely in the bathroom, Tyler drew out the contrap again. She switched it to the *Ghost Portal*, peered into the crystal lens and called softly for Zebedee. She needed to ask him about the missing pages and wondered if he might shed light on the strange failure of the bones when she'd tried to summon Mengele's ghost to the portal. Zebedee, however, was not forthcoming and so Tyler called for the old woman who had previously been of help. Izabella had seemed to be an expert on the contrap and its intricacies.

"Izabella?"

Mist swirled in a faceless whirlwind within the viewing glass. Tyler called again.

"Izabella?"

A figure formed slowly out the shifting fog and, for a moment, Tyler thought it was Izabella and that she might get some answers.

But she was very wrong.

"Zebedee, is that you?" she asked. "What's going on? Who are you?"

The figure grew in stature, features refining as it closed distance. A bearded face formed. The ghost of Leopold Bagshot Mcguire stepped forward and met her gaze coldly over the top of translucent, thick-rimmed spectacles.

"It's not often one meets one's murderer," he said. "I hope to repay your kindness one day."

Tyler shuddered and almost switched to the *Safeguarding Skull*, but had second thoughts, wondering if she still might learn something. And really, what was Bagshot going to do to her? He was at her mercy, captive within the contrap.

"You were murdered by the ghost of Travis of Normandy and by your own greed. I had little to do with it."

"You set me up and you know it."

"Someone had to stop you. You brought Hitler back from the dead, and half of the Third Reich."

"That's a gross exaggeration."

"Irrelevant. The point is you set in motion something that is now threatening the entire world. You had to be stopped before you did any more damage. Why did you do it? I mean, why would somebody do that?"

"What? Bring back Adolf Hitler from the dead? Because I actually believe the world would be a better place if he'd won the war. Because I truly believe it is for the best."

Tyler was speechless for a moment. She recognized something in Bagshot's eyes: a presence, a drive, a spirit.

The spirit of the oppressor...

"You really are a lunatic," she said, before turning the contrap and switching to the *Safeguarding Skull*. She put the contrap down but snatched it up again the next moment, switching to the *Tree of Knowledge*. She remembered Zebedee's warnings about the tree's use but right now she didn't care. She wanted answers and her frustrations outweighed her fears.

"Where are the missing pages?" she asked. Her words formed like ink within the mist of the crystal and spiraled into the murky distance until gone. A few moments later the answer floated into view, bobbing strangely.

Missing

Very helpful, I'm sure.

She tried again.

"Where are the pages torn from the book called *Ghost Haunting*?"

As before, the answer drifted back to her.

The pages are on the move

"Where are they going?" Tyler quickly asked, but the same answer came back.

The pages are on the move

She tried several variations of the same question but the contrap stubbornly repeated that same phrase and offered nothing more. Then Tyler tried something else, asking "Where is Adolf Hitler?"

Adolf Hitler is scattered as ash upon the waters

Tyler already knew this but she was struck by the fact that the contrap had given a half-reasonable reply so she tried again with a renewed hope, hoping to coax out some useful information.

"What is Adolf Hitler doing now?"

Adolf Hitler is dead

"Where is the ghost of Adolf Hitler?"
Surely this question cannot be sidestepped.
Two words formed in the fog to hover within the crystal.

At large

Tyler felt her knees go week and she steadied herself against the washroom wall, as more ghostly words followed, unprompted.

Tyler stared at them and felt herself slide down the wall, shaking.

"Who am I talking to?" she asked, trying to steady her voice.

No reply appeared.

"Who are you? Who is this?" she demanded, but the *Tree of Knowledge* had shared enough for one night. The hideous words remained in the lens, taunting her:

And he is going to kill you

PART THREE

C & R

Twenty-four hours later the shadowy Mr Flynn checked them into a stuffy, little hotel in Tel Aviv, room number thirty-five, on the third floor. During the long flight Tyler had been restless. She had mixed feelings about leaving behind both Mengele and Himmler to roam free, but she had discussed options with Lucy and Melissa and it seemed the best thing to do right now. In any case, the original plan was to obtain all of the artefacts they would need before going after the gloves. Incredibly, both Mengele and Himmler were still registering on the tracer monitor and, as long as that continued, Tyler was not overly concerned. She was even less concerned now that a more threatening presence was apparent.

Where is Adolf Hitler?

She slept fitfully and woke several times, sweating profusely, from visions of a monstrously distorted Hitler bearing down on her with murderous intent. The shackled, withered bodies of Jewish zombie-prisoners surrounded him, obeying his every command as he rallied them to attack.

When morning finally came she was hugely relieved and itching to get on with their next task.

Melissa gave the others a recap of Adolf Eichmann's story; his part in the mass murder of the Jews and others judged as unwanted; how he had become known as *the architect of the holocaust*; how he escaped after the war but was tracked down in Brazil years later by Mossad, secretly arrested and deported to Israel for trial; how he was hanged and cremated, his ashes scattered at sea. A small collection of his personal belongings, recovered by Mossad, had recently been put on display in the Beit Hafutsot museum, which Tyler and her team were planning to infiltrate.

They readied themselves, donning white lab coats and fake ID badges. Melissa put on her most sophisticated pair of reading glasses and adding makeup, high heels and a few carefully chosen pieces of jewellery, the girls checked their reflections.

"You could all easily pass for early twenties," said Weaver. "You look fabulous!"

They left the hotel early in the morning, hoping to enter the museum before too many other visitors arrived.

"The museum will be secretly guarded by Nazis, for sure," said Tyler. "But maybe we can fool them. If we're lucky they won't have had time to circulate pictures of us yet and we'll pass for the real R & C team."

"And if we're unlucky?" asked Melissa.

"The place will be overrun with armed gloves and we'll be shot to ribbons," said Lucy, busily scratching

Mengele's name on the money capsule containing his finger bone.

"Just be confident when you enter. If we're all skittish they'll smell a rat," said Weaver. "Are the artefact copies all ready?"

"I have them in my pocket," said Melissa.

The team rehearsed their parts for the infiltration thoroughly before leaving the hotel.

The museum, set back from the roadside behind a grassy lawn with a scattering of tall palms at its edges, was all but empty when they arrived in the early dry warmth. Inside, air conditioning cooled the atmosphere to a comfortable twenty degrees. The museum promised visitors exhibits that told the four-thousand-year story of the Jewish nation. A lone woman in a khaki suit, perched behind a wide reception desk and engrossed in a magazine, was surprised when Tyler interrupted her reading.

"Good morning," began Tyler, flashing an ID card. "Restoration and Conservation. Would you be so kind as to allow us access to the exhibits for assessment and cleaning?"

The receptionist took the three girls in with a long glance and blinked twice, but seemed reassured when Weaver threw her a charming smile. She said something in Hebrew but quickly realized she was addressing English speaking westerners.

"Right. Er, I was not expecting any cleaning crew. I have no..." She checked a desk diary for a relevant entry, found none. "Er, did you have an appointment? There is nothing in the book."

Tyler noticed the name badge on the woman's waistcoat: Elizabeth.

"Yes, yes. We are running to a strict schedule here. We don't have time for this."

Weaver interjected, keeping true to their closely rehearsed routine.

"No problem. Miss, if you would kindly call this number, I'm sure our headquarters will confirm the booking. We'll need access to all exhibits, new and old, if you will be so kind."

Elizabeth eyed Weaver and then the card he handed her and, after a moment's hesitation, reached for the desk phone. On the other end of the line a prearranged MI6 agent answered her call, confirming the Restoration and Conservation team appointment and the identities of the four crew members. Elizabeth checked their name badges as the agent gave a convincing spiel. It was enough to persuade her there had been some kind of mix-up and she ended the call to lead the team deeper into the museum.

"Where would you like to begin?" asked Elizabeth as she walked.

"The newer exhibits, please," Tyler said. "We generally start with the new and work our way back through to the ancient pieces."

"It shouldn't take long," Weaver added. "We'll do little actual cleaning or restoration today. It's mainly assessing the artefacts' condition to begin with. We'll arrange a follow up appointment if needed."

Elizabeth led them into a room holding modern items relevant to the Jewish nation's story and Tyler tried not to let it show when she saw the glass display case housing the Eichmann artefacts. She forced her eyes to follow Elizabeth's clipped footsteps. They passed into another chamber where Elizabeth stopped.

"Here we are. You can begin in this room and make your way round the rest of the building," she said.

Tyler and the team pulled on powdery latex gloves. Weaver propped open an aluminium case of brushes, bottles and other cleaning gear, all arrayed neatly in hinged compartments.

"You know where to find me if you need anything," said Elizabeth, dropping a large bunch of keys for access to each of the display cases, into Weaver's hand. The girls exchanged disbelieving looks as she left them.

Was it really going to be this easy? Tyler was uneasy. She checked about suspiciously, used the *Present Eye* to scan the place but found nothing foreboding.

When Elizabeth's footsteps were distant, the C & R team backtracked to the previous room and went to work. The biggest problem was finding the right key for the right case. Lucy worked her way through them, trying to match the tiny numbers to the numbered case before her. Weaver opened the glass lid of a case Lucy had already unlocked and began brushing down its contents. The case they needed access to was, frustratingly, still sealed.

"I don't understand," said Tyler. "Where are the Nazi guards? Where's Adolf Eichmann? He should be here, defending the artefacts." Through the glass, Tyler viewed Eichmann's keys, cigarette holder, penknife and comb, along with the syringe used to sedate him upon his capture. To one side stood the booth with bullet-proof glass, in which he sat during his trail.

So close...

"Maybe he's on his way. Himmler didn't show up until it was too late," said Melissa.

Albert appeared, standing beside Tyler, scratching his head.

"Maybe 'e finks there's anover artefact somewhere what you're more likely to nick," he said.

"Let's just get the artefacts and get out of here," said Lucy.

Tyler did not feel reassured.

"Albert, keep an eye out for the receptionist or anyone coming this way, will you? We'll try to make this quick, like Lucy says."

Lucy was halfway through the keys. Albert nodded and vanished.

"Here goes nothing," Lucy said, shoving a small key into the little brass lock on the side of the case. She turned the key and the lock clicked. She gently lifted the hinged lid. "We're in."

Albert reappeared, concern tensing his brow.

"Missy, someone's comin'! That girl made a call and two o'them carriages turned up outside. There's men comin' in right now!"

"Is there a back way out?" asked Melissa, panicking.

"Follow me," said Weaver, taking several steps towards the next room. "If there is, it'll be this way."

Tyler grabbed Eichmann's pocket knife while Lucy disassembled the cigarette holder and stuffed the black tip that had once been in Eichmann's mouth into a third money capsule she'd added to the chain around her neck. Melissa snatched the comb slipping it into her back pocket before replacing the items with the copies she'd brought. She lowered the glass lid and removed the key. They fled after Weaver.

Several rooms later, Weaver found a fire exit and shoved it open, triggering an alarm. They didn't care. They were outside and running, artefacts secured.

*

They reached their hotel in high spirits, laughing about how easy the whole thing had been. Tyler took out her list before reaching the entrance and felt good when she put a tick by Eichmann's name. Beneath that, two more names remained unchecked: Reinhard Heydrich and Joseph Goebbels.

"That was so easy," said Melissa. "So where was Eichmann's glove?"

"Nowhere to be seen," said Lucy. "Maybe he met with some kind of accident. Let's hope he's dead. Again."

"He could have been among the men the girl called," said Melissa. "Do you think they were Nazis?"

"Without doubt," said Tyler. "I reckon Eichmann had the place watched, or paid the staff to call if anyone unusual turned up. Just like Mengele."

It was Lucy who noticed first. Something was wrong.

"Hey guys, what's with this?"

Beyond the glass doors of the hotel nothing moved. A vase was smashed on the floor, glass fragments widely scattered amongst spilled flowers and water. Tyler and the others entered and looked about. The reception desk was unmanned, the place tomb-silent until the desk phone rang. Nobody answered it.

"Hello?" Tyler called. No response. She shrugged and was heading for the elevator when she saw blood smeared down the wall behind the reception desk. It led to a crumpled, lifeless body, beneath which blood continued to spread across the tiled floor. Tyler's stomach lurched and she subdued the need to retch. At her back, Melissa swore. The receptionist's throat had been cut. Tyler drew her Taser and the girls followed suit, unsure of what this meant. Had the Nazis done this? If so, why?

Weaver borrowed Lucy's mobile and called it in to the local police.

Tyler led the way to the elevator where a crimson smudge told her the killer, or killers, had entered. She pressed the call button and a moment later the doors opened. More blood streaked the interior walls, but the lift was otherwise empty.

"What's going on?" Melissa asked, nervously eyeing a smudged, bloody handprint next to the shiny steel control console.

"I don't know." Tyler hit the button for level three.

"We should check our rooms. Get our stuff. Get out of here," said Weaver as the lift moved.

"Sounds like a plan," said Lucy.

"Albert?" called Tyler. Albert appeared.

"I'm 'ere, Missy."

"Can you go ahead to our room? Check for danger?"

"I'm on my way." Albert said before vanishing. A moment later he returned.

"No one around, Missy," he reported. "Well, no one alive, anyways."

The lift arrived at the third floor and automatic doors opened to reveal bodies and more blood: unfortunate holidaymakers; American or European; cameras, shorts, back packs; their final vacation. The trail led to room thirty-five where the door handle was slick with blood.

Tyler approached the door.

"You did check inside the room?" she asked Albert.

"Like I said, no one alive." Albert shrugged.

Tyler wondered if she was asleep and stuck in a grim nightmare. Things seemed to have taken a very strange turn. First the unbelievably easy raid on the museum and now this. She took a deep breath and thrust open their door to peer inside. The room was in disarray, clothes strewn here and there, cases cast askew and upturned. She entered and read the large words scrawled in blood on the wall opposite the window.

GIVE ME THE DEVICE OR YOU WILL DIE

Weaver read it aloud. "Presumably whoever did this is talking about the contrap."

"She is," said Tyler. "Her name is Silvia Bates. She's a witch who's been after the contrap for a while now. She's also possessed by the ghost of an insane, Victorian murderer named Violet Corpe, thanks to me, so this is all my fault. She wants me dead."

Tyler felt anxiety rising as she stared at the words. Fear and guilt constricted her throat and she began to hyperventilate.

"It's my fault, Mel. All these people are dead because of me."

Melissa guided her out of the room with an arm around her shoulders, turned her away from the bodies in the corridor.

"It will be all right. It's gonna be all right. It wasn't you. It was Bates."

Tyler sank to the floor and huddled against the wall, shivering, head in hands. She listened to Lucy explaining more about Silvia Bates to Weaver, inside the room. The next minute Weaver was on the phone to Chapman organizing a private flight out of the country.

"Yes, Sir. She's fine. Just a little shaken," said Weaver. There was a pause and Tyler knew Chapman was talking. Weaver continued. "They're okay. We have the artefacts. We'll be leaving in a few minutes. Soon as we collect our things."

The girls packed hurriedly and left the hotel before the local police arrived. Tyler watched blue flashing lights heading to the hotel as their cab pulled away.

"Mr Flynn will meet you in Berlin. Chapman wants you to know there's no way Bates can know where we're heading. He's pretty sure she has no way of following or tracking us either," explained Weaver, looking back from the front seat. "Has little technology and no backup. So don't worry. You're perfectly safe."

Yes, I feel really safe. Six Nazi ghouls and a demented, possessed, murdering witch want me dead. I'm not sure I'll ever feel safe again.

Tyler felt exhausted. She slept in the car, waking with a start only when they pulled up at a private airstrip and it was all she could do to transfer herself to the small silver plane that taxied out to them from a long, low hanger. She checked down the road behind her for cars, fearing Bates was following, but no other vehicles turned into the enclosure. The others took care of the baggage and other arrangements. Their plan, to obtain the artefacts of the most dangerous gloves first, now beckoned them back to Germany. Tyler took a seat in the aircraft, strapped herself in and wished someone would turn off the radio that funneled unwelcome world news through to the passenger deck. The third story caught her attention.

"...reported a disturbing attempt to steal valuable exhibits early this morning from Tel Aviv's Hatfutsot Museum. Interpol has released a statement this afternoon suggesting the choice of exhibits targeted may be evidence of links to other similar break-ins, although in this instance the thieves failed to escape with any artefacts. Elsewhere, press has speculated the culprits are the same small group dubbed the *Thieves of Antiquity* known to be responsible for recent thefts of ancient objects in Northern Germany. Interpol has issued a warning to all museums worldwide to be extra vigilant at this time."

A hostess visited each of the girls with a narrow trolley of drinks. When she'd gone, Lucy raised her plastic cup to toast with the others across the aisle.

"To the Thieves of Antiquity." They drank.

Tyler managed to pull out her list before the drowsiness returned. The name she contemplated as she drifted into slumber, beneath the vibrating drone of the aircraft engine, was Reinhard Heydrich.

Screw you, Bates. I'm going to get them all and there's nothing you can do about it. And you're next, Heydrich.

PART FOUR

Invalidenfriedhof

"Reinhard Heydrich was Chief of Gestapo and an SS General during the Second World War. His role under Hitler's authority was to oversee the seeking out and elimination of anyone who stood in the way of the Nazi Party. He did this with secretive murders and deportations via his shadowy intelligence organization, the SD."

Tyler stifled a yawn. Lucy was less successful and Weaver tilted his head in mock exasperation.

"I know it's like school, girls, but you need to know your adversary in order to defeat him. May I continue?"

"Yessir."

"Right. In 1938 he helped co-ordinate organized killings of the Jewish population in Nazi Germany and parts of Austria. Heydrich also chaired the meeting, which made the decisions in finding *the final solution to the Jewish question*, in other words, the deportation and elimination of all Jews in German occupied territory. Hitler referred to him as 'the man with the iron heart'.

"On May 27th 1942 he was en route from his home in Panenské, traveling to Prague Castle through an area of the capital known as Liben, when his car was ambushed by two British trained soldiers: a Czech named Josef Gabčík and a Slovak named Jan Kubiš. Their mission to assassinate Heydrich, codenamed *Operation Anthropoid*, was viewed as almost certain suicide by the allies."

"Know how they feel," muttered Lucy.

"As Heydrich's open-topped Mercedes-Benz slowed at the specially selected hair-pin bend, Gabčík stepped out in front of the vehicle and tried to open fire, but his Sten gun jammed. The driver stopped while Heydrich fired at his attacker but, as he did so, Kubiš threw a bomb at the car, showering the area in shrapnel, some of which struck Heydrich. Some of it struck Gabčík, but the two assassins escaped after an exchange of gunfire, believing they had failed.

"Heydrich wasn't killed that day but the shrapnel wounds to his lower back proved fatal and he died from his injuries a week after the attack, on the 6th June. He died a German war hero and was to be buried with full military honours, when things took a bad turn for the German war effort and, at the last minute, formalities were postponed. He was put into a grave in Berlin's Invalidenfriedhof with a temporary marker which mysteriously disappeared later, when the Red Army took the city. The grave marker was never replaced."

"Can we get out now?"

Weaver snorted and shook his head as he slipped out from behind the steering wheel and opened the rear door for the girls.

"Thanks."

This far, the mission to acquire a relic of Heydrich had been simple, but now Tyler stood in the cemetery in Berlin, staring at a multitude of graves, feeling quite overwhelmed. She wondered if Heydrich would make an appearance and try to prevent them from getting his bones. If history taught her anything, he would not go down without a fight.

"It's around here somewhere, in section A, near the north wall of the Invalidenfriedhof," said Melissa, turning on the spot and looking around as though she might find an obvious place to start digging. She checked a compass and looked ahead at the great wall, grey in the dimness. "This is the north wall. The old photographs of the funeral ceremony show it was around here."

"That's *really* helpful," said Lucy. They had arrived at the cemetery in darkness at precisely one o'clock in the morning. It was now three minutes past and Lucy looked like she wanted to go already.

"Listen, we knew this wasn't going to be easy. I told you the exact place is unknown," Melissa said. "It's not like I hid the grave on purpose."

Albert drifted out of the surrounding murk and stopped near Tyler.

"Nuffin' untoward," he reported. "A few reveries 'angin' around their graves, but that's t'be expected. Nufin' t'worry about. They seem pretty quiet."

"Good," said Tyler. "Keep watch while we search for the grave. Heydrich's bound to show up at some point. He's probably got the place under surveillance, so look out for spies."

"Right you are, Missy." Albert floated off again into the night passing through crooked grave stones as he went.

Weaver looked to Tyler, who shivered in the bitter cold.

"What exactly can the contrap offer us?" he asked.

Tyler thought about this and didn't know where to start. In the end she told him every idea she could conceive.

"Well, the *Flight* symbol could take me up in the air. I could get a bird's eye view of the cemetery so I could maybe see if there's a place being kept free of other burials. The *Tower* could lead me to the grave because, when you are on the right track, the little tower in the crystal grows higher, but that could take a while and we don't have much time. *Tree of Knowledge* answers questions. It's not always that helpful but, in theory, it could tell us exactly where to dig. The *Present Eye* would allow me to look into the ground so long as there's a void of some sort although, on second thoughts, there wouldn't be a light source so that's not going to work as, unfortunately, it doesn't come with a built-in magic torch. And with the *Past Eye* I could look back in time and watch the burial actually taking place. I could see the body actually being put into the ground. But again, that can be immensely time consuming. And it gives me eyestrain."

Weaver raised his brows in frustration.

"I'm kind of regretting asking."

"You see my predicament," said Tyler.

He shrugged. "Where to start?"

Tyler viewed her surroundings, trying to distinguish the vast graveyard perimeter. Cast in moonlight, it appeared an endless sprawling of gravestones, stone crosses and tomb markers interspersed with shadowed trees. She shivered and drew up the hood of her black coat.

"You sure we're in the middle of the area?" she asked Melissa.

"As sure as I can be."

Tyler gazed at the contrap in her hand, set the switch to the *Tree of Knowledge* and squinted into the shifting fog within the crystal lens.

"Where is the grave of Reinhard Heydrich?" she asked. Words appeared and swirled away into nothingness. An answer soon floated into being, like ink coalescing in water.

Turn to your left

Surprised by a helpful response, Tyler turned.

Take five steps forward

Tyler took five paces dead ahead, sidestepping to avoid a stone cross. Soon more directions formed within the crystal, although the little voice in her head whispered words of caution.

Two steps to your left

Tyler did as the *Tree of Knowledge* said. She waited for more instructions that never came, so instead she asked, "Is the grave of Reinhard Heydrich right here, under my feet?"

He lies beneath

They were not digging long before Tyler called a sudden halt. The little voice in her head was now screaming a warning she could no longer ignore.

"Wait! Wait a minute. I'm not sure about this. I'm getting a really bad feeling."

Lucy glared at her.

"*A bad feeling...*"

"Yes, a bad feeling," snapped Tyler. "Something's not right. Zebedee warned me about using the *Tree of Knowledge*. I'm not sure I believe what it's telling me."

"Why?" asked Weaver. "What do you mean?"

"Zebedee said two of the known symbols could not always be trusted. And since Bagshot and Hitler went into the contrap, I trust them even less. I think we should stop digging and try something else. It could be Bagshot talking through the contrap, or someone worse. They'd have us dig up the wrong body and find an artefact that doesn't work."

"Not that the others are working anyway," Lucy mumbled, but then she brightened. "Can you speak to someone through the *Ghost Portal* and ask what would be the best way? I mean, ask Zebedee or Izabella. Someone who knows about it. Someone we trust."

"Good idea," said Melissa.

"Well, you're not the only one with a brain," sniped Lucy.

"*Whatever*. I think you should try it, Tyler. It has to be worth a shot." Beyond Lucy's line of sight, Melissa mimed shooting her in the head with two fingers.

Tyler peered at the star strewn heavens.

God help me.

"Okay, I'll try. But if I can't find anyone we'll have to use a different way."

Tyler switched the contrap to the *Ghost Portal* before turning it over to look into the lens. She called Zebedee, softly. She tried again and again during the following minutes but he never showed. She was growing extremely frustrated, and calling Zebedee some choice names under her breath, when another figure appeared through the spectral haze. Izabella's rotund form timidly drew closer until Tyler could see the flowery, printed pattern of her tent-like dress and the greyness behind her afflicted eyes. Tyler stepped away from the others so she could talk without distraction.

"Hello, Izabella. I'm glad I've found you. I need your help."

Izabella squinted back at Tyler and for a moment Tyler thought she might bolt, but Izabella remained there studying Tyler with interest.

"So, you put Hitler into the contrap," Izabella said at length, in her clipped Russian accent.

"Er, yes. I did," confessed Tyler, unsure if this was a good or a bad thing to be admitting.

Izabella nodded slowly.

"Very well. Someone should have done that a long time ago."

Tyler was pleased and a little relieved.

"You helped me before. Will you help me now?"

"What is it you think you need to know, child?"

Tyler thought this a strange way to phrase a question.

"I need to know the best way to use the contrap to locate the grave of Reinhard Heydrich."

"You wish to know how to use the contrap? You should know about the counter spell. You put Hitler in, but did you release another spirit? If you neglected to do so the contrap will now be unbalanced."

Tyler grew more irritated. This *was* something she wanted to learn more about but it wasn't helpful right now.

"I did release a ghost from the contrap, but I don't know if it's balanced or not. It may've been unbalanced when it came to me."

"I *could* tell you the spell, but perhaps I shouldn't," Izabella said as though debating with herself. "The contrap is a powerful object. It should not be used in ignorance."

Tyler visualized Bagshot's spirit being sucked from his body on the bridge.

"You're right. Please tell me."

"I'll tell you the words you need to balance the contrap, but you must firstly promise you will only use it for the good of others. I know things now, terrible things. You learn them when you die. We are all accountable for every little thing we've ever done. I'm forbidden to tell you more but, believe me, every selfish act that hurts another, for these we are accountable. Promise me you will only use it for good. And that you will destroy it when you're done."

Tyler checked over her shoulder to be sure the others were not eavesdropping. They were talking amongst themselves.

"I promise!"

"So be it. The words are *Compenso Pondera*. These words will balance the contrap without the need to release or absorb further entities."

Tyler scribbled the words on the back of her hand in Biro.

"Was that how the ghosts first got there?"

"It *was* with the aid of this spell that many of the ghosts were acquired. If the contrap is left unbalanced it becomes dangerous. It randomly vomits out ghosts and sucks in the souls of the living. This is quite undesirable, you will agree. But using these two words after an exchange of essences, you can make the contrap safe and put whoever you need inside it. But be warned. It is a *dark* thing to do against a person's will, living or dead."

"Thank you, Izabella," said Tyler. "I'll use it with care."

"You're welcome, child. I must go now. I'm quite tired from all this talk." Izabella turned to leave. "I wish you well."

"Wait!" called Tyler. "I need to know more! I have more questions!"

Izabella turned back slowly, leveling weary, intelligent eyes at Tyler.

"*More* questions?"

"I need to know where Hitler is. And why didn't Mengele's skeleton work as a summoning artefact? Has the contrap stopped working? And I need to…"

"I'm sorry, I really must go," said Izabella, shrinking into the fog of the crystal. She muttered as she went away, "You're a bright girl. I'm sure you'll work it all out."

Tyler peered into the murk trying to locate Izabella, but she had gone. She noticed something way off in the far distance and blinked. It looked as though a long, low ship had cruised into sight. However, shrugging this notion off as nonsensical, she switched back to the *Safeguarding Skull*. She fought the urge to hurl the contrap at the cemetery wall but swore vociferously instead.

She turned to the others and almost despaired. Lucy argued with Melissa and threw Tyler dirty looks at regular intervals. Tyler glanced back at Weaver for support and caught his wistful gaze.

Really? Now?

Some minutes later she had calmed and was able to focus her mind firmly on her mission. She still needed to locate the grave of Reinhard Heydrich, and Izabella had been of no help at all, so Tyler set the switch to the *Tower of Doom*. When Tyler took a step forward the tower within the crystal began to crumble. She turned to her right and took two steps. The tower stopped falling.

Well, that's a start.

She made an incremental adjustment to her path, shuffling further to her right. This time when she moved forwards the tower rose, almost imperceptibly, but it rose. In this manner she tracked her way towards a position in the graveyard where the tower within the contrap stood tall and complete. There she stopped and called to the others as, inside the crystal, the huge black birds circled about the shimmering full moon.

"It's here. It's right here." She took a spade from Melissa and heeled it into the ground to mark the spot. It was some four metres from the place where they'd begun digging earlier, with a large stone grave slab in between.

The four exchanged unsettled glances but together they began digging again. They had reached a depth of around a metre when Albert returned suddenly, looking panicked.

"Someone's coming! You need to get out now!"

Memoria Gravitas

The girls and Weaver stopped digging to confer in urgent whispers.

"Who's coming?" asked Tyler. "Where are they?"

"What do we do now?" asked Melissa. "We don't have time to fill in the hole!"

"We have time to run," stated Lucy.

"What's up with *you*? I thought you'd be right at home in a graveyard," said Melissa.

"They're over there." Albert pointed behind him, but Tyler could see nobody in the vast reaches of the cemetery. "They was right behind me!"

The team found themselves waiting and watching rather than fleeing.

"Was it men or gloves? Or ghosts?" asked Tyler.

"Dunno," Albert shrugged. "I ain't sure." He peered pensively into the distance. After several moments had passed and nothing had happened, he looked at them all, irritably.

"Wait 'ere. I'll go see wha's 'appenin'. Maybe they've gone away." Albert cautiously followed his path back into the depths of the cemetery. When he'd been gone for a while and all was silent, Melissa began refilling the hole.

"Wait!" said Tyler, feeling jittery. "Just wait a minute. Where's he gone?"

Melissa stopped shoveling.

Lucy pointed to their right suddenly.

"What's that? Over there. Someone's coming!"

They watched as a ghostly figure appeared from the night, but it was only Albert returning.

"Guess it were a false alarm," he said when he reached them.

"Dig," said Tyler. The girls and Weaver returned uneasily to their work, casting wary glances at the surrounding graveyard. They dug in pairs, taking turns to rest, as the pit was too narrow for more than two to comfortably work.

Two hours passed and the diggers were exhausted, but their excavation was approaching one and a half metres in depth.

"Any time now," said Weaver. "If we're in the right place we should hit something soon." He peered at Tyler, his current digging partner. "Why don't you take a break? I'll finish this off." Tyler thought she detected a certain warmth to his tone.

Lucy also noticed and shot him a glare.

Tyler climbed out of the deep hole with a hand from Lucy.

"Hands off," Lucy warned, close to Tyler's ear. "He's mine!"

Tyler stood and held up her hands resignedly. "Hey, I'm not interested. Right?"

In the hole, Weaver dug, unaware of the whispered exchange.

"Where's Albert?" asked Melissa. "He's been gone ages."

"I sent him to patrol the cemetery perimeter," said Tyler. "Do you think he's in trouble?" She scanned the graveyard, turning on her heel. Dark trees, graves, walls and the outlines of faceless buildings beyond borders. No Albert.

"I'll go see if I can find him," said Lucy.

"Do you think that's wise?" asked Melissa. Before Lucy could respond a hollow thud rose from the open grave and Weaver shouted.

"I've hit something!"

The girls peered into the grave at Weaver, who was scraping soil from a small patch of wooden surface.

Albert suddenly appeared close to Tyler.

"Reveries!" he hissed. "They're coming! Run!"

All about them spirits issued from the murk; ghostly, unfocused figures, closing in, drawn by some unseen force.

"No!" cried Tyler. "We're nearly there! Albert, do something!"

"I'll try to draw 'em off," said Albert. "Use the contrap!"

Reveries floated closer, a wall of blank-faced entities. Mouths gaped. Eyes slowly acknowledged prey. Translucent arms rose towards the girls. Some were old soldiers in Prussian uniform: riding boots, tri-cornered hats and dark military coats trimmed in red. Some were young and would have been handsome in life. Right now, all were ugly. Others were clearly German soldiers from the Second World War, complete with rounded helmets and ghost MP 40 machine guns. Officers carried ghost pistols.

Tyler took out the contrap and switched to the *Ghost Portal*, pointed it at the closest reverie, the numb-looking ghost of a German soldier, and pulled the little lever down clockwise around the edge.

"Why are they coming for us?" asked Melissa. "Why now?"

The German soldier closed on Tyler's position, hands mauling towards her. She felt something deep inside; a deadening of awareness, a softening of perception, and she knew the reverie was sapping her will. Suddenly it seemed much less important to do anything.

Why should *I fight this? What's the point? What are we doing here again?*

She shook herself, knowing she could not afford to think like that.

"Phasmatis Licentia!" she commanded, and the reverie soldier became a dazzling, blue, morphing light that spun through the air to enter the open portal, where it vanished.

"Get the bones!" shouted Lucy to Weaver. "We've got to get out of here!" She leapt into the grave and desperately clawed dirt away from the lid with her hands, searching for an edge. Weaver had cleared a wide area with his spade and he slid its tip down one side.

"Here!" he said. "Help me lift it!"

They hauled at the old sodden wood.

"It's not shifting!" Lucy shouted in frustration.

"Well, get off the bloody lid!"

Next to the hole, Melissa and Tyler circled on the spot, back to back. More reveries were gathering but

Albert had drawn a flock away. Tyler lost sight of him among the massing ghosts.

"We just need some finger bones," urged Lucy, unaware that a Prussian reverie was toppling into the grave above her. She screamed as Tyler uttered the words.

"Phasmatis Licentia!"

The reverie was sucked into the portal with a rush and a shriek.

The coffin lid was soft and Weaver's spade had penetrated. He realized there was a good chance of breaking through with the iron spade tip and hacked urgently. Moments later he and Lucy prized the top half of the coffin open and rummaged around in the dirt ridden remains inside, the bare skull of Heydrich grinning at them, his decaying Nazi dress uniform still evident in muted tones. A worm oozed from his nasal cavity.

Tyler sucked more spirits into the contrap and, remembering Izabella's instruction, read the words from the back of her hand.

"Compenso Pondera."

She continued to take aim at lurching reveries with growing concern for Albert. She glanced into the grave and glimpsed Lucy tearing the skeleton's hand loose.

"Albert? Albert, where are you?" Tyler shouted.

Albert did not respond.

Behind her, Lucy and Weaver scrambled out of the hole, Lucy grasping a fist full of slimy hand bones.

"GO!" she cried.

The four backed away from the grave as Tyler took out reveries that stood in their path. The further they ran from the hole, the less interested in them the reveries seemed to be. By the time they found Albert at the edge of the graveyard the numbing ghouls had ceased to follow.

He was standing, gazing at a blank wall, unmoving and when Tyler spoke to him he appeared not to hear.

"What was all that about?" asked Melissa, looking at Albert with concern and then at the others in turn. "Why did they turn on us?"

"It's like someone set them on us," Lucy suggested.

Tyler turned back towards the north wall, set the contrap to the *Present Eye* and scanned the graveyard.

"It's Heydrich. He's here. Heydrich set the reveries on us. I don't know how, but he did it."

"Maybe he has some kind of power over them," said Melissa.

"Perhaps that person Albert first saw was someone watching for us. A guard. They could've then alerted Heydrich," suggested Lucy.

"Could be," said Tyler. She considered trying to summon Heydrich there and then, but what she saw dissuaded her. Through the contrap's lens, Tyler watched the gloved ghost of Reinhard Heydrich standing amidst a sea of reveries and looking back at her, his skin an eerie blue. No, not looking at her, staring *through* her with murderous eyes as though he could perceive her naked soul.

*

Tyler was in a morbid mood and she had let the others know. This time they had plumped for a small guesthouse not too far from the Invalidenfriedhof. Tyler sat alone in its reading room, although she could still hear the others talking through the closed door. She had left Melissa scanning the bedroom for unwelcome guests.

"It's not our fault. We weren't to know," said Lucy defensively.

"It's not like we wanted him to get *reveried*, or anything," agreed Melissa. "I don't know what we're supposed to do about it."

"I'd help if I knew how."

"Me too. Of course I would. We all would."

Tyler took the contrap from her shirt and, switching to the *Ghost Portal*, called for Zebedee. With Albert stuck in a reverie trance in the graveyard and Izabella's leaning towards unhelpfulness, she really had no choice. She simply needed Zebedee, but she wasn't holding her breath and was surprised when he appeared soon after she called him, as though he'd been hiding around the corner, waiting for her.

"Good day to you, Miss May," he said with a bow and a wave of his long-stemmed pipe. "How may I help you?"

"It's Albert," said Tyler. "He needs help. The reveries got him."

Zebedee's carefree demeanor evaporated as Tyler explained all that had happened.

"Where is he? How many were there?"

"He's in the graveyard. I'll take you. There were more than I could count. Like an army."

"An army, indeed! How perfectly awful. Lead the way, my girl. Lead the way!"

Tyler was about to turn when she noticed way off in the distance, beyond Zebedee, the object that looked like a city that she'd glimpsed earlier. It was grey and ghostly like everything she'd seen within the contrap and it rose from a carpet of mist, though at this distance she could see little detail.

"What's that?" she asked. "What's that behind you?"

Zebedee frowned and glanced over his shoulder.

"Oh, that. That's the moving city. Memoria Gravitas."

"A city? I didn't know there was a city in there."

"Oh yes. There's always been a city in here. Not a real city, I should say. It's more an abstract mass of collective, morphic memories that naturally gravitate towards one another to gregariously cluster."

"Naturally," said Tyler.

"Quite fascinating really. Wouldn't you say? Sometimes it's part feelings or, more accurately, a rendition of a remembered place conveyed by feelings or emotions - as in the emotion or feeling one once had about that place."

"So it's not a real city but a collection of memories."

"That's correct, though the affect is the same. The difference is it tends to move around. It shifts all the time, you see. Memories aren't quite as solid as brick and mortar and one person's memory is slightly different from the next, so you see, even if two individual ghosts had a recollection of the same place, in here that place would appear strange; not quite true to the original. In fact it's sometimes downright off-centre. Parts of it come and go as they please and often when they return they've changed."

"How odd," said Tyler. "Anyway, we need to go." She tucked the contrap into her shirt, put on her coat and left the guesthouse. She walked through busy streets until reaching the solitude of the graveyard, where the absence of visitors gave the place a lost feel. Albert hung right where she'd left him, transfixed like an opaque zombie. Tyler took out the contrap after double checking that no one was looking her way. From her position she couldn't see another living sole.

"I'm going to let you out, Zebedee," she whispered into the *Ghost Portal*. "Do what you can to help him." She pulled the lever on the contrap anticlockwise and murmured, "Phasmatis Licentia." There came a whirl of blue mist and light, accompanied by a sudden hissing, and then Zebedee Lieberman was hovering before her, still puffing merrily away on his pipe.

"Compenso Pondera," said Tyler.

"Oh, it's nice to be out and about again!" sang Zebedee, rather too loudly for Tyler's liking.

"Shush! Keep it down, will you!"

"Oh, yes, sorry. Well, I'd like to do a spot of sightseeing but I suppose we'd best take a look at young Albert." Zebedee strode over to study Albert and circled him. "He's in a bad way. If he's truly become a reverie it could be an awful long time before he can be brought back to us."

"Has he become one of *them*?"

"It's too early to say, but he's going to need a lot of looking after if he's ever to be the same chirpy lad he was. I'll see what I can do, of course, but honestly, only time will tell."

"Should I put you both back into the *Ghost Portal?*"

"It would be a good idea, except, I fear Albert is too frail. To put him into the device now would only weaken him further. He should not be moved. Not yet anyway."

"But the reveries! Won't they…"

"The reveries acted in a very unnatural fashion when they attacked you and Albert, and there's no sign of them now. Oh no, I think he'll be quite safe. In any case, my dear girl, it seems to me they've done everything they can to the poor fellow, unless they get the contrap, that is. Then they could put him into the Shivering Pool...

"I'll stay with him and make sure he's all right. Don't fret. And when he's recovered and strong enough to move, we'll find you. I promise."

"Zebedee, why were we able to see the reveries in the graveyard? Albert told us they were ghosts with very little power and he said ghosts with little power would not be visible to us."

Zebedee considered this soberly for a moment while striking a ghost match and relighting his pipe.

"What Albert said is quite correct. It seems to me the reveries were able to draw power from somewhere or someone. You did say that a glove was present?"

"Reinhard Heydrich. He was watching us."

"I think, perhaps, therein lies your answer. It could be Heydrich has found a way to control the reveries though, I shudder to say, this does *not* bode well. This does *not* bode well at all."

*

Tyler was so worried about Albert that she couldn't sleep that night. She peered into the portal hoping to catch a glimpse of the distant city, but it had vanished without trace. She took out her list and ticked off Reinhard Heydrich's name.

With twenty seven bones in the human hand, Lucy's fist full of remains had rendered a choice of artefacts once cleaned and disarticulated. The girls had each taken a single finger bone as before. Lucy had tucked hers into a new money capsule, scratched Heydrich's name upon it and strung it around her neck with the others so that it looked like a chain of four silver bullets. The overall appearance blended well enough with her gothic image to pass unremarked. Weaver took the remaining bones as a further failsafe.

Tyler viewed her list and added notes.

Artefacts Acquired

Heinrich Himmler	√	*Finger bones*
Josef Mengele	√	*Finger bones*
Adolf Eichmann	√	*Penknife, cigarette holder & comb*
Reinhard Heydrich	√	*Finger bones*
Joseph Goebbels		

She'd given up trying to conceal the artefacts after Himmler had known exactly where to look. Albert had warned her that the gloves could probably sense things like that; things like bits of their old bodies that still survived and, if that was true, what was the point in hiding them away?

She spread out three transparent plastic evidence bags on her bed and looked at the artefacts inside: two phalanges and a folding pocket knife. Each was labelled with a name. They didn't seem much when she weighed the effort they had taken to collect. What was more, she was seriously concerned that the summoning power of the contrap had died. If *that* were true, their entire mission was a waste of time, yet something deep inside told her she was doing the right thing. Against all odds, admittedly, but the right thing, nonetheless. She steeled herself for what was to come and focused on the list. In the morning they were to catch a flight to America.

Joseph Goebbels, you're next.

PART FIVE

The Rise of Nazism

Tyler was rudely awoken by her mobile. She fumbled for it on the bedside table as it buzzed frantically like a trapped wasp.

"Yes?"

"Good morning, Ghost. I trust you slept well?"

"Like the dead, Mr Chapman."

"Just as well. You've a long flight ahead of you and you're going to need your wits about you. I've made a minor tweak to your plans…"

"Wait. Give me a minute." Tyler rubbed sleep from the corners of her eyes and tried to focus. She hauled herself into a sitting position on the bed and yawned. "Okay. I'm listening."

"Right. You'll find your tickets waiting for you in the guesthouse in-tray along with a passport for Weaver. You'll note Weaver's is in a separate envelope. That's because I'm sending him on another mission. He's not going with you to Massachusetts. He's going to California."

"What? Why?"

"Listen, I know you girls have thought this through carefully but I've never really agreed with Goebbels being placed at the bottom of your list. In *my* book he's one of the most dangerous of the six names you recovered from the NVF. He was often regarded as Hitler's right hand man. He wrote the speeches and governed what and how information was fed to the public. In short, he was responsible for convincing the German nation to follow a homicidal lunatic into war and in many ways the Second World War is his fault. To think he's out there now somewhere, resurrected and plotting God knows what... Well, let's just say I'll feel better when he's been safely *dealt with*. Anyway, I'm sending Weaver to the Hoover Institute for Goebbel's diary while you girls go for the papers in Massachusetts. If one of you fails, there's still a good chance the other will recover a usable artefact. I want Goebbels brought down, at any cost."

"Okay, I'll tell the girls. Thanks."

She dropped her phone on the bed.

Nuts. With Zebedee tending Albert and Weaver on his mission we're on our own again. Back to the unholy trinity.

She dressed and went to break it to the others.

"He can't do that!" Lucy snarled. "We need him. He's one of the team now."

"He can do whatever he wants. He's the boss," Melissa reminded her.

Weaver said nothing but looked from one face to another, unshaken by the news. Lucy turned to him, glowering.

"Hey, don't blame me," Weaver said. "I don't make the rules. I go where I'm sent. Do what I'm told."

Lucy wasn't interested.

"Whatever. I'm just saying it's a bad idea. We stand a better chance together."

Weaver went to her and grasped her hands.

"It will work out. You'll see. You girls are a great team with or without me. Chapman knows that or he would never have sent you anywhere."

Lucy threw her arms around him and hugged him tightly, reminding Tyler of a child hugging a father. "I don't want you to go. It's been... I've... We've been safer with you around." She straightened up and held his gaze. "Don't go."

"I'd stay with you if I could," he said. He took her hand and kissed it.

*

Tyler inserted a micro tracer into the syringe and eyed Lucy, who hadn't ceased pacing since Weaver had collected his tickets and left to catch his flight.

"Who's first?" Tyler asked.

"Why are we doing this again?" Lucy moaned.

"If we get separated or captured these tracers could save our lives. Chapman will be able to search and locate us. Feel free to refuse. It's your funeral."

"I'm touched by your concern," said Lucy, thrusting her forearm at Tyler. Tyler shoved the needle into her arm, squeezed and withdrew the syringe.

"Son of a..." Lucy hugged her arm and winced.

"Oh, don't be such a baby," said Tyler.

"You've got one hell of a bedside manner."

Tyler injected herself with the next tracer and nearly fell off her chair with the pain.

"You're not jabbing me with that thing," Melissa stated. "I'll take my chances without a tracer, thank you very much."

"Lucy?" Tyler gave the nod.

"On it." Lucy pinned Melissa down on her bed and yanked up a sleeve while Tyler prepared to inject. "You gotta have it. It's for your own good."

"This is gonna sting a little. Ready?"

"Uh uh. NO!" Melissa fought, but Lucy was stronger.

Tyler injected a micro tracer into Melissa's arm. Melissa screamed and bucked, head-butted Lucy out cold with the back of her head.

"Sorry," said Melissa, when Lucy came round several minutes later. "Didn't see you there…"

*

The Museum of World War II was a pale cream building of ten thousand square feet and contained the most complete personal collection of Second World War artefacts open to the public. The girls found it easily on its quiet, tree-edged street and entered through the Doric columned doorway flanked either side by the stars and stripes. They acted like casual tourists, perusing galleries of relics and mannequins dressed in aged military regalia.

The first part of their tour covered the war trials in Japan, the next, the prisoners of war and the collapse of Germany. They passed into a chamber dedicated to D-Day and the allies in Europe before moving into areas on Italy, Russia and Africa. Each section displayed clothing, documents, posters, weaponry and other trappings of conflict.

Tyler searched the milling visitors for the sickly bluish tint of the gloves but found none. No sign of a black trilby moving among them anywhere.

It was not until they'd ploughed their way through exhibitions on Pearl Harbor, the Holocaust, occupied Europe, the Resistance, the Battle of Britain and on Munich that things became truly interesting. Melissa was slow to move on from any displays showing documents, absorbing every written word.

"What's the deal, super brain?" Lucy complained while Tyler waited and people watched.

The last sections of the museum were given over to Germany in the 1920's, the German military and, finally, the Rise of Nazism. This was the area Tyler had been waiting for and she was pleased to find it was annexed in a corner of the building, tucked away. Joseph Goebbels' speech notes comprised four sheets of white paper, bearing a list of twenty-nine numbered points he had planned and covered during a speech in 1933.

There it was: four paltry sheets of paper in a glass case, taunting her. Goebbels' handwriting was an even scribble, sagging towards the base of the page at the end of each line. Tyler smothered a sudden urge to smash the glass then and there, to scoop up the pages and run. She checked for CCTV cameras and found only one trained on the glass cabinet. The place had an alarm system too; motion sensors were dotted around the building and would be active whenever the place was closed. Still, the security measures were not as rigorous as she'd feared and she relished the thought of ticking off the very last item on her artefacts list.

Tonight, she told herself.

Lucy leaned in to whisper.

"Hey, *Moriarty* – don't drool on the glass, will you. Take it easy or you'll give the game away."

"Yeah, right," said Tyler, suddenly aware she'd been staring at the speech notes for an age. She looked away and feigned interest in a bust of Goebbels instead. Lucy was right. They didn't want others to know why they were there, especially any Nazi spies who might be watching. Tyler checked about but saw nobody who was obviously observing them, only tourists and enthusiasts with what she considered to be a tasteless fascination with war. She risked a last glance at the display case, noting the lock at the base and the fact that the glass lid was probably going to take the three girls' combined strength to lift.

*

Their pre-booked guesthouse, a comfortable, homely place with Americana adorning the walls, was less than two miles down the road from the museum. Licence plates and county road signs dotted the corridors and the stuffed heads of an impressive variety of wild animals watched over doorways with sad, vacant eyes. Melissa looked from creature to creature despairingly as she wheeled her case in Mr Flynn's wake.

"Don't worry," whispered Tyler. "We won't be here long."

Several other guests were making use of the common rooms, so the girls kept all talk relating to their mission to their spacious three-bed room.

"We've got all this money," said Lucy. Her mobile beeped and she grabbed it from the bedside table to read a text. "And it's a private collection. Why don't we just find the guy who owns it and make him an offer he can't refuse. *Buy* the speech pages? Why do we have to steal everything?"

Melissa looked at Tyler, who didn't seem interested in replying, and so took it upon herself.

"If we make our intentions obvious, the NVF may out-bid us, or worse, nick the artefacts before we do."

"Right. Of course." Lucy was busily texting.

"Don't worry. We'll drop an anonymous donation off to the owner. We'll pay for what we take, and for any damage, as before."

"I wish Albert was coming with us," said Tyler. "I'd feel better about it knowing he could go ahead and check it out before we go in."

"You'll just have to use the contrap," said Lucy, pulling a jacket on.

"Where are you going?"

"Oh, nowhere. Just need a breath of fresh air. Won't be long." Lucy waved her fingers in farewell.

"Hey, we should stick together!" said Melissa. "Mr Chapman told us to…"

Lucy shoved her iPod earphones in and gave a cheerless smile.

"Sorry, can't hear you," she said loudly before exiting the room.

"What the heck's she up to?"

"*God* knows," said Tyler. Right now she was too tired to care.

"Maybe she's missing lover boy."

*

Jetlagged and exhausted, Tyler still couldn't sleep. *I can sleep when I have the last artefact safe and sound,* she told herself. She studied a large sash window pensively before unlatching it to haul it up. The room was on ground level and the window led out onto a patio a short drop below. Beyond were trees and grass, several other houses, a road and then level fields. She closed the window.

When Lucy woke, Tyler was pacing the floor of the bedroom. Melissa was researching Goebbels on her laptop. Tyler made a strong cup of coffee and plonked it on Lucy's bedside table.

"Two sugars, right?"

"What you do that for?" asked Lucy, bleary eyed.

"You have to wake up. What were you doing out to make you so tired, anyway? No, forget it. We have work to do." Tyler resumed her pacing. "We need to talk, to go through our plan."

"What plan?" Lucy took her phone from her pocket and checked for messages.

"Our plan for tonight, when we go into the museum to get the papers."

"Tonight? Why tonight? We only just got here." Lucy struggled to sit up, took her cup and inhaled coffee fumes.

"We go in tonight. We fly out tomorrow."

"But we're in America. Can't we spend a few days looking round? Do the tourist thing? We've got to have a break at some point. This whole thing is nuts!" Lucy sipped her coffee warily but nodded her approval.

"Hey, this isn't bad. You should make me coffee more often."

"Yeah? Well don't get used to it. We have a map of the museum layout from our recon visit. We know where we're going and where to find the papers. It will be simple. We'll go down there tonight and I'll break in using the contrap. We'll take the papers and get out quick, just like Tel Aviv."

"Why don't we use the C and R team routine like Tel Aviv? That would work, wouldn't it?" asked Lucy.

"Too risky," said Melissa. "This is a private collection. There's a much better chance someone there would know we'd not been booked to come in. It wouldn't work."

"And it would mean putting it off until tomorrow," Tyler pointed out.

"And *that* would be a tragedy," mumbled Lucy.

Tyler checked her watch.

"It's ten past five now. We need to eat and get ready. We'll set out around one a.m. Okay?"

"*Brilliant*," said Lucy, replacing her cup and burying her head under her pillow.

*

They left the guesthouse via the bedroom window so their movements would not rouse the owners and other guests. Outside, the night air chilled them. Dressed all in black, adrenaline pumping, they found the cab Melissa had ordered waiting for them half a mile away as planned, its engine running. The driver was no ordinary cabby but an MI6 operative who knew not to waste time asking questions. Tyler looked him over. Middle aged, in good shape, a thin, angular face topped with a buzz cut. He seemed alright. At least his skin did not glow an unnatural shade of blue.

"Where are you bound?" asked Tyler, just as she'd been instructed.

"*Portsmouth*," the driver replied, relaying the mission password.

They climbed in knowing it was safe, gave no names and said nothing more. He already knew where they wanted to be taken.

Lucy checked her cell phone again.

"All phones set to vibrate?" asked Tyler. The others nodded. Lucy was texting.

"Who are you texting at this time of night?" asked Melissa with a sideways glance at Tyler.

"None of your beeswax," said Lucy, her fingers ceaselessly tapping.

She was still texting when the taxi pulled over.

"We're here," said Tyler. "You need to put that away now. Whoever it is, they can wait 'til later. We need all eyes on the job."

"Alright, alright!" Lucy put her mobile away.

The girls sat in the car for a further minute while Tyler viewed the vast museum through the *Present Eye*, grateful that the dark, still building was only a single storey. She scanned through rooms of exhibits, cypher machines, guns, dressed mannequins and display cases. Then she glimpsed it: a pale, translucent shape, shifting in the shadows, waiting for them.

Massachusetts Ghosts

The ghost glided slowly about the unlit museum and Tyler considered the way they moved. It seemed to her they could walk like the living when they chose, or hover and glide when it suited. She squinted hard, trying to make out features, needing to know exactly what she was dealing with. It didn't appear to be in uniform or wearing a German World War II helmet. In fact it was quite nondescript; just a grey shape moving amongst the collection, though she had the impression it was male. Was it one of Heydrich's unholy reveries, or only a harmless drifter, drawn there by an associated museum piece? She told the girls what she saw.

"So what now?" Melissa asked.

Tyler was undecided. She still wanted to go ahead with the mission but knew the others would not be so keen.

"This changes everything. I say we hold off," said Lucy. "Wait until Albert is back. He can check it out for us. Albert would tell us what sort of a ghost's in there, whether it's dangerous or not."

Tyler knew Lucy was right, but she didn't want to admit it. She couldn't bear the thought of putting off the mission for, what? Two days? Ten weeks? Who could say? How long might it be before Albert was back with them?

"Listen. We don't even know Albert *will* return to us. He could be a reverie forever. He might be unfixable." The reality of her words struck home and she fought back her swelling emotions. What if Albert was gone for good, damned to be a reverie for all time, stuck in a graveyard in Berlin? Forcing herself to focus on the here and now, Tyler scanned the surrounding grounds of the museum through the *Present Eye*. Nothing, living *or* dead.

"It must be a guard," she concluded. "The gloves have posted a ghost guard here. It's the only explanation. He's waiting for us to try something."

"Makes sense," Melissa agreed. "This *is* the biggest collection of World War II relics in existence as far as my research shows. There could be numerous artefacts in there that we could use against the gloves. This is where the NVF found Hitler's reading glasses remember and probably the medals they used to bring back the other gloves with the GAUNT machine."

"Well, we'll just have to deal with it," said Tyler, opening the car door.

"Hey, hey! Wait a minute! What are you doing?" babbled Lucy. It was the first time Tyler could recall her appearing afraid.

"We have to go in. And the longer we hang around out here, the bigger the chance we'll be spotted and it will be *too late* to go in. Chapman put me in charge of the team so you have to do as I say. Now come on. We're wasting time!" It was also the first time she'd ever had to pull rank and it didn't feel good.

Tyler rolled down the balaclava she'd been wearing like a hat to cover her face. She led the way from the car to the museum's large doors. Behind the girls, the cab waited for their return, the unspeaking driver tracking their progress.

Tyler peered into the museum doors' locking mechanism via the *Present Eye* and probed internal latches with her lock-pick. She froze when it clicked audibly. It was a small noise but in the stillness of the night it felt like an explosion. She waited for a moment to be sure the sound had not alerted anyone to their presence. When she set back to work the lock clicked twice in quick succession making Melissa jump. The girls looked at each other.

"I think that's it," said Tyler. She slowly reached for the door handle and shivered as something passed right through the door and herself, chilling her insides. She turned to see the museum's ghost guard darting away into the night.

"OMG, I nearly died!" said Melissa.

"Well, I guess there's no cause for stealth any more. The clock's ticking. How long do you think we have before that ghost alerts Goebbels?" Tyler asked no one in particular.

"I don't know," said Melissa.

"Three minutes, tops," stated Lucy. "Move!"

They entered, shoving the doors out of the way and paying no heed to CCTV cameras or alarms. If all went according to plan, there would be no time for any security unit or police to respond and their identities would be hidden by their balaclavas and uniform black outfits. Tyler knew the clearest thing that would be seen on any CCTV footage would be their Maglite beams sweeping around the rooms. She had checked for motion sensing lights during the reconnaissance. There were none and she was relieved to find no security guards on site.

They shot past exhibits of no interest, needing only to reach the zone displaying Goebbels' speech, but they were slowed by the mass of objects along the way. Military gear, cases, gasmasks, flight consoles, mannequins, small arms and other clutter. Melissa turned a corner and shrieked when she came face to face with a German soldier looming over a massive gun on a tripod. She gawked at it for moments before convincing herself it was only a dressed mannequin. She passed the anti-tank gun and the accompanying camouflaged Jeep hurriedly to catch up with Tyler.

"These freakin' mannequins are *well* creepy," she said.

"Tell me about it," said Tyler. They turned a corner and found the display case with the documents. Tyler began to pick the case's tiny lock but thought twice about it, hefting the bronze bust of Goebbels from its plinth instead and smashing the protective glass into a million shards.

"Subtle," said Lucy.

"Just keep your eyes peeled," said Tyler, picking through lethally sharp debris. "You two keep watch. I'll get the pages."

Melissa and Lucy disappeared into the depths of the museum as Tyler carefully brushed small fragments of glass away from paper. She lifted the first of the four pages.

A man's voice came from loudspeakers set high around the building's interior.

"I've been expecting you."

Tyler went ridged as an icy tremor traversed her spine and she knew she was listening to the gloved ghost of Joseph Goebbels. The voice continued as Tyler searched for its origin.

"The pages you are now collecting are, of course, forgeries. Do you think I would leave it to chance; to give *you* the chance to claim the documents and make an end of me? No, this is something I would not do. The real pages are in a safe place where you will never set foot."

Tyler let the page fall back amongst the ruined case.

"You could be lying to me," she shouted, not knowing where Goebbels was. "You could be saying that just to make me leave the pages behind."

"Is that why you have just replaced the page you held, little girl?"

So, wherever you are, you can see me well enough. CCTV? The security room near the entrance, perhaps?

"I shall not - how do you say - beat about the bush, little girl. You have by now realised what it is I want from you."

Tyler unconsciously tucked the contrap further into her shirt.

"Yes, of course you have understood. And yes, you have walked into a trap that I myself set for you. You think you are clever, little girl, but in your arrogance you have proved otherwise."

"There's nothing clever about what you've done, Goebbels, or what you're doing," retaliated Tyler.

Where are Lucy and Melissa? What are they doing?

She'd expected to hear them running back but, except for Goebbels voice, the place was silent.

"Come, come little girl. Hand over the device. If you do this, I may consider releasing you and your friends without a fuss. You can go home, play with your dollies, or whatever it is you little girls play with…"

"You'll have to kill me first," shouted Tyler. She took a page and put it on the contrap, setting the switch to the *Ghost Portal.* Goebbels had to be close by. If the page was an original, it would make a powerful summoning artefact and he should surely be drawn in like a paperclip to an electro-magnet. But nothing happened. "Why don't you come out and face me like a man? You're a coward, just like the rest of your kind. Can't even face the world unless you're hiding behind a gun. Oh, I forgot, you're not really a man are you. More of a zombie freak." She ditched the paper.

She heard Goebbels chuckling into his microphone. The sound gave her the creeps.

"You are correct in *that*, at least. I *do* have a gun. It is a rather good one! Would you like to see it?"

Tyler edged her way back through the museum, hoping to find the other girls, dreading finding someone else. She drew out the contrap and, with shaking hands, set the switch to the *Ghost Portal* and held it out before her at the ready.

"You know, we already have ghost spies *everywhere.* Your battle is really quite futile. If only you knew." More chuckling. "We know much about you and your friends, about the contraption you so proudly wield. We have many resources you know nothing of. When the NVF released us from death they elevated us to the status of gods. We have secret Nazis worldwide, worshipping us as though we were deities, just waiting to do our bidding. And they shall! When the time is right they will rise up! We have many plans already coming to fruition. You really should give up. It is the only logical thing to do."

Another voice reached her from somewhere in the darkness of the museum.

"Don't listen to him! He's just a loser! Don't forget he was the Minister for Propoganda. He's full of bull." Melissa's encouragement was punctuated by a cry of pain. Someone, or something, had silenced her.

Tyler ran a few paces forwards, peered around a corner into the next room. Mannequins. Mannequins everywhere, looking like ghosts in the shadows. Melissa was right about them. Tyler tried to close on the place she thought she'd heard Melissa's voice come from, but in the terrifying darkness and maze of exhibitions she felt herself begin to slide. Her breathing accelerated. She fought it consciously, willing her chest to slow, telling herself over and over, 'It will be alright'. She crossed the floor and caught herself before risking a glance into the next chamber. In a glass cabinet across the way she glimpsed movement. She froze and squinted, trying to make sense of the reflection. She quickly set the contrap back to the *Present Eye* and looked through the wall to get a better view. There were Melissa and Lucy, standing terrified. Two ghost soldiers trained MP40 machine guns on them, holding them prisoner. A trickle of blood ran from Melissa's forehead and down her left cheek and Tyler could hear her now, sobbing softly in fear of another blow. Even through the contrap's lens, Tyler could tell the MP40s were not transparent like the ghosts. The guns were real.

Ghosts with guns…

Tyler took a deep breath and edged closer to the corner. She set the contrap back to the *Ghost Portal* and uttered the words before rounding on the spectres.

"Phasmatis Licentia!"

Machine gun bullets rained about as the closest ghost opened fire, though it was unclear to Tyler exactly what he was aiming at now. The gun made an unnatural arch, riddling the floor, the walls and the ceiling with bullets, devastating irreplaceable museum pieces as the ghost became a vaporous miasma and was drawn towards the portal. The second ghost fought with his gun, which appeared to have failed. While the first vanished with a sucking scream, Tyler turned the contrap on the second.

Lucy seized the moment and kicked through the remaining ghost to send his gun flying across the room. It landed out of sight, skittering into darkness.

"That's the problem with the MP forties," explained Melissa to the disarmed ghost. "Just like the Sten guns. They frequently jam due to residue build up in the magazine feed."

"Phasmatis Licentia." The ghost spun into tendrils of light and was gone a moment later.

"Let's get out of here!" said Tyler, heading for the door.

"What about Goebbels?" asked Melissa.

"What about the papers?" Lucy asked.

"Worthless. We'll think of something else."

As they closed on the entrance hall a slender figure stepped out of the shadows to block their way, and levelled a gun. Lucy and Melissa raised their Tasers.

"Do not come any closer. I can assure you, this one will not misfire," said Goebbels. "Drop those toys you carry and I'll give you one last chance before I use it. Give the device to me. Now." He fired a shot over their heads as if to prove his gun worked. "The next one will be aimed lower."

The girls let their Tasers clatter to the floor.

"Alright!" said Tyler, wondering if she was close enough to use the contrap. By her reckoning she was beyond reach and, without an artefact to summon with, she figured Goebbels would easily have time to shoot them all dead before she could get the portal close enough. "Okay. You can have it!" She let the contrap dangle on its chain so that Goebbels could see she was not attempting to use it on him.

"Good girl. Now throw it over here and keep your distance."

"NO!" shouted Melissa. "DON'T DO IT!"

Lucy drew a knife from beneath her shirt and, in one fluid motion, launched it at Goebbels. The blade lodged deeply in his shoulder before he could react and for a brief, pain-seized moment he lowered his gun. Melissa charged him and the others followed. They ran for the door in a hail of badly aimed bullets as Goebbels rolled to the floor and tried to recover. Then they were outside and sprinting for the car, bullets zipping around them. Tyler looked back to see Goebbels hunched in the doorway taking pot shots.

"Where is it?" shouted Lucy as they ran for the trees. Tyler searched the night but the cab was gone.

The Texan

Tyler looked up and down the street, taking shelter behind a tree with Lucy and Melissa. A bullet thwacked into the trunk inches from her head. Still no sign of their MI6 operative. Or the cab.

"We have to get out of here or we're dead!" she said.

"Don't worry," said Melissa. "He only has a Luger. Eight rounds in the magazine, one in the chamber, so a total of nine, max. He's used at least six so he only has maybe three shots left before he needs to reload."

"Excellent! One bullet each," Lucy pointed out.

"Just trying to be positive."

"Yeah, well don't."

A dark car roared out of the night at high speed and skidded to a halt alongside the girls as the passenger door flew open. Across the road, Goebbels had stopped firing and disappeared inside.

"Get in!" shouted their driver.

The girls ducked into the cab as Goebbels returned to the entrance armed with a machine gun to light up the night. Spent shells scattered on the museum steps as he emptied the gun, but soon they were away from the museum and Goebbels was out of sight. Tyler felt a little safer.

"Where were you?" Lucy demanded of the driver.

"My apologies," he said. "The police were showing an interest. After the second drive by, I decided to move on. My directive was that you were to be left undisturbed, but I was watching the site through a night-scope and I set off as soon as you left the building."

For once, Lucy said nothing but made a small noise in the back of her throat.

"What she means to say is, thank you," said Melissa. "You probably just saved our lives.

"Do you have the pages, Tyler?"

"I left them behind." Tyler watched the nocturnal world pass by her window. "They were copies. I tested them. Goebbels had already removed the real speech."

"So?"

"So let's hope Weaver's having more luck with the diary."

*

Chapman listened sympathetically to Tyler's report.

"Glad you made it out alive, Ghost. Don't worry about the speech notes. We had to try. Perhaps Weaver will win out with the diary. What does Cog say about the whole thing?"

"She has another plan already laid out. Some idea about scuba diving in a lake outside Goebbels' old house."

"I thought she might. Very well. I'll be in touch and will confer with Cog. There is one other possibility. Some privately owned letters of Goebbels' have come up for auction. Needless to say, we're putting in a very competitive bid. I'll let you know if we're successful. Take a day off, Ghost. Get some rest."

*

Breakfast was pancakes and maple syrup, a full English or cereal. The girls shared the dining room with two couples, seated at their respective lace-clad tables. The owner and manager of the guesthouse was a tall man named Gerald, who not only cooked and served the breakfast, but also made considerable conversation as he did the rounds.

"Are you enjoying your visit to Boston?" seemed to be a favourite opening line.

"Oh yes. We met up with friends yesterday. What fantastic weather. Such a big blue sky," explained a well-spoken, fifty-something lady in a smart jacket and pristine jeans with creases down the front.

The girls sat in silence, eating, not wanting to talk about their mission in public but having nothing else to discuss. Melissa eyed Lucy with suspicion while Tyler obsessed about how they might acquire another Goebbels artefact. Lucy shoveled syrup-swamped pancakes into her mouth and if she was aware of her companions' discontent did not let it show. Their silence rendered it almost impossible for them not to listen-in on the banter around the room.

Nothing much of any interest was said until a balding man in a tweed jacket casually mentioned to Gerald that he and his wife had, the day before, enjoyed a thought-provoking visit to the Museum of World War II. Tyler's ears pricked up immediately.

"Oh? And is the war of particular interest to yourself?" asked Gerald, delivering a rack of fresh toast.

"It is. I'm a bit of a fanatic, in fact," he replied in his broad Texan drawl.

This snippet of information seemed to kindle a thought in Gerald's mind. His brows raised and he pursed his lips.

"I wonder," he said, thinking aloud. "I wonder if she would show you…"

"If *who* would show me? Show me what?"

"I have a great, great aunt living close by. We call her Grandma. Don't ask. It's a long story. She's a bit of a crackpot but she does have the most remarkable private collection of Nazi memorabilia. I could make a call. Would you be interested if I were to arrange a visit? It's not big stuff, you know, like Jeeps and tanks, but sometimes it's the smaller bits and pieces that hold the most interest."

"Why, yes. I'd be much obliged, Sir," said the balding man. "Very much obliged! I'd be grateful if you'd make that call."

Tyler, Melissa and Lucy exchanged conspiring looks.

"Right you are. I'll see what I can do."

The girls spent most of that day spying on the Texan and Gerald, hoping to learn the address of Grandma, but with little luck.

"We should pack up and go to Goebbels' old house," said Melissa. "We're only timewasting here."

"But this place is just down the road," argued Tyler. "We're already here. We should try it first. We might get lucky."

Lucy nodded. Melissa shrugged.

"Alright, but don't say I didn't warn you."

Tyler followed Gerald's movements ceaselessly as he busied himself with laundry, kitchen work and cleaning. She took a much needed break when he left the house for several hours, but spent her time worrying he might have decided to actually visit Grandma instead of phoning. To her relief he finally reappeared in the porch heavily burdened with grocery bags. She shadowed him again and almost blew her cover rushing over to hear what was said when he picked up the kitchen phone. She righted herself and slipped through the hallway to eavesdrop at the corner by the kitchen door.

"Yes, yes. It's me. Gerald." Gerald repeated himself loudly. Whoever he was talking to was clearly deaf. At least this made *her* job easier.

"Yes. Yes it is."

Tyler waited while Gerald listened.

"Can I…"

More waiting.

"Yes, of course, but…"

Clearly a bit of a talker.

"Yes, but, Grandma, I have a favour to ask. I have a friend in town for a short spell, shares your interest in the war. I was wondering if he could drop by. You know, take a quick look at your old collection."

Gerald waited for what seemed an insurmountable length of time before replying to Grandma's tirade on the other end of the line. When he spoke he sounded quite depressed.

"Yes, Grandma. Of course. It's not a problem." Gerald waited. "That's fine. Goodbye, Grandma."

Grandma had said no. Well that scuppered plan A.

She had to find another way. She watched as Gerald disappeared through the doorway and crept to the phone. Carefully picking it up she dialed the last caller service number and scribbled down the mechanically voiced digits into a notebook. Back in their room she handed it to Melissa.

Plan B.

Melissa texted the number through to Chapman for an address trace and minutes later Chapman came back with a local address complete with zip code.

"Here you go, Tyler."

The address popped up on her laptop screen along with an image of the property owner, a senior citizen in her eighties named Edith Schumacher. Edith had a shrunken look, wrinkled, tanned skin and thinning, white hair. In the photo on the screen she looked bewildered as if not quite sure what the photographer was up to.

"She looks harmless enough. A bit like my old Nan. By the way, Mr Chapman said to remind you it's your day off."

Tyler ignored the remark. She planned to take a day off once the five marauding gloves and all their accompanying ghosts were safely within the contrap and when she'd destroyed the contrap for good. In fact, she planned to take the rest of her life off.

Lucy peered over Tyler's shoulder at Grandma's photo.

"Perfect! This'll be like taking candy from a baby," she said.

Melissa shrugged.

"You obviously haven't met my neighbours' kid."

*

Grandma's place was a massive, old, colonial style house with verandas and window shutters, once painted white. The size of a tithe barn, it towered into the night sky ominously as Tyler surveyed its vast outline.

"Nobody say, *haunted house*," quipped Lucy. "It's the original *house on the hill!*" She drew her Taser and checked her belt pouch was fully loaded with cartridges.

"It's not just me then," said Melissa. "It does look like a, well, you said it." She turned to Tyler. "Are you sure this is a good idea?"

"Go back if you don't want to go in. I'm happy to go it alone. Perhaps *happy* is the wrong term..." Tyler set off for the house. She knew that Grandma was asleep upstairs but it was too dark in the house to see anything with clarity through the contrap. She'd learned that, although the house from the outside was clearly two stories high, it also had an attic and a cellar. Her plan was simple enough: break in and have a damned good nose around while the old bird slept. If they could find something pertaining to Goebbels, they would take it and leave. If not, no harm done. No one would ever know they had been there.

A colonnade ran the length of two sides of the house, meeting at a corner, and Tyler padded softly up from the rickety wooden steps to creep along it to a battered door. Behind her the girls followed, slowing only when Melissa put a foot through the rotting planking with a loud crunch.

"Sshhhh!" hissed Lucy. She glared at Melissa.

Tyler looked defeated.

Really?

"Not my fault!" whispered Melissa. "It's rotten!"

Tyler viewed Grandma's bedroom through the contrap to be sure the old woman had not awoken.

The door was in no better shape than the walkway and Tyler thought it would give way with one hearty shove from Melissa's shoulder. The whole frame shook as Tyler tested it, but she picked the lock anyway, not wanting to leave a trail of damage. She entered and stood in the hallway for a moment, looking around. Even in the darkness she could tell the place was a shrine to the German war effort. Walls were heavily massed with oil paintings of officers, and propaganda posters characterized war heroes shouting encouragements in Gothic text. Over the front door at the far end of the passage arched an impressive display of military daggers and swords. Further down the wall, most obvious of all, was a vast red flag bearing a black swastika in a white circle, its edges burned and tattered.

"I think we're in the right place," whispered Lucy, casting her Maglite's beam around the walls and illuminating the swastika. The light revealed peeling paint, decaying plaster and water marks streaking the walls, broken pipes and several holes in the floorboards. Lucy tried a door and the doorknob came off in her hand.

"Wow, this place is falling apart," she whispered.

She wriggled the doorknob back onto its spindle, pushed the door gently open and stepped into a dingy sitting room.

Tyler found a large, freestanding display case under the stairs in the hall and ran her torchlight over its contents. Shell casings, mortars and grenades, guns, badges and medals bedded on a folded flag.

"Hey, girls," she whispered. "I think I found something. Come look. Do you think this is the collection? There's loads of stuff inside."

Lucy poked her head out of the sitting room.

"Er, that's just the warm up act. You should take a look in here!"

They gathered in the lounge and swept their lights around in awe of the relics they saw.

"What? She must be a *real* fanatic," said Melissa. She found another door and peered into a different room before creeping in.

"Try *lunatic*," said Lucy.

Tyler didn't know where to start. There were just too many objects.

"Bit of a hoarder, wasn't she?"

"Er, guys." Melissa reappeared in the doorway. "There's more. It just goes on and on. And it's all Nazi stuff. The woman clearly has some issues."

"Okay, we'd best make a start."

"Let me guess," said Mel. "We're gonna split up, right? That's what always happens in the films just before the girls in the haunted house get slaughtered…"

"This is *way* too weird to be in a film," muttered Lucy. "But yeah, we're all gonna die."

Tyler had a strong urge to bash their heads together.

"We'll cover more ground if we split up. There are four levels to check out. I'll do the ground floor. Mel, you get the upstairs and Lucy can search the loft. Collect anything you find that could have a direct association with Goebbels."

"But, Tyler, this feels like we're just stealing," said Melissa.

Tyler took a deep breath. There wasn't time for this.

"We *are* stealing. We're the *Thieves of Antiquity*, but we're stealing for all the right reasons. We can always return it later if it's useless."

"Right. Sorry."

Lucy shrugged and Melissa nodded. They headed back out to the stairs leaving Tyler alone to search. She began systematically working her way around the room and soon decided there was nothing there that could be directly linked to Goebbels. She needed to find documents, letters or more speech notes. An autographed photo would be good but she figured that was probably too much to hope for. She tried to think what else might hang around for posterity after Goebbels' influential years but in the end she just moved on, searching her way from room to room. After several minutes pawing through a shelf of German books and papers she was discouraged to realize that any of these things might have had an association and she had no way of knowing. That was the problem; it had to be a clear and obvious association that anyone could see, otherwise it could be dangerous. She could walk right past his coat or his watch or his handgun and never know. She was contemplating this with mounting irritation and moving into yet another cluttered chamber when the floor beneath her feet gave way and she plummeted with surprising speed into utter darkness.

Grandma

An acrid smell filled the air. At first Tyler could see nothing, but her eyes slowly became accustomed to the new darkness until she could make out dim shapes and forms. She was cold from the armpits down, her hands and arms splayed outwards for some reason that she could not yet grasp. Tyler had no inkling where her torch had ended up but knew one thing: Her left thigh hurt like hell. She reached down to feel it and her hand plunged into a thick, greasy, cold liquid. Stretching out, the tips of her fingers found cold, rusting sides of an old tank. An oil tank she was in. A few feet above her head she could make out the holes she had made in the floor and the lid of the tank. Bits of decaying wood and iron were scattered over her and covered the slick surface of the black oil.

This must be a part of some antiquated heating system, she figured. *Manky, old oil.* But knowing that did not help her escape it.

The hole above was too high to reach. In normal circumstances she would have jumped high enough to grab hold but, buried in this gloopy, grasping oil, she could barely jump at all. The sides offered no help either; no hand holds and her hands were slick and slippery.

From the floors above echoed a sudden thumping followed by a scream. A gunshot made her jump.

What's going on? Where's Lucy? Where's Melissa? Who's shooting?

Tyler started to panic.

"Mel?" She called softly at first and then louder. "Mel! Mel, I'm down here! I'm trapped!"

She waited. More footsteps and thumping. Two more gunshots and muffled shouts.

What the hell is going on?

Help me, Mel!

"MEL! MELISSA WATTS, GET DOWN HERE NOW!" she screamed at the top of her voice. She tried again to leap up and catch the edge of the broken tank lid. It was no use. Her arms fell back into the sludge and she felt something hard slipping under the surface. She grabbed it before it sank completely.

My torch!

She wiped what oil she could from the glass and switched it on. It lit her claustrophobic prison instantly. It also illuminated the pallid, lucent heads and shoulders of the five ghosts sharing her small space. The German ghost-soldiers watched her intently.

Tyler screamed and dropped the torch. Terrified, she flailed around in the darkness, seeking her Maglite, her breathing rate rising. She scooped up the torch and swept its glass clean again with slippery fingers.

Ghostly faces stared, mouths gaping.

"MELISSA, GET ME OUT OF HERE!" she shouted from the very base of her lungs. "THERE ARE GHOSTS IN HERE! GET ME OUT! GET ME OUT! GET ME OUT!"

She watched the ghouls feverishly but tensed further when hollow footfalls sounded from somewhere across the unlit room. Someone, some *thing*, was descending the wooden steps into the cellar. She tried desperately to control her respiration.

"Mel? Lucy? Is that you?" The footsteps closed and Tyler had a very bad feeling. Her head swam from both the oil fumes and her escalating terror. Her heart thrashed like it wanted to leave her body. A shadowy face loomed over her, peering through the broken lid.

"What you doing in *there*?"

"Mel! Thank God it's you! Get me out! Now! There are five ghosts in here and they're looking at me like I'm dinner. Hurry up!" Tyler shuddered uncontrollably. She reached up to grasp Melissa's hands as more chaos sounded from above.

"What is that? What's going on up there?" Tyler asked, hauling herself up to the jagged, rusting lid with Melissa's help.

"Oh *that*…" said Melissa, matter-of-factly. "We woke *the beast*. That's Grandma, by the way. Turns out she's not as harmless as we thought. Turns out she's a psychopathic, Nazi head case with a foul mouth and a shotgun."

Tyler swore. "We need to leave."

"My thoughts precisely. Although I was hoping she might shoot Lucy first. Can't we leave them together just a little longer?"

Tyler slid down the side of the oil tank and tried in vain to scrape herself clean. Black, viscous oil oozed from her clothes and boots.

"Ew," said Melissa.

"Come on," said Tyler, heading for the precarious looking staircase, but Melissa caught her arm to slow her, swinging her torch around the room. The walls were lined with shelving and every possible space was occupied by relics. Among the multitude of objects, Tyler saw books, bound in what looked suspiciously like skin, ceremonial SS daggers and, most disturbingly, a chair made from what Tyler could only imagine were human bones.

"Look at this place. The woman's crazy. Why would anyone..."

Tyler was mesmerized by the sheer number of artefacts.

"Mel, there *has* to be something here that would work. So much stuff..."

"You're probably right, Tyler. But you said it yourself; we have to go and, anyway, we could search through this lot for years and still not find anything. It's not worth it. Let's get out."

"Right," said Tyler, feeling defeated. She forced herself up the creaky steps, her injured thigh screaming. She reached the hallway moments after Melissa, just in time to see Lucy bolting down the stairs towards them.

"Don't shoot!"

Grandma's thundering footsteps and her tirade of obscenities chased Lucy. Tyler and Melissa froze, dumbstruck as she shouldered the outer door off its hinges. The frame splintered as Grandma blasted two shots at them.

Lucy didn't stop.

"DON'T STAND THERE. RUN!"

*

Lucy squealed.

"Sorry," said Melissa. "Are you sure you don't want to go to a doctor?"

"No thanks. Too much fuss. Just get them out and sterilize it with iodine."

The girls were in their bedroom at the guesthouse, Lucy bent over her bed, face down in a pillow trying not to scream, her ruined combats balled in a heap on the floor. Melissa twanged her latex forensics gloves, enjoying every second.

"Okay.   If you're sure."   Melissa steadied her tweezers, aiming for one of five shotgun pellets embedded in Lucy's rear.

"I'm sure."

"Brace yourself. This is going to sting."

"Ow! *You mother... Stupid, senile, Nazi witch...*"

"Now, now, Lucy."   Tyler, suppressed giggles. "Melissa's only trying to help."

"I was talking about the old woman," spat Lucy, needlessly.

Melissa plucked a lead shot from Lucy's flesh.

"OW!"

"You want some more paracetamol?" offered Tyler.

"No thanks. Better not or I might O.D."

"Two down. Three to go," said Melissa. She let the lead ball plink into the waste bin. "I hope you don't get lead poisoning."

Lucy glared at her.

"So, *that* didn't work." Melissa grappled with the third pellet. "Can we try my idea now?"

"One thing's for sure," muttered Lucy. "I'm not going back to Grandma's. There has to be an easier way."

"My way *is* the easier way. It won't be guarded and it's highly unlikely they'll be any crazed, Nazi grannies hanging around."

"Gets my vote," said Lucy.

When Lucy was purged of lead and her wounds sterilized and dressed, it was Tyler's turn for treatment. Melissa drew out several large splinters from the long gash on Tyler's thigh. After that, too, was cleaned, sterilized and bandaged, the girls gathered around Melissa's laptop. Melissa showed them numerous website articles on Nazi relics from lakes in the Salzkammergut region of inner Austria and pointed out one article in particular that talked about searching in the deep mud at the bottom of Lake Grundle, where one of Joseph Goebbels' old houses stood on the shoreline.

"In recent years divers have hauled up SS daggers, Lugers, propaganda leaflets, large-caliber machine-gun bullets, an anti-aircraft gun, metal cases of sterling currency forged by the Nazis, bazooka shells and launchers," she explained. "The mud at the bottom of the lakes is devoid of oxygen and so the finds come out perfectly preserved. The guns that were recovered were still good enough to shoot.

"It seems to me that people can't live by a lake without, at some point in time, throwing something into the water. I'd say the probability that Goebbels did the same is quite high." She pointed out an image of a lakeside house. "All the finds have come from lakes in this area. There it is."

Tyler looked at Goebbels' old house with interest. The image showed a huge, attractive Austrian villa with a tall peaked tower at one corner. The house faced onto a beautiful lake of shimmering water and was backed by a range of snow-dusted Alps. It was an image that haunted Tyler as she lay in bed, drifting into an uneasy slumber.

*

She was woken once more by a call from Chapman. She checked her watch: 7.32 a.m.

Tyler groaned. She'd had less than three hours rest. She leaned on her bad leg and groaned again. It hurt more than it had the night before.

"Ghost?"

"Here, Sir."

"Still no word from Weaver and I'm afraid our shot at the auction has evaporated. I'm trying to get to the bottom of it but the sellers have pulled out and gone underground, along with Goebbels' letters. Sorry, but we still need you to acquire a suitable artefact for Goebbels. You've done very well so far; better than anyone dreamed. It's just this last one."

"We're on it, Mr Chapman. We're going to need flights to Austria. We have to get to Lake Grundle. Austrians call it Grundlsee."

"I'll have that organized asap. Mr Flynn will escort you there as before. Good luck, Ghost."

*

Tyler viewed the narrow area between Joseph Goebbels' old home, now known as Villa Roth, and the slick, still water of Grundlsee. With the contrap set to the *Past Eye*, she tugged the little lever around the edge and watched time in reverse, days cycling backwards. She'd been there for several hours, working her way back through the years until she was quite sure she had reached 1945. She slowed the speed only when the slim figure of a man emerged from the grand villa. She had watched him come and go several times now, once with his family and twice only with a woman for company, presumably his wife, but this time was different. This time he was alone and was carrying a small wooden box. Tyler held her breath as she watched Goebbels walk slowly down the steps leading to the narrow gravel beach and the water's edge. She had hardly dare hope for what she saw him do next.

Goebbels strolled along to the beach, looking wistfully across the lake. He opened the box, took a gun from his pocket and placed it in the box before closing the lid and hurling it high into the air. Tyler followed the box's arc until it entered the water about twenty metres from shore. She gently adjusted the contrap's lever and watched again. She watched over and over until she could pinpoint the exact spot where the box had hit the water.

"There," she said to Melissa and Lucy. "It went in right there."

*

The lake water was icy cold despite a thick layer of neoprene. Tyler adjusted her wetsuit and checked her oxygen gauge. Just over half a tank left. Good for another fifteen minutes. Grundlsee stretched out around her, its unspoiled shoreline a picturesque curve scattered with tress and punctuated by the occasional exquisite dwelling.

The place had an inert restfulness about it. Lucy surfaced next to her, disturbing calm waters.

"Anything?"

Lucy shook her head and peeled off her diving mask, sweeping her hair back and forth to shed water.

"Lots of mud. I can't stay out here much longer. I'm freezing to the bone."

"Me too. Take a minute. One more dive and we'll call it a day. I really need to sleep." Tyler waved to Melissa, now watching from the shore in the shadow of Villa Roth. Next to her on the beach several upturned rowboats rested, their oars alongside.

Tyler spat on the inside of her mask and spread the saliva around with her finger tips to prevent steam-up. She pulled her mask down and wriggled it into position, gave Lucy a nod and plunged beneath the surface into an aquamarine netherworld.

She descended, working arms and legs hard to pull herself deeper. The day was still bright above the water but the light penetrated less the lower she went and silence engulfed her. A moment later Lucy's dark outline came into view and they exchanged the okay sign. They dropped another two metres to a bank of chocolate mud where touch replaced the sense of sight by necessity. Probing mud, Tyler searched for any kind of object that might have been discarded by Goebbels, while hoping she would lay her fingers on the wooden box. Lucy worked a few feet to Tyler's right, lost to the soup. Each time she pushed her hands into the soft, sucking mud, clouds of silt plumed up into the water to reduce visibility. Tyler gave up trying to see what she was doing. As her hands investigated, her mind wandered. Lucy's behaviour troubled her. Tyler thought back over their last few operations. Before they'd broken into the Museum of World War II, Lucy had been texting madly, refusing to reveal the recipient's identity. The next minute they were set upon by Nazi ghosts and Goebbels himself had arrived. She had also taken herself off several times along their journey and had offered no real explanation why. It didn't sit comfortably with Tyler. It was awful to admit it but right now she didn't trust Lucy. She checked to her right but could see no one, not even a vague shape that had been there moments before. She shrugged. Lucy was a law unto herself.

Tyler felt something hard in the mud and tugged until it came free. She ran gloved hands over its length but, deciding it was only a piece of an old branch, discarded it. She was returning to the mud bank when hands grasped her about the shoulders.

Lucy?

Tyler tried to turn but the hands held her firmly and she could find no purchase on the gloop beneath her knees. She panicked. Lucy was a spy and had come to kill her. Down here no one would see. Nothing could be proven. Lucy would kill her and then tell of a tragic diving accident in which one of her best friends had perished.

Tyler fought back, managed to break clear of one hand. It bought her enough freedom to turn halfway and then drop her upper body to kick out as hard as she could at Lucy with her good leg. She felt the weight of a body as she made contact. A gratifying stream of bubbles issued from her attacker. Lucy's hazy form was swallowed by murk. Tyler pushed herself away and headed for the surface, desperate to get her head above water.

The House by the Lake

Lucy surfaced a few metres away, tore off her mask and shouted furiously.

"What the hell was all that about? You nearly killed me! Jeez!"

Tyler trod water, grimacing at her.

"What do you mean? You were trying to kill *me*. Just keep away from me!"

"I was trying to kill you? Why would I do that, you numbskull?"

Tyler did not respond. She simply studied Lucy's face, trying to discern if this was all part of an act.

Lucy had a moment of clarity.

"Oh, I see. You don't trust me! You really think I'm trying to kill you. You've got me all sussed. *Really*?

What? So I can take the contrap? I get it! You think I'm a Nazi. Well that's great. Thanks. After everything I've done. Well, I think I've had enough fun for one day." She headed for shore not waiting for a response.

Tyler watched her go, glad to be above the water line.

"Wait," she called out. Lucy turned, pain in her eyes.

"What? You not done insulting me yet?"

"No. I mean yes. I mean... Just wait a minute. If you weren't trying to kill me, why did you attack me?"

"I didn't *attack you*. I was just trying to find you, for goodness sake. I couldn't see a damn thing. I was just trying to tell you I'd had enough and was going to head to the surface."

"Really?"

"Yes! *Really!*"

"Okay," said Tyler after a moment's contemplation. "Sorry. I may have overreacted."

"You can say that again." Lucy swam to shore, scowling all the way. Tyler watched her go, feeling foolish and awkward.

"I still don't trust you, Lucy Denby," she said to herself.

Sunlight bouncing from the lake surface made her squint. She looked away but movement caught her eye. Someone other than Melissa was watching them. A figure shadowed by a rank of pine trees some way off to the left of the villa, lowered binoculars and looked back at her.

Who is that?

The next moment the figure vanished behind some low shrubs. Tyler waited and scanned the bank, searching, but the presence was gone. She looked back at the villa and watched Lucy stalk past Melissa and go inside.

Suddenly Tyler knew exactly what she needed to do.

*

Chapman had arranged for Villa Roth to be empty and so it was, for the near future at least, the girls' to use as they pleased. One condition applied: they were to leave it as they'd found it, down to the last speck of dust. The returning residents were not to know the house had been used and so a complete photographic record of each room had been kept to aid them in replacing everything just as it had been when they'd arrived. The girls gathered upstairs in the large bedroom they had sequestered.

"Are you sure?" asked Melissa.

"As sure as I'm seeing you now. Someone was watching us. You wouldn't have seen them from where you were on the beach, but I saw someone spying on us."

"That's a shame," said Lucy, glowering out of the window at the lake. "Since we came here so we could hunt for an artefact without anyone spying on us. Kind of defeats the purpose, don't you think?"

"Yes," snapped Tyler. "I get that."

"Do you think it was one of the gloves? Maybe it was just a birdwatcher or something," said Melissa, clearly unsettled by the news.

Lucy laughed cynically.

"Oh, shut your face," said Melissa. "Why are you always so completely unhelpful?"

"Deal with it." Lucy gave her a flat grin. "Think I need to be alone." She left the room, slamming the door behind her.

"I *really* thought she was trying to murder me."

"Who knows? Maybe she was and you just fought her off."

"Maybe." Tyler sat down and examined the gash on her leg. She sterilized it again and put on a clean dressing. Soaking it in freezing cold lake water for an hour hadn't helped.

"Mel, I had an idea when I was out there watching you on the shore, but to make it work we'll have to convince Goebbels that he needs to come here. We'll need to let our little spy think we're *really* on to something. Maybe we can get Goebbels worried enough to make an appearance."

"I'm listening."

*

The next morning Tyler received a reply from Chapman.

"Twenty-four heat signatures on the shores of Grundlsee. I've accounted for all of them except two who appear to be loitering purposelessly in a copse near Villa Roth. I think they're the ones. As you face the lake, they'll be off to your right."

"That's exactly where I saw the spy yesterday," said Tyler.

"Then it's a fair bet they have a shelter close by, or perhaps they've set up a hide in the woods, or are staying in one of the other houses. Either way, I'd say you're being observed."

"That's all I wanted to know. Thanks."

"Anytime."

Tyler ended the call and turned to the others.

"We're on."

Back on the gravel beach, Tyler went through the motions of searching with the contrap, only this time for the benefit of those spying. When she thought she'd been searching long enough for the spies to have seen and realized what she was doing, she mimicked her actions of the previous afternoon, following the arc of Goebbels' wooden box as it trailed through the air to land in the lake. She repeated the action.

"Hey, guys!" she shouted. "I think I found something!" Lucy and Melissa ran over in mock excitement.

"Where?"

"What is it?"

"Goebbels threw something into the lake. It landed over there. We just have to fish it out!"

"Then what are we waiting for?"

"Let's go get it!"

Job done. Unless the spies were deaf and blind or had no perception of what the contrap could do, they would soon be reporting the right kind of message back to their superiors. Now all the girls had to do was dive again to search for the box, which they'd planned to do in any case. Then they would wait for Goebbels to show. If he came anywhere near the villa, it would no longer matter whether they had reclaimed the box or not.

Tyler fetched her scuba gear.

*

Later that night the girls enjoyed a rare couple of hours forgetting their cares. It seemed unlikely that Goebbels would be able to react as quickly as to arrive before the next day or two and so the girls felt safe enough for now. Yes, they were no doubt being spied upon.

But what's new?

They relaxed and even Lucy chilled-out enough to join in a few rounds of cards. Their second dive had turned up nothing, not even an old beer bottle, but Tyler didn't care. She looked out over the dark, reticent water and knew in the pit of her stomach the gloved ghost of Joseph Goebbels was on his way to Austria.

*

The fragile sense of respite slowly dispelled over the following day. If Goebbels was coming they would soon know about it and who could tell what they might face? If their plan had failed, he was not coming and they would be stuck once more without an artefact. Back to square one. Nobody wanted that.

Tyler contacted Chapman hoping for something positive on Weaver's mission but there was no news and it seemed that Weaver had simply vanished again. Tyler pictured him in another prison cell and part of her lurched at the thought. Lucy clearly feared the same, or worse, repeatedly checking her mobile for messages that never came. She became more withdrawn and distant as the evening deepened and at nine o'clock announced she was going to bed.

Melissa took the first shift. At one a.m. Tyler woke her to take over the watch for Goebbels' arrival. Tyler sat cross-legged on her bed as Melissa settled down to sleep and wondered if it would be tonight, nerves churning her gut. She left the two girls sleeping and climbed the staircase to the top room of the tower, which served as a perfect lookout. It had only one blind spot where the house met the tower and masked part of the aspect, but otherwise the tower room gave a panoramic view.

Tyler tried to make herself comfortable. An hour of utter boredom passed and she needed a break from peering into the night through the room's twelve arched windows. She took out the contrap, set the switch to the spiral symbol and turned it over to look into the crystal lens.

"Is anybody there?" she asked, before realizing the cliché and irony of her question.

In the lens, mist twirled. She knew neither Albert nor Zebedee were there.

Hitler should be in there somewhere though, along with Bagshot, Kylie Marsh, Travis of Normandy and, oh yes, several Nazi soldiers.

Bad idea.

She turned the contrap and set it back to the *Safeguarding Skull* before any unpleasant entities could show themselves. As she did this a soft rumbling sounded from somewhere outside and she searched the night for the source of the noise. A light was shifting smoothly through woodland where she knew a roughly maintained road ran down to the lake, not far from the house. Its presence caused a knot in her stomach. Switching the contrap to the *Present Eye*, she focused in on a moving car as it flashed briefly through trees, headlamps lighting up the night. She glimpsed men inside it and the tell-tale blue glow of a glove. That was all she needed to see. Goebbels was on his way. It was happening tonight. It was happening right now.

Tyler dashed down stairs and shot breathlessly into the bedroom, adrenalin coursing.

"Get up! He's here! Goebbels is outside!"

Lucy groaned. Melissa awoke, screwing her face up as though in pain.

"He's in a car coming this way. He has men with him."

Melissa slipped out of bed fully dressed while Lucy pulled on a tight fitting black top and strapped on her knives and Taser holster.

"Ready," she said. "Shall we go?"

Tyler was unsure how far the visitors might have gone in the short time she'd left the tower room, but it didn't really matter. They would come. Now or in five minutes; what was the difference?

The girls crept downstairs, leaving lights off and peering from windows whenever they could. Outside a half-moon struggled to pierce a blanket of deep cloud. Through a kitchen window, Tyler scanned the forest where she'd seen the car but found no lights and no sign of any vehicle. She had a really bad feeling they were being played.

Oh well, too late now.

Searching again and finding nothing, she doubted her own sanity and wondered if she'd been seeing things. Had she really seen a car carrying a glove? She shook herself. Of course she'd seen him. It was Goebbels, for sure. Or was it? What if Mengele or Himmler had come in his place? Or one of the others? What if Reinhard Heydrich was, at this very moment, herding a battalion of reveries towards Villa Roth? She knew then she *was* undoubtedly losing her mind. She knew she must be crazy to ever think she stood a chance against the gloves. After all, they had powers she knew nothing about.

A sudden noise from the front door shattered her nerves and left her shaking. She wanted to run back upstairs to get the tracer monitor to see if the glove was Himmler or Mengele, or neither, but it was too late for that. They were right outside. She could hear them testing the doors, rattling windows.

"I need to know who the glove is," she yelled. "Lucy, I need the artefacts! I left mine upstairs." Banging from the side of the house nearest the lake increased her urgency.

Lucy holstered her Taser, unfastened the chain from around her neck and threw it, along with the capsules, across to Tyler.

"Here. I'm gonna check around the side." Lucy slipped into the hall and out of sight. Tyler checked the shiny metal capsules on Lucy's chain. She had four, each labeled with a glove's name excepting, of course, Goebbels. She heard a door open, followed by quick footsteps. Her pulse quickened as adrenaline flooded her body, bringing the jitters. Hands shaking, she unscrewed one of the capsules and was relieved to find a finger bone protruding. Then she fastened the chain around her neck and toed her way out into the hall after Lucy.

"Mel?" she whispered, expecting to hear a reply from somewhere close by. She began to worry when no answer came. "Melissa!" she hissed more loudly. More thumping echoed from a door on the other side of the villa.

Melissa Watts, where are you?

She shuffled through an open doorway to look across an empty lounge and out through windows across the lake.

"Lucy?" she called, no longer caring for stealth. Still no reply. She flicked the contrap switch to the spiral symbol, ready to use the *Ghost Portal*.

"Melissa, where are you?" She heard anger in her own voice. Anger and fear. Leaving the room, she turned into the hall and crept to the door where she had previously heard the banging. The door stood wide open to the night now and she was met by a view of the black crystal waters of the lake beyond the steps and the gravel beach. She thought Melissa and Lucy might be waiting for her outside, unable to hear her calling so, with trepidation, she stepped out into the night. Nothing moved. Not even a night bird over the black lake. A sudden noise behind her made her reel about and she screamed, briefly glimpsing Goebbels' bluish face and a boat oar swinging at her head. The oar struck. The world waltzed.

Dizzying pain.

Blackness.

Dead Again

When Tyler came round she knew that something was very odd indeed. She was freezing and in a darkness that was otherworldly. She thought she'd gone deaf until she realized she was underwater. For several cloudy moments she wondered if she was actually dead, because she was breathing and yet she was without her scuba gear or any source of air. She was breathing water and that meant she must surely be dead, or at best, in her dying moments.

So this is what it feels like.

A thought struck her: There was only one possible way she knew of that a person might breathe water and not die, and that was with the protection of the contrap. She remembered with a jolt the last thing she'd seen: Goebbels knocking her out with a paddle. Her hand flew to her chest. The contrap was there, but how? Why had Goebbels not taken it from her?

I'm not dead. I'M NOT DEAD!

Panic struck as a ghostly form closed on her in the murky water and she tried to move away, only to find she was tethered to a large rock by a rope binding her ankles and holding her in the depths. The ghost came nearer and Tyler concluded she must be dreaming or experiencing some kind of waking nightmare because nothing made sense.

The ghost was close now but she still could see no face, or name the figure, because it looked away as though hearing a call from the surface. Then she knew the face as it turned and found her in the pitch and she would have squealed with excitement had her throat not been so occluded with water.

Albert? Albert!

Albert smiled. He looked at her for a long moment as though savouring a view he had missed and then pointed to the rope anchoring her feet. Tyler nodded her understanding. She needed to untie the knots herself. Albert would most likely not be able to do that. It didn't matter. Her hands were unbound and so it was easy. She freed herself and swam for the surface, broke into air and ejected a great lungful of water. She coughed, purging lungs of icy water and dragging in great gulps of air, which, at first did not seem to want to be breathed, but she did it and did not really mind. Albert was there.

"Wait, Missy!" he whispered into her ear as she slowly recovered. "'E's still 'ere! 'E's in there." Albert, half submerged, pointed to Roth Villa. "It's Goebbels."

That was all she needed to know. She swam to the shore while her burning lungs eased and hauled herself out of the water. Albert's words had flooded her with a new sense of purpose and all pain was forgotten. Tyler stood, streams of water pouring from her sodden clothes, and scowled at the villa.

He's in there. And he thinks he's killed me.

She strode up the steps from the beach and slipped the contrap's switch from the *Safeguarding Skull* to the *Ghost Portal*. She slapped it firmly against the door post of Villa Roth and immediately heard a scraping, struggling sound from within the house.

"Come out, come out, wherever you are!" she shouted. Unnatural thumping and scraping noises issued from the lounge. He was there, trapped against the wall as the summoning tore at him. Tyler took the contrap from the post and the scrabbling ceased. Several steps into the hall she placed the contrap onto the doorpost of the lounge door. She pulled the lever to open the *Ghost Portal*, using the house as the summoning artefact.

"Phasmatis Licentia! Goodbye Reich Minister for Propaganda."

For a split second Goebbels appeared before her, face warping into neon blue essence and spinning into threads in the air. There came a rushing sound which climaxed as he flowed into the portal, squealing and shrieking. And then he was gone. Silence. Tyler released the contrap's lever and listened to it rotate with its soft clicking.

"Compenso Pondera," she whispered. She was about to leave the house in search of her missing friends when a voice from the lounge startled her.

"Hello?" It was the voice of a young girl.

Tyler peered around the doorway. Standing in the middle of the room was a naked, ashen girl, covering herself as best as she could with only her hands and arms, shivering and looking nervously about. Around her were scattered Goebbels' old clothes.

"Emily?" asked Tyler. "Are you Emily Stanford?"

The girl nodded. Tyler took a sofa throw and wrapped it around the girl. Clearly terrified and very confused, Emily nodded again.

"Who... Who are you?" she asked.

"My name's Tyler May. You're safe now. You don't need to worry."

Emily leaned forward and vomited. Tyler caught her before she collapsed and helped her into a chair. There came running footfalls from the hallway and Lucy appeared in the doorway, leaning in.

"Tyler! You alright?" she asked. "Who's this?"

Lucy's chain and four capsules lay on the floor where Goebbels had last stood. Tyler picked these up and handed them back to Lucy as Melissa arrived, breathless.

"I'm fine," said Tyler and she meant it, though she felt she was in shock. "Here, these are yours."

Melissa noticed Albert, who had walked through the lounge wall to stand next to Tyler.

"Albert! You're back!"

Albert cast Melissa a wink. Tyler found another throw and put it around Emily's shoulders, hugging her close. The girl was shivering and deathly pale.

"Albert saved me," explained Tyler. "Goebbels knocked me out with an oar and ditched me in the lake, but Albert rescued me. I'm not sure quite how he did it, but that can wait. Girls, this is Emily Stanford. She was gloved with Goebbels."

"You mean..." began Melissa.

"Yep."

"You got him?" asked Lucy in disbelief. "You mean you got Goebbels?"

Tyler nodded. She was also shivering and felt weak at the knees.

"Goebbels is gone. Right now we need to look after Emily. Where are the others, the men who came with Goebbels?"

"Heading for the hills," said Lucy.

"We tasered them until they begged for mercy," boasted Melissa.

"Beggin' your pardon, Missy," said Albert. "But it weren't just me what saved ya'. Oh no. It were Mr Lieberman too." He nodded to his side where a shadow seemed to grow from the wall. Zebedee Lieberman entered the room and gathered form to stand with Albert. He clenched his pipe in his teeth and removed his top hat to give a brief bow.

"At your service, Miss May."

*

"So how did you two save me exactly? I still don't understand." Tyler cupped her hands around a steaming mug of hot chocolate. She didn't know what time of night it was. She didn't care.

Emily had eaten a small meal and had sipped hot chocolate. After that she'd curled up beneath a duvet and fallen fast asleep in the girls' room. Zebedee had told them she should be alright but to expect her to need a lot of rest for the first few days of her recovery.

"I stayed with Albert for a long time, never leaving his side. The reveries showed no further interest in him, so it was easy to remain in the graveyard. I talked to him, for that is all you can do with a patient who's been reveried. For a long time he did not respond and I wondered if he would ever recover, but after a day or so he turned his head and looked at me. It was not much, just a small sign, but I knew then that all was not lost. I spoke words of encouragement and comfort to the lad, just trying to bring him back from the void, and eventually he spoke to me.

"He gradually regained the will that the reveries had stolen from him. When I knew he was strong enough, we set out to find you, homing in on the contrap, knowing that it would eventually lead us to you. We were passing over mountains and closing on the house when we saw you and Goebbels out by the front door. Alas, we came too late to stop Goebbels from striking you out."

"But we knew we'ad t'do somfin'."

"We were quite stumped for a moment or two, but then young Albert here had a flash of inspiration. A rather good one, I should say!"

Albert shrugged as if to say *it was nothing really*.

"We both know about the contrap but Albert immediately knew what he needed to do." Zebedee tapped out the smoldering remnants of his old tobacco and refilled his ghostly pipe with fresh as he spoke. "He had me distract Goebbels right away. I mean before Goebbels had a chance to search you for the contrap. While I led Goebbels on a merry dance, Albert took the contrap! Just like that! He lifted it right off you and carried it away for safe keeping. I've rarely seen a ghost move things in the real world like that before. I was amazed!"

"But I…" began Tyler. "You must be a powerful ghost to do that, Albert."

Albert shrugged again.

"Guess it were my 'motions," he said.

"He *is* a strong ghost," stated Zebedee. "At least, he proved to have some strong emotions when you were in peril. In fact, I'd say it was most likely his love for you that made him strong enough to lift the contrap and bear its weight. Of course, he also carried it back to you once Goebbels had searched you and found nothing but Lucy's chain of artefacts. He put you in a boat, weighted you down with that rock, and was shoving off into the water when I distracted him again so Albert could return the contrap to you. He set the switch to the skull symbol and tucked the device well into your coat so that Goebbels would not see it and the rest, as they say, is history."

"Thank you," said Tyler to both of the ghosts. "Thank you for all you have done." She went to Zebedee and, although she could feel nothing when he offered her his hand, she took it as best she could and kissed it. She laid a gentle kiss upon Albert's brow in the same manner, feeling nothing but cool air upon her lips.

"Thank you, Albert. You saved my life."

"It were nuffin' really. I couldn't let 'im hurt ya' now, could I? Not my Missy."

*

Tyler cried as she lay down to sleep. She cried out of sorrow for the horror forced upon Emily Stanford. She cried from exhaustion and pain. She also cried out of joy and relief. Goebbels was no more, Emily was safe and recovering and Albert had returned. She didn't know who she loved most: Albert himself, or Zebedee for returning him to her. She cried all the more because Albert was still a ghost and would be forever untouchable. She turned her head and found him in the darkness of the bedroom.

Unaware that she watched him, he stood by the window, looking through a gap in the curtains like a sentry on duty.

Albert Goodwin was watching over her. She rolled over and slept soundly.

*

The next day the girls packed and put Roth Villa back as they had found it. Mr Flynn picked them up in a cab and escorted them to Salzburg Airport where they caught a flight home to England. After a brief physical examination at MI5 headquarters, Emily Stanford was released back into the care of her parents in Watford. Tyler, Melissa and Lucy also underwent a physical assessment for duty. It was while Tyler was lying in an MI5 examination ward, hooked up to a variety of machines, awaiting test results, and having recently received twelve stitches in her torn thigh and numerous jabs, that Agent Weaver appeared in the doorway, one arm in a sling. Lucy and Melissa were with him, Lucy hanging off his good arm. And she was actually smiling.

"I got the diary," said Weaver, waving a thick brown envelope and finding a chair next to Tyler's bed. "Of course, it's completely useless now."

Tyler grinned.

"Well done," said Weaver.

"You too. Glad you made it back in one piece. Well almost." Tyler pointed to his damaged arm. "What happened?"

"Nazi spies were waiting for me when I left the library with the book. There was shooting. Guess I'm lucky it was only my arm."

"Does it hurt?"

"Not really. Not if I keep it still. I'll be out of action for a while though, just until it heals."

"Chapman's sending us back to school," said Melissa, examining Tyler's heart rate monitor. "Maybe for good."

"He didn't say that," said Lucy.

"No, but it's a feeling I got when he spoke to us," explained Melissa. "I'm not sure he wants us to continue."

"Let's not jump to conclusions," said Weaver. "He may just want you to rest up for a bit. You've had a traumatic ride. A break would do you good. You've all worked hard."

"And we have schoolwork to catch up with," said Melissa.

Lucy groaned.

Tyler thought about this. School, homework, exams, gym class and county gymnastics training, Mum and Dad, home, normality; it all seemed alien to her and, although she'd longed for it, fought for it even, now that it was here facing her she was unsure if she wanted it any longer.

"Hey, I forgot!" She delved into a bag at the side of her bed and pulled out a crumpled piece of notepaper and smoothed it out.

"Oh, here we go." Lucy rolled her eyes. "Always with the lists..." The others sniggered.

Taking a pen, Tyler put a tick next to Goebbels' name on the artefacts list. She added notes and reread it.

~~*Adolf Hitler*~~	*gloved with Kylie Marsh*
	(deceased)
Heinrich Himmler	*gloved with Freddy Carter*
	(alive)
Josef Mengele	*gloved with Steven Lewis*
	(alive)

Reinhard Heydrich	*gloved with Susan Ellis (alive)*
~~*Joseph Goebbels*~~	*gloved with Emily Stanford (alive) SAFE*
Adolf Eichmann	*gloved with Harry McGrath (alive)*

Artefacts Acquired

Heinrich Himmler	√	*Finger bones*
Josef Mengele	√	*Finger bones*
Adolf Eichmann	√	*Penknife, cigarette holder & comb*
Reinhard Heydrich	√	*Finger bones*
Joseph Goebbels	√	*Villa*

Find out what has become of Adolf Hitler

Two down. Four to go. Tyler was nowhere near ready to take a break.

The Box

It was odd to be back home. Comforting, yet somehow claustrophobic. Her parents ran around, full of concern and wanting to know what she'd been up to, treating her like a war hero. She gave them the bare facts and, when she tired of going over it, cited the Official Secrets Act and sequestered herself to her bedroom.

To Tyler's frustration, her gym coach would not let her train until her thigh had fully healed. She skulked around the school yard feeling more out of place than she'd ever felt before. Lucy also appeared to be struggling to adapt back into normality. Tyler watched her from across the classroom in what seemed a surreal throwback to another time and another life. A time before the contrap. Lucy was withdrawing into her dark, gothic shell. She appeared to take pleasure in flaunting her distain of the dress code: purple lipstick, no school tie, knee-length boots and an outright refusal to remove the chain bearing the artefacts in money capsules. The first day back, she'd been sent home. Now Miss Sedgewick no longer seemed to know what to do with her. She considered Lucy with a vexed expression and eventually plumped for a week's worth of detention. Lucy glared out of the window at deserted playing fields, uncaring.

Tyler sympathized and realized this was a new development. She, too, felt like a caged animal, holed up in the school and forced to rest. Melissa was the only one of them who seemed at ease with the situation, apparently enjoying school life and the work she was set.

Tyler completed homework with due diligence but lacked enthusiasm. She made many lists. Lists about boring everyday things. But, ever more so, her lists took on a new function. The petty items featured less and less until eventually the lists solely concerned healing her leg and getting fit; being ready for when they would be in the field again. She lived for that moment and *that* moment alone. She was chatted up by boys in the school canteen as usual but none of it mattered. How could it when four children remained trapped with the gloved ghosts of Nazi war criminals?

There were other questions too. Questions too weighty to be forgotten for long. She revisited them repeatedly.

What has become of Hitler's ghost?

Why did the bones of Josef Mengele not work as a summoning artefact?

At Zebedee's request, she had put him back into the contrap.

"Some strange things have happened lately. I think at least one of us should return to the contrap just to keep an eye on things," he had said. "Even more so, now that Goebbels is in there."

Albert had asked to remain free to continue watching over Tyler and the other girls. She saw him frequently in moments when no one else was around. He would come to her each night before she went to sleep and whisper reassuring words to her. Then he would remain like a sentry, watching vigilantly from her window. When she woke in the mornings he was the first thing she saw. His presence helped her sleep and she began to feel fitter and more able. She trained outside of school hours to get back to her prior fitness level, despite her coaches contrary directives. When four long weeks had passed and her leg was healing well, her MI5 mobile, which had lain silent all this time, buzzed into life. She snatched it up eagerly from her bedside table.

"Yes?"

"Ghost? Are you well?"

She sat on her bed and looked at Albert, who watched her.

"Bored. What's new?"

"I've been monitoring the tracers you planted on Mengele and Himmler. Incredibly, they still seem to be unaware of them. Guess you struck lucky. I've had operatives following them both but I've had to pull my men out for... political reasons. Himmler made at least one visit to the mountainous Urubici region of Santa Catarina, which is very odd, because there is nothing there apart from snow and mountains. My man was prevented from tailing. I could use your talents again, Ghost. I need someone who can slip under the radar. I'm thinking three teenage girls might go unnoticed.

"The gloves we're tracing were quite stationary for several weeks. Mengele never left São Paulo with Himmler never far away. This morning they began moving again. Feels like they're preparing for something. I want you to get over there and tell me what they're up to. Obviously, if the chance offers, deal with them, but your primary mission is to recon and report only. Okay?"

"When do we leave?"

"Tomorrow night. A car will come for you at six. Be ready."

"Right."

That night Tyler met with Melissa and Lucy in Melissa's bedroom to talk. They were pleased to be back together despite ongoing frictions and the undesirable task at hand. Far better than hanging around. Melissa punched in a code and the tracer monitor appeared on her laptop screen. She expanded the displayed region until a green dot came into view, followed closely by an amber dot. She touched the screen to focus on São Paulo and the surrounding area.

"Green's Himmler. The amber is Mengele," she reminded the others.

"Mengele's still in São Paulo," said Tyler. "I think we should check him out first, but I need to speak to Izabella again. See if I can get some answers."

"Can you do it before we leave for Brazil?" asked Lucy.

"Depends. I've tried but she's not always around. And when she *is* around she's not always that helpful. I asked Zebedee already but he didn't really know anything about Mengele's bones or why they didn't work as an artefact." She consulted her list. "Steven Lewis is the kid gloved with Mengele." She looked back to the screen and pointed. "That amber dot is also Steven Lewis and he's waiting for us to set him free."

"So why not Himmler?" asked Lucy.

"I'm more concerned about Mengele because something weird is happening with him and I don't like it. If nothing else, we can spy on him, maybe learn something."

"Okay. Mengele it is," agreed Lucy.

*

The mist shifted ominously, setting Tyler on edge. More on edge than usual. As the list of undesirables in the contrap grew, so did her reticence to look inside. She still hated the thought of bumping into Kylie Marsh and now Goebbels was in there somewhere. Consequently, she'd put this off for far too long. She sat on the edge of her bed, glad of Albert's company.

A tall figure walked towards her from the distant murk of the crystal. Tyler gulped fearfully, but then sighed with relief when she recognized a friend.

"Good evening to you, Miss May," said Zebedee with a nod.

"Zebedee, thank God..."

"Were you expecting someone else?"

"Oh, you know, Nazi ghosts and the like, but I'm glad it's you. Listen, we're going after Mengele and I *really* need to talk to Izabella. Could you find her for me?"

"I shall try. I believe I saw her a while ago, heading for the city. Or was that yesterday? No, no, I distinctly remember seeing her..." He tapped his chin thoughtfully with the tip of his long pipe. "Oh well. I'll find her. You wait right there."

Zebedee strode away and was soon consumed by smog. The next moment, Travis the Norman soldier appeared, sneering at Tyler and trying his usual tricks to coax her into the portal. He looked as grimy as ever and particularly pleased with himself. She told him where to go and was surprised when he left. She kicked off her boots and slipped beneath the duvet on her bed meaning only to make herself comfortable.

"Missy, wake up. She's 'ere. Izabella's 'ere for ya."

Tyler bolted upright.

"Oh. Thanks, Albert." She looked into the portal to see Izabella peering impatiently out of the lens.

"Well, child? You dragged me all the way out here to keep me waiting in this confounded fog? What is it? What, in the name of the pope, do you want with me?"

"I have some questions you might be able to help me with. I need to know where Hitler is. You know I put him into the contrap, but is he still in there? Albert says he searched and couldn't find him anywhere. The *Tree of Knowledge* told me he has escaped, but I don't trust it."

"You have *lost* Hitler, now? Well, child, if *you* do not know where he is, what makes you think I should know? Eh?"

"I don't know. I just thought… Zebedee told me that ghosts know things. That they know all kinds of stuff…"

"Yes, yes, yes. He's quite correct. But *this* we do not know. We don't know where Hitler is." She waved a hand. "Next question please."

"Right," said Tyler, glancing sideways at Albert, who could only shrug. "I need to know why a summoning artefact doesn't work. I tried to use Mengele's bones as an artefact but he just walked away. Why was that? I used

Goebbels' old house on Goebbels and that worked fine, so the contrap *is* still working."

"Of course, of course. The contrap is still working and so you have answered your own question. If the problem was not the contrap, it was either the artefact or the ghost."

"But the artefact, I mean the bones, were proven to be the true remains of Mengele. They did DNA tests and everything."

"Therefore it was neither the artefact nor the contrap that was the problem, child. Use your head! Really, you had no need to bother me with all this. You are bright enough to know your left from your right, are you not?"

"You mean the problem lies with Mengele's glove."

"That is the only logical conclusion. Now, if you are done with the questions, I must rest. I am really quite exhausted!" Izabella turned to leave but paused as though undecided. She turned back to Tyler.

"By the way, you do know about the box, don't you?" asked Izabella slowly.

"The box? What box?" Tyler did not have a clue what the old woman was talking about.

"The *lead* box."

"What lead box?"

"I see. Well, you should know about this if what your friend, Mr Lieberman, tells me is true. He said you are going after the others…"

"I am."

"Then you will surely need a lead box. You see, ghosts can sense the contrap and so wherever you go, if you carry it upon you, they will also sense you. They will know when you have arrived. They'll know when you have left. They'll sense when you are close by. It would be a crippling thing to go after them and all the time be warning them in this way where you are and what you are doing. Do you agree?"

"Yes," said Tyler, crestfallen, knowing now that this is exactly what she had been doing from the start.

"Then this is what you must do. You must make a lead box big enough to conceal the contrap. The box must have a hinged lid that can be properly closed. It must be well crafted. Keep the contrap hidden in the lead box at all times unless you mean to use it."

"The lead will stop the ghosts from sensing the contrap?"

"It will indeed, child. Lead is the only element that has the power to do so. Now, I must retire. Good luck to you, child." Izabella shook her head despairingly. "I think you may need it."

Tyler was buzzing. This knowledge could help them; *would* really help them. She remembered the lead box among the relics from Himmler's shrine and phoned Melissa, pulling boots on with one hand while waiting for her to pick up.

"Tyler?"

"Mel, where are the cases with the stuff from Himmler's shrine? I mean the basement where they put Himmler's remains. All the stuff with the swastikas."

"I have it here. Still haven't examined it properly. Why?"

"Never mind. I'll see you in a few minutes."

Melissa met Tyler at the door with a steaming mug.

"Your usual, Madam."

Tyler explained about the lead box.

"The stuff's over here," said Melissa opening a cupboard door to reveal the two suitcases. They dragged them out and riffled through their contents. There it was: a small but heavy, grey, metal box. It was no ordinary box and Tyler understood why they'd found it with the Nazi artefacts. The surface of the box was dull, pitted and scratched, its corners worn and rounded from years of use.

"What does it mean?" asked Melissa.

"They *know*. Don't you see? Somehow they know all about it. They're after the contrap and they already had this box, ready and waiting. Look at it. It's old. Really old."

"You think one of them knew about the contrap back when they were alive?"

Tyler stared at Melissa. The implications were overwhelming. Tyler lifted the contrap from around her neck and placed it into the box. It fitted perfectly, with a comfortable amount of room in the corners to accommodate the chain.

Made for it!

She closed the lid.

"Whatever the case, we know about it now and *we* are using the box. This time they won't know we're coming."

PART SIX

The Inconstant Smile

July 21st: São Paulo Airport.

Tyler hauled her suitcase awkwardly from the luggage carousel and extended the handle to wheel it. She turned her phone back on, jetlag firmly setting in. She felt shaky and tired. Disorientated and dizzy. Weary of standing in queues at flight desks, customs and passport control. All around, São Paulo airport bustled with excited holidaymakers and lone businessmen and women. Tyler jumped when her mobile immediately rang. It was Chapman.

"Thank God I got you. He's there in the airport. Check your tracer monitor. Mengele's with you."

"On it," said Tyler. She'd never felt less *on it* in her life. She glanced to her left where Mr Flynn awaited his bags.

"Okay. I'll be keeping an eye on your movements. Good luck, Ghost. And be careful."

"Mengele's here," Tyler told the girls while pocketing her phone. They looked at each other, bemused.

"Duh. We know that," said Melissa. "That's why we came."

"No. He's *here*." Tyler took out the tracer monitor and switched it on. She found the amber marker and zoomed in so the map on the monitor showed little else beyond the airport's perimeter.

"Look. We're the dot with three rings, right. Mengele is…" She looked up, gauging their position. "…just over there." She searched the crowd on the other side of the baggage carousel and soon found him. Mengele was wearing his trademark trilby and helping a tall, smartly dressed woman to reclaim her baggage. The woman's figure-hugging, dark-grey business suit and high heels only added to her commanding persona. Mengele appeared to be at her beck and call. Tyler knew at once that she'd seen the woman before.

"Last time I saw her, she was wearing a Nazi uniform in the NVF headquarters in Whitechapel," she explained to Melissa and Lucy. "I saw her through the *Present Eye*. She was the first one to arrive that morning we went spying. Come on. They're leaving."

Ahead of the girls, Mengele and the woman headed for the airport exit. Tyler thought quickly. Their specially transported black, armoured cases would be waiting for them at the customs office, courtesy of Chapman.

"You guys stick with Flynn. Grab the cases. I'll stay on the happy couple." She threw on her rucksack, the artefacts and the contrap safely stowed in its lead box, inside. Leaving her suitcase with Melissa, she followed

Mengele and the woman. Melissa also had a lead box containing her artefacts and Lucy had personally coated the inside of her money capsules with molten lead to prevent the gloves from sensing their contents and, so far, the lead seemed to be working. Mengele did not know Tyler was there. At least, if he did, he had given no sign of it. She watched them leave the airport and claim a waiting cab, Mengele politely opening the door for the woman. Tyler found a cab and told the driver to follow at a distance, waving a wad of bank notes under the driver's nose.

Mengele's cab led her through the well-lit streets of São Paulo, soon pulling over for the couple to climb out. They paid the driver and entered a tall, drab residential block. Tyler waited for a few moments before testing the door. Locked. She could go no further without breaking in. Too risky in broad daylight and in a busy street.

She scribbled the address on the back of her hand and returned to the airport to find the girls.

I know where you live, Josef.

*

The next morning the girls headed out from their hotel in central São Paulo to stakeout Mengele's place. Tyler led the way and pointed out the door where she'd last seen Mengele and the woman.

Melissa sipped Coke while Lucy drank cappuccino and wore dark glasses, her face a permanent 'talk to the hand' expression. Tyler's hot chocolate was going cold as they sat in a café across the street and watched from the window.

"Why don't you use the *Present Eye* to spy on him?" Lucy suggested.

Tyler's gaze flitted briefly to Melissa, who, by the look on her face, seemed to be thinking the same as Tyler.

"That would give away the fact that we're here watching," said Tyler, wondering if Lucy already realised this, or if she was just being a bit slow.

"Oh, yeah. Right," said Lucy. "Well, *this* is fun. Are we going to sit here all day?"

"Not if you don't want to. It only takes one of us to keep a watch. We can always take turns. You can hit the beach if you like," Tyler offered.

"Okay. Then I'm going for a walk," said Lucy. She drained her cup and left.

"Good riddance to bad…" began Melissa, until Tyler gave her a look. "Well… She's *so* miserable. Honestly. She *could* make an effort. It's not like she was any happier before we came out here. She hated being back at school. Do you still think she's a spy? I mean, one who's not on our side?"

"I don't know. I think we should keep an eye on her. And if we learn anything really important, we should probably keep it between you, me and Chapman."

Melissa nodded.

"Agreed."

Several hours later, Mengele and the smart woman surfaced. Melissa and Tyler followed, maintaining a distance, incognito. Tyler was a natural. Melissa, on the other hand, was as covert as a rampaging elephant, creeping about unnaturally, nervously looking around and staring at their mark. Tyler was amazed that Mengele and the woman hadn't noticed them.

When the couple entered a restaurant and found seats, Tyler could stand it no more and sent Melissa away, saying that one of them should go back to the café in case Lucy returned and wondered what was happening.

An idea struck her as she waited alone.

She had a great view of Mengele's table and all that stood between her and the glove was a vast restaurant window and a scattering of chairs and tables; nothing that would give any real resistance to the tug of a strong summoning artefact. Tyler casually leant against a lamppost and searched her bag for the lead box. She drew out the contrap, along with a distal phalanx. She opened the *Ghost Portal* and placed Mengele's bone on the contrap before looking up to observe his reaction. He frowned musingly. He looked for a moment as though he was in pain and he turned to look directly in Tyler's direction, but she had expected this and had drawn her baseball cap down low to shield her face and she left her post and strolled away looking like any other holidaymaker. She knew there was something different about Mengele. The summoning artefact had again failed. So what had changed? How was Mengele protected from its power?

Tyler did not know, but she intended to find out.

*

Tyler threw herself onto her bed, utterly frustrated. She had put the contrap away and given up for the day. Tomorrow would bring more of the same: stakeouts, tailing, creeping, wondering. She talked with Albert long into the night as the others slept, mulling over everything that had happened, trying to find some small detail she might have missed; some tiny morsel of information that might prove crucial and provide an answer. Without that answer, she knew Mengele was untouchable and the knowledge smoldered in her head, an unreachable subterranean fire.

*

At midday, Tyler again used the contrap. Mengele had been out briefly in the morning, but his short trip proved only to be a walk to the newsagents for a paper. She watched him reading it now from her uncomfortable plastic chair in the café. Mengele's new friend had left earlier and had yet to return. Lucy and Melissa were following her to see if she went anywhere interesting.

Mengele lit a cigarette and smoked, luxuriating in an exquisite lounge chair like a lord. She watched him take a final drag, stub out the butt, fold his paper and stand. He looked around the room as though searching, or perhaps listening and she knew he had sensed the contrap. He was close enough; just across the street, three floors up, and with only two walls between. Tyler recognized a detail that she remembered from a previous encounter. Once before, in the São Paulo Institute for Forensic Science, she had witnessed a sudden mood swing when they had almost come face to face. There Mengele had smiled one moment and, quite suddenly, snarled the next. He did the same thing now as Tyler watched, startled. It was *very* odd. The Mengele she'd encountered in the woods of Watford, on the car park roof and on the streets of London, was a man with a smile so persistent it was irritating, yet here he was, switching moods like a cat in a lightning storm.

Mengele crossed to the window overlooking the street and peered out, his sickeningly confident smile returning. He knew she was there, close by. Tyler slipped the contrap back into its lead box and closed the lid. She turned away from the café's large, plate glass window in time to hide herself from his searching eyes, once more just one of the crowd.

Catch me if you can, Josef.

*

Melissa finished typing in the address and hit send.

"Done. Chapman should have the address now. The *Novo Velocidade Financas*. It's the NVF all over again. It translates roughly as New Velocity Finances, so it's a pretty sure bet she was visiting to invest some money or to take some out. It's obviously some kind of international Nazi bank of evil."

"Whatever she was doing there, it's Chapman's problem now," said Lucy. "We've done our bit."

"Yeah," Tyler found herself actually agreeing with Lucy. "I'm ready to move on. We're getting nowhere here. So how did you get her name?"

"We followed her to the building and waited outside while she went in, but we watched through the window. We saw exactly where she went. She stood at a kiosk and spoke with a woman on the other side. She wrote something and handed something over, a bank card or something. When she'd finished her business, she left and Lucy followed her back to the block. I went into the Novo Velocidade Financas and pretended I was lost. All I did was ask the woman behind the kiosk where the bus station was, but while she answered, I took the top sheet of paper from the desk jotter there, pretending to make notes on what she was telling me."

Tyler looked again at the paper in her hand. It was a plain white page of A5 notepaper, but Melissa had carefully passed a soft pencil across it to reveal the indented words written on the preceding sheet. Most of it was unreadable and it looked as though several messages had been scribbled one upon the other, but one name was clear enough.

"Valda Braun," Tyler read aloud. She'd seen that name before, written on an address label of a box containing Adolf Hitler's reading glasses, addressed to the secret Nazi headquarters in Whitechapel. "And you think she is actually Valda Braun?"

"It could be her," said Melissa.

"It does seem like a heck of a coincidence," said Lucy. "It has to be her, surely."

Tyler gave a nod.

"Where next?" asked Melissa.

"We'll go after Himmler," said Tyler. "Hope he doesn't have the same kind of protection that Mengele seems to have."

"You can only try, Missy," said Albert.

Tyler's phone rang. She put Chapman on speakerphone, knowing that Melissa had swept the room for bugs and the fingerprints of spies. The room was clean.

"Thanks for the name and the addresses. You've done very well, team. I'd like to congratulate you. There'll be a full investigation into Novo Velocidade Financas. In fact, I think you deserve a proper break. Things are getting, well... Put it this way, you're not safe out there right now. I'd like you to come in for a while, at least until we've investigated and we know more about what we're dealing with. First indications on Novo Velocidade Financas suggest this thing's massive and there's some serious money behind the NVF over there. But it's complicated. I'm sorry, but I have to call you in, girls."

The girls looked at one another, astonished.

"You can't call us in," said Tyler. "Himmler is here. We can get him. I know we can! He's right here in the city."

"It's getting out of control, Agent Ghost. It's for your own safety. I'll have other agents sent in once we have enough intel to make some informed decisions."

Even Lucy raged at the idea.

"You *can't* call us in. What if we refuse?"

"You can't refuse, Agent Pointer. You're working for the British Secret Service. If you refuse to come in, you'll be brought in, forcibly."

"Well, I'm not going anywhere," said Tyler. "Not until we have Himmler."

Drop Zone

Tyler stared at the phone in her hand.

"You just hung up on Chapman! Was that wise?" asked Melissa.

"He'll call back," said Tyler. She waited.

"Maybe not," said Lucy.

The phone rang. Tyler answered the call, making an effort to be cool, speakerphone on.

"Hello."

"Hello, Ghost," said Chapman. "That wasn't very clever."

"You have to help us. We're going after Himmler and you have to help us."

Silence. Tyler could almost hear Chapman's brain whirring.

"If you do this, you're on your own. No traceable link to the security services."

"Suits us."

"And this would need to be a black op. No record of the mission. No support if it all goes wrong. I don't know... It's tantamount to suicide."

"Sounds perfect," said Lucy. "I like the odds."

"You do know Himmler is no longer in São Paulo?" asked Chapman.

"What?" said Tyler. She gestured for Melissa to call up the tracer monitor on the laptop.

"Himmler is heading back towards the mountainous Urubici region of Santa Catarina as we speak."

Tyler viewed the screen as a green tracer tracked southwards, almost parallel to the coast.

"Right. Well, I'm going after him. You can either help me or try to stop me but that's how it is."

"Anyone asks, I don't know you."

Tyler put her phone away and grinned.

"He's gonna help us," she said. "Knew he would."

*

Albert was waiting for Tyler to fall asleep, watching the world go by from the hotel window.

"Do you think I'm going to die?" Tyler asked him.

He turned and smiled.

"Everybody dies in the end, Missy. You'll do just fine. An' anyways, I'm comin' with ya' an' I ain't gonna let ya' die. Not yet." When Tyler said nothing, he spoke again. "We're all comin' with ya'. Even Zebedee. We're gonna get Himmler's glove. You'll see."

"I'm glad you're with me, Albert."

Tyler drew out the contrap from her nightshirt and switched it to the *Ghost Portal*. She called for Zebedee and he was soon there, tapping his cane through the ever present mist. She told him the plan. "We're setting out tomorrow," she concluded.

"That is good," said Zebedee, looking very serious. "If you need me, I'll be right here. If you need anything at all, just call."

"You don't think I'm making a mistake?"

"My dear girl, why would I think that? You have every chance of success. Every chance…"

"We don't really know what's up there in the mountains. Himmler's been up there before but no one followed. That mission was called off."

"It'll be fine, my dear. Just keep your wits about you. We have Albert and your friends, Melissa and Lucy, and of course, don't forget our secret weapon!"

"Oh yeah, the contrap."

"My dear girl! I was talking about *you*."

*

A little over twenty-four hours later, the girls were out in a seemingly endless wilderness, broken only by the private airstrip around them; nothing else man-made for miles around. An operative in black handed out white mountain-survival jumpsuits in near darkness.

"Here, you'll need these. It gets cold in the mountains." The man was well-muscled, his hair clipped so short that he almost appeared bald. Black body armour made him look bigger and more intimidating. The girls were never given his name, nor did they ask for it. "You've jumped before?"

The girls nodded. They had each parachuted five times during their short term of training to earn their *wings* at Brize Norton.

The special ops stealth plane was a sleek, black bird resting in the night. They pulled on jumpsuits and nervously climbed the metal drop-down steps. Tyler viewed the aircraft's seats, harnesses, racks of gear and exits. Everywhere she looked there was high-end military equipment. Consoles glimmered above their heads and over the cockpit doorway. Rows of lights lit the passenger hold, but nothing much showed up beneath their glow. Most of its content was black, excepting the girls' jumpsuits which gleamed brightly. They found seats. When a second man offered them each handguns, Melissa recoiled.

"Don't worry," he reassured her. "They're untraceable."

"Okay. Yeah," said Melissa. "That's what was worrying me..." She mouthed to Tyler *'We've got guns!'* Melissa didn't want guns. Lucy took the Walther P99 offered to her without hesitation, clipped on and adjusted the leg holster.

"Here," said Melissa. "I don't really want this."

Lucy took Melissa's gun and strapped it to her other thigh while Muscles passed around parachute packs.

"I know it's best practice to pack your own but we don't have time for that on this op. Get them on. Jump time twenty-three hundred hours. Takeoff in five." Muscles left the aircraft but paused briefly on the steps to turn.

"By the way, your mark appears to have reached a destination."

Tyler took out the small tracer monitor and watched it flicker to life. She closed on the green marker, now stationary, in the middle of an area mapped as nothing but ridges and peaks.

"What's he doing?" Melissa wondered aloud.

"Who knows?" said Tyler. "The only thing we know is it's not going to be anything good."

They finished buckling on chutes and strapped themselves into their seats. Muscles boarded, secured the hatch and headed into the cockpit. The takeoff g-force churned her stomach. Tyler gripped her seat and closed her eyes, glad she'd been too nervous to eat before they'd set out. Once airborne and traveling at, what Tyler considered to be, a frightful speed, Muscles returned to the hold, armed with a map of the area. He positioned it so all could see, and then pointed.

"Here's your mark. He's high, very high. More than eighteen hundred metres. It's one of the tallest peaks, which is a problem. We need to keep as low as possible to avoid radar, so we won't be dropping you right over the target. This valley here is our best bet. We'll fly up the valley and slow enough for your exit. You'll have to make your own way to the mark from there. Don't count your drop metres. Engage the 'chute as soon as you're clear of the bird, or you'll all die. You have your tracer monitor?"

Tyler nodded, nausea rising in her throat.

"Good. Not long now. Oh, one more thing. The pilot tells me he flew over this peak two weeks ago. Reckons it's a dead zone. Says it nearly brought him down. It's another reason he's refusing to go anywhere near the peak."

"*A dead zone?*" asked Melissa.

"Anything electronic cuts out. Nothing works. Said all he saw was rock and ice, so who knows what's down there." Muscles left them looking fearfully at one another.

"A dead zone," repeated Melissa. "If that's true, none of our gear will work out there. Great."

"Do you think we should turn back?" asked Lucy, leaning in.

Tyler considered this and recalled Zebedee's encouraging words from the previous night. She thought again about why they were doing all this.

"No. We don't turn back. Do you know how many people were killed in World War II?"

"More than sixty million," stated Melissa over the soft drone of the aircraft. "Although, actually, there is some debate over it. Some argue that figure is very conservative and that the true figure is closer to seventy million…"

"If we do nothing, these Nazis will bring war," said Tyler. "It will happen all over again. *They* told me it will happen all over again unless the gloves are stopped. We must stop them. We're the only ones who have the contrap and that's the only way that we know of to separate the gloves from the kids."

"Who told you it will happen again?" asked Lucy.

"Kinga and Danuta. The twins from the *Ghost Portal*."

"We *will* stop them," said Melissa.

"We'll stop them," echoed Lucy. "You'll see."

It seemed to Tyler that their exit call came only minutes later.

"Time to go," shouted Muscles from the front of the plane. He hit a locking mechanism and slid open the hatch, exposing a frantic wind. "We gotta do this quick or you'll end up in the mountainside."

Lucy went first, launching herself into darkness and mayhem, apparently without a second thought. Muscles counted to four and shoved Melissa out of the door. Tyler figured Chapman must have warned him she was likely to delay the moment.

Tyler counted with him and jumped before he could touch her. Then she was tumbling and trying to focus on a spiraling world. The world slowed as she stopped spinning and she remembered she needed to open her 'chute. No time for free falling. She tugged on the canopy release and was yanked upwards as the 'chute billowed open. The wrench on her shoulders bruised and temporarily winded her. Below her she saw a vast expanse of snow-covered ground, grey in the night, featureless, all but masking a perilous incline. Moments later she landed, tumbling down the steep valley side in a foot of snow. She rolled to a stop and gasped for air, waiting for the world to cease spinning. A ferocious, icy gale tore at her.

When she found her feet she stumbled a few yards realizing that to go any real distance in this snow would take a vast effort. This was not going to be easy. She released herself from the grounded parachute to search for Lucy and Melissa, but she saw only the inky black, starlit sky and a cruel, frozen, mountainous landscape surrounding her. She caught sight of a glimmering light way off in the distance and, as she squinted, other small lights became apparent. She knew at once this must be the place where Himmler was holding up. In dismay, she realized it was miles away and their odds of success were decreasing rapidly. She discarded her helmet and drew up her hood, shed her backpack and dug around for the tracer monitor. Fixing her position to confirm the green marker was up ahead in the direction of those glinting lights, she became concerned. Lucy and Melissa were not there. Tyler had been the last to jump and so should be the closest to the target. The others would be behind her, somewhere down the valley. She risked calling their names, cupping gloved hands about her mouth and staring into the snowy void.

"Melissa? Lucy?"

Tyler waited, listening intently. She thought she heard a sound but it was not Melissa or Lucy. At least, she hoped it wasn't. The cry, if that's what it was, sounded like an animal and it came from up ahead towards the peak. She peered in that direction but saw nothing but the grey of snow, softening away into pitch. She checked the temperature on her phone app.

-11°C

No dead zone yet.

She scraped ice from the surface of her goggles before realising it was also on the inside. The wind stung her eyes as she polished the glass. She noticed she had no reception on her mobile and so tried the comms. No response from Lucy. Out of range.

"Mel! You alright?"

"Yeah. Where are you?"

"Can you see the lights?"

"Yes."

"Head for them. I reckon that's where Himmler is, so if you head for the lights you should come to me. I'll wait here for you."

"Right."

Fifteen minutes later a grey shape emerged from the landscape and Tyler ran to meet Melissa, never more pleased for company.

"I think I saw Lucy behind me. She shouldn't be long."

When Lucy caught up she was tired from the hike and so they rested before setting off towards the peak where the lights glimmered. Cold from standing around, Tyler was glad to be moving again, although progress was frustratingly slow, wading through deep snow and climbing the slope. She thought it best not to mention to the others the strange noise she'd heard coming from the mountain side. Melissa was already unnerved and struggling with the ascent. She didn't need more to worry about.

"Did anyone bring a flask of hot chocolate?" Melissa asked when they'd been walking for half an hour.

"Yeah, I got a whole picnic in back," said Lucy. "Complete with table and chairs."

"Oh well. I have chocolate. Fancy a piece?" She broke off chunks and passed them around with gloved hands.

"Thanks," said Lucy. "How far do you think we've gone?"

Tyler looked up ahead at the lights in the distance. They didn't seem any closer than before.

"Oh, quite a way. Maybe half a mile," she said, realizing just how unprepared they were for a survival hike in the mountains.

Lucy couldn't hold it in any more.

"Why the hell didn't they give us snow shoes?"

They trudged.

Two hours later, Tyler stopped and turned. They had been working hard and the lights were much closer.

"We'll rest a while. Then do the final push. It can't be far now." She gazed up the rising mountain ahead of them and saw snow, ice and rock. At the uppermost reaches of the mountain she could make out the faint suggestion of a vast building. The lights were fewer now, but those remaining were clearer, brighter; yellow lights in the shape of narrow arched windows. Tyler counted five. They brought to mind images of castles with arrow slits placed strategically around the walls and towers, and then Tyler knew what she was looking at. It was a castle of some sort. It couldn't be anything else.

"It's a stronghold," she said. "A castle, hidden away up here."

"Not exactly on the tourist route," said Lucy.

"How are we going to get in?" asked Melissa.

"I'm not sure," admitted Tyler.

Another hour of battling the slope brought them as close as they could get without being easily seen from the windows high above them, Tyler judged. The castle towered over them and they could see how it had been cunningly built on the summit's edge so that its towers overhung the mountainside. Its walls matched the same grey tone of the snowy mountain so that from a distance, the castle might be easily missed. Tyler dumped her backpack in the snow and took out the lead box. To Melissa's horror, she opened the lid.

"What are you doing?"

"I need to take a closer look. Find a way in."

"But they'll know we're here!"

"Too bad." Tyler took out the contrap, set it to *Flight*. "Wait here. I won't be long." She drew the contrap's small lever clockwise around the side and ascended into the greyness.

Dead Zone

A harsh wind pummeled her. Tyler battled it, flew upwards past the few windows that were still lit from within. The castle was a strange design. To her it seemed simultaneously modern and inexplicably ancient.

New Gothic, she decided.

The towers and turrets were roofed in a pale stone, a pattern of camouflage built-in to blend with the surroundings, with or without snow. Once she had risen over the structure, she could see the full effect of this ingenious concealment. It appeared to be little more than an outcrop of rock at the mountain's peak.

She flew around the entire site, seeking a way in, some unguarded entrance more easily assailed. She saw the land beyond the mountain ridge and noted an uncluttered strip of rock: a road, well-disguised, and leading away to a low, flat expanse. Squinting into the night she discerned several white helicopters sheltered beneath a small overhanging cliff face. The helicopters were netted over with more camouflage.

So that's how you come and go, Himmler...

Tyler dropped onto a parapet, remembering that she was revealing her position the whole time she had the contrap out of the box. She boxed it and crept along a narrow, high walkway to a small door that seemed as good as anywhere to stage a break-in. She was just about to pick the lock when she noticed a broad chimney top across the roof from her. If she entered through the chimney, she would not need to pick a single lock and she wouldn't meet anyone along the way either, at least, not until she exited from the fireplace below. She unboxed the contrap to flit over the roof and perched briefly to check for any signs of heat or smoke. There were none.

When Albert suddenly appeared she nearly slipped from the roof.

"It's alright, Missy. It ain't lit nor nuffin'."

"Okay. Thanks. Are there any people in the room at the bottom?"

Albert shook his head somberly.

"No livin' ones."

"Ghosts? There are ghosts down there?"

Albert gave a slow nod.

"Nuffin' to worry about, though. Not in the room down there, anyways."

Tyler peered down the chimney. She didn't like the way it smelt. She was wondering why the Nazis might need a chimney as large as this one when it occurred to her that she should not linger on that question. Whatever the reason, it would serve as a way in.

She descended the flue. Inside, the air was warmer but the smell stronger. A greasy, burnt stench. She dropped quickly, taking care not to graze her arms on the stone sides, and guided herself out of the arched chamber at the base, shoving open a heavy iron door that stood between her and the outer room. Free of the chimney, she alighted and turned, taking in the large concrete vault around her. Albert was at her side as she boxed the contrap.

"You say there're ghosts in this room?" Tyler asked.

"Aye, many," said Albert, mournfully watching entities beyond Tyler's sight. "But them's good ones. Innocent victims."

"You can tell the good ones from the bad?"

"Oh yeah. It's like a feeling ya' get. Most of the time ya' can tell, anyways."

Tyler looked about, unsettled. The stone chamber was tall with vents built into the walls but was empty and devoid of embellishment. It emitted a desolate aura; not a space for the living to dwell.

"Why are they here?"

"Lord knows," said Albert.

"We need to find a good way in for Melissa and Lucy."

Albert nodded curtly.

"Follow me." He crossed the chamber and passed through a heavy, wooden door. Tyler inched the door ajar to peek through after him. No one around. She threaded her way through the castle behind Albert, checking for people ahead. Once, Albert backtracked quickly, warning her there were people on the stairway ahead, but mostly the way was clear and it seemed the place and its inhabitants slumbered. They eventually came to an expansive, ground level entrance that spilled out onto the mountainside. From the inside she was easily able to unbolt the vast door and escape but, needing to return, she disengaged the two lock catches and left it unbarred, knowing it would remain open as long as nobody noticed the bolts were not drawn. She slid out into the cold, easing the door closed behind her.

A trampled track in the snow denoted a route upwards, curving to the right to bent around the castle's side, towards the road and the helicopters. A second narrower path, laden with untouched snow, dropped left, away from the castle and into the valley below. She unboxed the contrap and flew back to her shivering friends in the shadow of the castle. Twenty trudging minutes later, Tyler was back at the door, this time with Lucy and Melissa. They entered into the quiet of the castle, relieved to be out of the cold and the pounding wind, but feeling more like refugees than a black ops team.

Tyler checked her watch: 2.51 a.m.

That was good. They had some time while people slept. She hoped Himmler was still dreaming.

She unzipped her snowsuit, slipped it off and shoved it into the bottom of her bag, hoping she'd live long enough to need it again. The others did the same, peering around nervously. The vast entrance hall offered a choice of four closed doorways, each at the top of three steps. Tyler located Himmler's green marker on the trace monitor. He was somewhere in the depths of the castle but Tyler had no way of knowing which of the many floors he was on.

"Come on. We'll try this way," she whispered. Figuring he would most likely be asleep in one of the upper rooms she looked for a stairway but the door she chose only led onto a corridor. She entered anyway, not knowing where it might lead and not recalling the way Albert had previously taken her. The other girls followed and Tyler whispered for Albert. A moment later he was at her side.

"I need your help again. We have to find Himmler. Can you go ahead and warn us if you see anyone? We need to get upstairs."

"Right you are, Missy."

Albert disappeared around the corner at the end of the corridor. A moment later he was back, shaking his head.

"No stairs," he shrugged.

"Should we try another door?" asked Melissa.

"Okay," whispered Tyler, indicating for them all to head back but when Melissa reached the door they'd just used and pushed it, she turned round and shrugged.

"What?" said Lucy.

"It's locked."

"How can it be locked?" whispered Lucy. "We just came through it."

Tyler rummaged frantically in her bag for her lock pick and tried to unlock the door.

"It's no good," hissed Lucy. We don't have time for this."

"Just give me a few seconds," said Tyler desperately trying to free them.

"It does seem a bit odd that the door would just lock itself behind us like that," whispered Melissa. She scanned the corridor nervously.

Tyler wrestled with the lock but it would not budge and she realized a secondary mechanism had engaged. One beyond her reach.

"It's no good. I can't do it. We'll have to go on."

"This is *not* cool," said Melissa.

"You know, I love the way you constantly state the obvious," sneered Lucy. "Jeez, this is frustrating."

They followed Albert right, into another hallway with many doors on both sides. Hoping for a way upstairs, they walked silently until they reached another junction.

"Which way?" asked Albert.

Tyler checked the monitor. Himmler was somewhere off to their left.

"Left," she whispered.

"I'll check out this way," said Lucy, slipping past Tyler and jogging down the passage to the right.

"Lucy!" Tyler hissed after her. "What are you doing?" But Lucy either did not hear or chose to ignore her. She reached the end of the passage, took a left and was gone.

"Did you see that?" said Tyler. "Why did she do *that*? We need to stick together."

Melissa peered down the unlit corridor after Lucy and raised her eyebrows philosophically.

"Oh well," she whispered. "If the girl wants to get herself killed then who am I to stop her?"

They waited and ticked off the minutes until Albert returned, looking pleased.

"This way, Missy. Take the next left. There's a staircase beyond the next door."

Tyler followed and found it just as he'd said. She opened the door and climbed the first five steps before turning.

"Wait! Don't let it…"

The door closed behind Melissa with an audible click followed by a clunk.

"...shut?" asked Melissa. "Oops." She turned and tried the door only to find it, too, had mysteriously locked. She screwed up her face. "Sorry."

"Never mind." Tyler climbed onwards but three steps from the top her tread triggered a trap and the staircase folded beneath her feet.. She gasped and slid downwards until, a moment later, the slide ended and she plummeted into a black void. Vaguely aware of Melissa's scream nearby, she fell and collided with a steep surface. They were on another slide now; a steeper one, which ended shortly to deposit them into nothingness until they landed heavily in darkness on a cold concrete floor.

Tyler groaned, rubbed a bruised shoulder and tried to straighten her left leg which had ended up twisted at an awkward angle. It wouldn't budge and she didn't know why until her hand found a wall and then another wall. She reasoned she had fallen into a corner until she found more walls and Melissa, who shrieked at her touch. They were in a small and incredibly dark pit.

"Can you reach your torch?" asked Tyler. "I can barely move."

"I think so."

Tyler could feel Melissa fumbling in the darkness next to her. She worked her leg into a more comfortable position while Melissa searched blindly.

"Got it!" said Melissa moments later, but the click that Tyler awaited brought no light.

"Dead zone," Melissa reminded her.

"Oh *great*. We're doomed. *Dead zone* is right."

Tyler felt for her mobile. Also dead.

"Nothing's working. They must have some kind of device that kills anything electrical."

"So how do they switch the light on? Boil the kettle?"

"Who knows? Maybe it only works on stuff that's not plugged into the mains."

"Do you think they heard us when we fell?"

"I think it's safe to assume they did. You wailed like a banshee."

"Oh. Sorry."

"It doesn't matter. They know we're here. If they didn't sense the contrap already, they'll have heard the stair trap being triggered. And anyway, I think they've known all along. Don't you think it was odd how Lucy ducked down that corridor? Almost like she knew exactly where she was going, and the next minute we're caught in a trap."

"She's one of them!"

"It's the only explanation," said Tyler. "I didn't want to believe it but..."

"But what about all the times she's helped us?"

"Maybe she used to be on our side but they got to her, turned her."

"The contrap!" said Melissa suddenly. "The contrap still works here. You already proved that. We can still use it. Maybe we can still get out."

Tyler felt for it and took it out. Unable to see, she switched settings randomly until the crystal glowed. The *Tower of Doom*, bizarrely, was surprisingly tall.

"It's grown!" She showed Melissa. "Almost complete. That doesn't make sense." This amazed Tyler because she had an overwhelming notion they had already failed bitterly in their task. She watched it dubiously. "Maybe the dead zone's messing with it."

Albert joined them, materializing from the wall.

In the soft glow from the crystal they assessed their grim surroundings; steep concrete walls rising to a wooden ceiling far beyond reach and, in the centre, a closed trap door.

"Do you think you can open it?" asked Melissa gazing upwards.

"You can do it, Missy. I knows ya' can," said Albert.

"I can try." Tyler put the contrap's chain around her neck and set the switch to *Flight*, but this dimmed the glow of the stone, leaving her to work almost blind. Even so, she guided herself up into the far reaches of their narrow cell to hover beneath the wooden trap. She was practiced enough to hold the contrap and its small lever steady with only one hand, but trying to reverse the heavy wooden trap above her head one handed was still impossible. It was a dead weight. Albert drew close to take a look and also tried to push up the door.

"Sorry. It's too 'evy for me," he said. "Might'a moved it if I weren't dead."

"It's no use. It won't budge," she admitted at length. She descended, halting to investigate a dark area of wall. Not wall, but a passage leading steeply upwards, another shoot from a trap elsewhere.

"I'll be back in a minute," she called down to Melissa before heading up this shaft with Albert close behind. At the end of the shaft, she waited briefly for Albert to check the way was clear. She found the trap here was easily opened and soon she was through and standing in an antechamber surrounded by more doors and searching for a rope. Room after room revealed nothing of any help. A thought hit her: All she had to do was get the contrap to Melissa, and Melissa could then fly out of the pit exactly as she had. She hurriedly packaged the contrap in her bag and dropped it down the shaft. Moments later she heard a reassuring thump and Melissa's muffled complaints.

"Use the contrap!" she hissed down the shaft and soon Melissa's face appeared in the open trap.

"Well done!" whispered Tyler as Melissa rose out and ungainly settled both feet on the floor. "I knew you'd figure it out." Tyler slung the contrap around her neck rather than boxing it. There seemed little point in trying to hide it anymore and she figured it might be their only defence. Any minute now she expected a host of Nazis to come swarming down the stairs and passages.

Melissa sighed, relieved to be out of the pit. She leant against the paneled wall of the corridor and squealed when it shifted. A secret door slid briefly open and swallowed her before sliding shut again.

Why am I not surprised?

Tyler felt along the wall pressing every ridge and panel hoping to find a door-release mechanism. A panel depressed with a dull click and the door slid open once more.

Tyler stepped forward into the dark unknown.

Here we go again.

Room of Pillars

On the other side of the wall panel Melissa was frozen to the spot listening at a closed door at the far wall of the small chamber. It was unlit except for a strip of light streaming from under the door. An antique rug and two leather armchairs were arranged around a large, cold, stone fireplace. Tyler rushed to Melissa, opening her mouth to speak but Melissa drew a cautionary finger to her lips.

"Shhh. People. In the next room," she whispered.

Tyler inched quietly closer to listen and heard a man's voice.

"Yes, Sir. Indeed it is."

"Alright then. Inform him now and tell him I shall await him in the antechamber," said another man in a more authoritative tone.

"Very well, Sir." They heard footsteps leaving the adjacent room. Then a third voice.

"Things will be different now that we have the device, of course."

"Very different. These petty timewasters will soon learn a thing or two. That's for sure."

"I'll have the furnace primed. Have they found the way yet?"

"Not yet. It won't take them long though. We'll be informed when they do."

"Of course. Well, I must go and make preparations. Our master will wish for a suitably regal ceremony, I'm sure. He won't be pleased at the disturbance but that can't be helped. He will want the moment to be remembered in just the right way. Come. We shall prepare."

Melissa turned to Tyler.

"They think they already have the contrap. They said they have the device," she whispered as more footsteps faded from next-door.

"Well, they're kind of right," said Tyler. "They have us pretty much trapped in here."

Melissa returned to the hidden door and tested it. Locked tight. A one-way latch. She crossed the chamber again and put her ear against the door to listen intently. When she was sure the men had left the room, she tried the handle. She grunted, clearly exasperated.

"It's locked isn't it? Just like all the others. And secured with a secondary mechanism."

"Oh my word! This place is a nightmare!" Melissa concluded. "What is it with these doors?"

"My thoughts exactly," said Tyler. "They know we're in here. They know they have us trapped and therefore they have the contrap. We need to escape fast or it's game over. We need to find a way out."

"Maybe there's another trapdoor."

"There has to be. The place is loaded with them."

They searched fruitlessly, the voices from the corridor outside shaking them.

"They're coming!" whispered Melissa. She had worked her way round the chamber checking everywhere for a hidden exit. At the stone fireplace she noticed a recess to one side within the vault and found, concealed, a small wooden door. She called Tyler over as footsteps on the other side of the wall grew louder. The little door reminded Tyler of a priest hole she'd seen in a sixteenth century house back in England. Albert dashed ahead and soon came back to report.

"Seems alright. There's a staircase that winds down for a bit, then it comes out in a great big room. Ain't no one around that I could see, alive or dead."

The door to the corridor behind them rattled as a key turned in the lock.

Tyler ducked through the priest hole and raced down the spiraling stairs, Melissa close on her heels. Albert was right; the stairs opened onto a massive stone chamber, but it was like nothing she'd ever seen before. The room, tall, circular and domed in the centre, resembled a cathedral. All around the edge stood a ring of stone pillars, creating a pillared walkway that encompassed a vast open space. Tyler noticed the floor; polished, sleek marble, with a huge swastika of black stone inlaid in a white circle dead centre. Around this symbol ran a jagged line, forming a ten-pointed star. Tyler found this strangely familiar but could not fathom why.

"Congratulations." An amplified voice boomed from an unseen sound system to echo about the empty stone vault. "You have made it. Well done."

Tyler and Melissa exchanged puzzled looks. The voice continued.

"It is good to see you again, Fräulein, although you have caused us all manner of irritation since our last rendezvous. I really should have finished you in that toymaker's little shop. But never mind."

"Himmler!" whispered Tyler.

"This is the end of our little game of cat and mouse," Himmler continued. "As I'm sure you will have already realized, we have won, but you shouldn't think of yourselves as the losers. It was foreseeable that we should triumph. I'm afraid your cards were marked from the start. Yet mankind will forever be in your debt, for bringing it to us. You are trapped and this time there are no hidden doorways for you to find. No disappearing steps or secret levers. No more amusing tricks, just an ostentatious room where you may, or may not, die.

"I do, however, have one offer to lay before you for consideration. *We* will come out of this little situation, one way or another, with the device, of course, but there are still things to be dealt with here. And so you will surrender the device calmly and without a fuss, place it in the centre of the swastika and walk away from it. If you do this, I give you my personal guarantee you shall not be harmed. I cannot say the same if you so choose to try to fight to the bitter end, as they say. However, I am not an unreasonable man. I shall give you ten minutes to think about it. If you have not presented the device at the end of this period, you will be left here to die, slowly, of starvation. Unless I decide to gas you, or shoot you, or... I could go on all day, but the upshot of it is you will die unpleasantly one way or another and we will take the device."

"Don't do it, Tyler! They're too scared of you and the contrap to face us. If you give it up they'll just come in and shoot us!"

"I repeat," said Himmler. "We do not wish to harm you. Lay down the device and you may go free."

Melissa shook her head slowly.

Tyler turned to her.

"This feels like the end, Mel. I don't see how we're going to get out of this. I think... I think they've won." She walked to the very edge of the room, set the contrap to the *Future Eye* and pulled the lever. Through the lens she watched the next few hours play out at speed, curious to see what the ghosts in the contrap thought might happen, desperate for a spark of hope.

Light from the small high windows grew and bent around the room as the day wore on and she could still see Melissa and herself standing, sometimes sitting, waiting stubbornly. She watched the first night come and go and still the two figures did not yield the contrap. Then a second and a third. Days and nights passed. The two figures thinned and became drawn through malnutrition, too weak to stand. She watched as her defeated self deposited the contrap at the centre of the swastika and crawled away to cower at the edge of the room. Then they came; a squad of men armed with automatics. She watched herself and Melissa being ruthlessly gunned down, baulked at the scene and looked away, but an itching desire persuaded her to continue and she drew the lever further round the contrap to speed up the rate. Days zoomed by, then weeks, then months. When she slowed again she saw a vast gathering of captains and generals: a ritualized ceremony where a shadowed figure presided, presenting medals of honour to knightly warriors. It sickened Tyler.

There is no honour in Nazism. Never has been, never will be.

The shadowed man rose from his seat to address the gathering.

"My friends, my loyal companions, we reach the night of victory at last. Long have we awaited this moment. Tonight we celebrate! For the new dawn will see in the rule of our people across Europe and America. Russia will soon follow and then the rest of the world!" He raised a glass. The gathered generals followed suit. "To victory in the West!"

She closed her eyes and released the lever, listened to it clicking softly back to the top of the contrap and opened her eyes.

"They've been tracking us somehow ever since we came into the castle," she said. "They knew we were in that room. They probably knew we were listening to them. They were just waiting for us to find that little door and the staircase. It will be sealed shut by now, of course."

"What did you see?" asked Melissa.

"Nothing," Tyler lied. "Nothing important, Mel. We did well. Don't you think? I mean, we got Hitler. We got Goebbels. We did alright for a couple of girls..."

Melissa threw her arms around her and hugged her tightly.

"You're the best friend a girl could have, Mel. Let's make a pact. If all else fails, we'll put ourselves into the *Ghost Portal*. At least they won't be able to kill us. And we'll be together."

"Deal."

They were quiet for a few moments.

"We shouldn't give up, you know, Tyler. We should fight till the end."

Tyler felt weak, broken.

"You're right," she said, wiping tears from her face. "You're right. You always are. We can't give up."

"We'll work it out, Tyler. We always do, remember?"

Tyler laughed through her tears.

"That's what I always liked about you, Mel: your optimism. Okay, think about this logically."

"Yes?"

"We still have the contrap. The contrap is working despite the dead zone, so we can still use it anyway we please."

"Yes," agreed Melissa. "You could fly up there and see if you can get out anywhere. That's probably the first thing we should try."

"Right! Yes. I'll do that. Wait. Albert! Where's Albert. He might be able to help us."

"I haven't seen him since we used the spiral staircase," said Lucy.

"Albert?" called Tyler, but Albert didn't appear.

"You could release Zebedee from the contrap and he could go for help. We could tell him to find Chapman. Chapman would send a rescue squad for us. Don't you think?"

They both knew the truth. Chapman had declared it a black ops mission. *He* had not sent the girls. *He* knew nothing about it. *He* would deny all knowledge of the mission and let them stew.

"He'd want to help us, wouldn't he?"

Melissa nodded. "He would. But I don't know he'd be able to. He did warn us it was too risky."

"Okay, I'll send Zebedee."

Tyler set the contrap to the *Ghost Portal* and called for Zebedee. He appeared a moment later and she wasted no time setting him free from the portal.

"Phasmatis Licentia. Compenso Pondera."

"Oh course I'll go, dear girl," said Zebedee when Tyler had explained what they needed him to do. He left them, walking through the chamber wall.

"Now to find a way out," said Tyler. She hoped she'd not over-used the contrap in the last few hours. She needed it now more than ever before. She switched to *Flight* and ascended the vault to the dome. She tested the lower row of windows encircling the dome, then the second row, but they were all small, narrow and thick. Tyler kicked at one with all her might, but only succeeded in bruising her foot. She took the gun from her thigh holster and shot at a window from a metre away but the glass did not even chip. The bullet ricocheted, zipping dangerously close to her head and she quickly ditched that notion. The windows were made to be unbreakable. Most likely bomb-proof, she figured. She toured the heights of the dome, disappointed to find no weaknesses anywhere. The lower parts of the chamber seemed stronger still and far more robust. The metal doors at ground level, if that's where they were, had no handles or keyholes or any signs of locking mechanisms on their side of the chamber. Only when Tyler used the *Present Eye* did she see the thick steel rods that crossed within to bar them closed. Even the low doorway through which they had entered from the spiral staircase was now blocked by that same kind of door. They were in a tightly sealed unit. No wonder the Nazis had sounded so confident. Tyler sat next to Melissa on the unforgiving marble floor and put her head in her hands.

"Nothing. Any other ideas?"

"Lucy's out there somewhere. If she *is* on our side she might rescue us. She might find a way…"

Tyler nodded somberly.

"Let's hope so." She checked her watch: 3.17 a.m. Melissa wandered around the walls, triple checking doors, seeking anything that might help, killing time. Tyler's frustration peaked.

I should be asleep in my bed at home in Watford, safe and sound.

"Albert!" she called aloud. "Where are you, Albert?" Her voice echoed about their massive crypt and died.

Tyler had a thought. She'd been so focused on the strength of the doors that she'd missed the obvious. What about the walls? What if they had a weakness, a stone thin enough to break through and escape into another room or a corridor? Anywhere would be better than this place. She used the *Present Eye* to search through the substance of the chamber, methodically checking her way around, starting at ground level. It would be easier to work the wall here, rather than an area high up where only one of them could work one-handed.

She found nothing and quickly gave up on the idea.

"There has to be something we're missing," she muttered in frustration.

"Maybe we could hide the contrap and put ourselves into the *Ghost Portal*," joked Melissa. "They'd think we'd just vanished along with the contrap."

Tyler gave an amused shrug.

"That would be sweet," she said, but although there was clearly no place to hide the contrap, the notion started her thinking. She looked into the portal, hoping, against all probability, to find someone helpful who might advise her.

"Isabella? Isabella, I need help!" she called. She waited for what felt like hours until a soft stirring melody drifted from the other side of the lens. The tune sounded familiar because she had heard it once before.

"Marcus? Is that you?" she asked, desperately trying to see through a mass of fog. The mournful tune loudened and the figure of a young boy emerged. Marcus ceased fiddling and lowered his violin and bow. The *silent fiddler*, Albert had called him.

Marcus looked up to meet Tyler's eyes.

"Marcus, I need your help. Can you fetch someone? Can you find Izabella for me? I need to speak to somebody who knows about the contrap."

Marcus surprised her by shaking his head, slowly. No. He couldn't, or wouldn't. Tyler didn't know which. Marcus raised an arm to point into the dense fog at his back.

"What?" asked Tyler. "What is it?"

As Marcus held out his arm, two other forms inched out of the cloud. Tyler squinted, desperate for help, dreading an appearance of her enemies trapped in the portal. The figures approached and Tyler gradually recognized the twin girls, Kinga and Danuta.

"You have called for help," said Danuta.

"And we have come," concluded Kinga.

"Great," said Tyler, wishing Izabella had heard her pleas. She prepared herself for more doom and gloom warnings of a biblical tone.

"You must act," stated Danuta. "You must act swiftly."

"Yes, I know, but what am I supposed to do. We're trapped. I need to know something more about the contrap. There has to be something that can help us."

"We know little about the contrap, yet you know all you need to know," said Kinga. "This is what we have come to tell you."

"I know all I need to know? *Really?*"

"Indeed. This task is yours to fulfill," Kinga stated.

"The task has been appointed to you, for *only you* would choose to do what needs to be done," said Danuta. "Use the knowledge you possess. Save yourselves."

"And save untold masses from the oppressor. The oppressor *must* be defeated."

Tyler thought for a moment before approaching Melissa.

"Wait a minute! You can put me into the portal and release me the next minute. As a ghost I would be free to go and search. I could search the place; maybe learn something we could use..."

"Tyler, have you heard yourself? That's lunacy. And probably suicide, too."

"No. It could work. Think about it."

"But even if you could come out of the contrap without being sucked straight back into your body, without your spirit, wouldn't your body would die? By the time you've searched the castle and come back, you'll be dead. You'll be stuck as a ghost forever."

Tyler considered this briefly.

"I don't know what else to suggest."

"You're nuts. I always knew you were."

"You know CPR, right?" asked Tyler. Melissa nodded. "So you can give my body chest compressions while I'm out, mouth to mouth, whatever it takes. Keep me alive. How long do you think a person can be dead for before they get brain damage? How long would I have, theoretically?"

Melissa stared at her.

"You're serious. You're *really* serious. *Only you*, Tyler. *Only you* could come up with such a crazy idea."

Only you...

Tyler nodded, now understanding that this was exactly what she should do.

"I'm no expert but I'd say a minute," said Melissa. "Maybe two, tops. I read an article on cases where people have fallen through the ice on rivers and been pulled out several minutes later to be revived with good results, but the article said the icy temperatures helped prevent brain damage while the brain was deprived of oxygen."

"You're amazing, you know. How do you know this stuff?"

Melissa shrugged.

"I read."

"Shame it's not colder in here."

"It's cold enough..."

"Two minutes?"

"Two minutes, tops."

"How much of the castle do you think I can search in two minutes?"

"Not much."

"You think I'm crazy."

"I *know* you are. This is pointless. *Here lies Tyler May. She died being ridiculous.*"

"I have to try something. Maybe I'll find Albert. I can put myself into the portal easily enough, but you'll have to free me from it. You know the words right?"

Melissa looked at Tyler with resignation and nodded.

"Right. And you pull the lever this way to open the way in and that way to open the way out."

"Got it."

"I won't have a watch that works when I'm a ghost, not if Zebedee's pocket watch is anything to go by, so I'll just have to count the seconds. Ready?"

Melissa shook her head.

Tyler pointed the crystal at herself.

"Okay, here we go. Phasmatis Licentia."

Trust

The world about her immediately began to implode as light all around streamed into a blinding, engulfing blaze. She had the strangest sensation of being simultaneously stretched and sucked, forcefully drawn away from her core, as her spirit left her body. The stretching became a terrible rending that stole her breath and brought a moment of sheer panic. Then a release. She was free of flesh and dashing through icy air one moment, the next, through a shard of clear crystal. Finally she saw the familiar mist spiraling all about her and she knew she was inside the contrap.

Tyler looked down to see the last sparkling remnant of fiery, blue essence evolve into ghost.

Her ghost.

She was aware of an unfamiliar nexus with her surroundings, a bond, an unrelenting tug that held her there. She lifted a hand before her eyes to study it, unsurprised to find she could see right through it. On the other side of her translucent, grey fingers she noticed a hole in the surrounding shadow-land; the crystal lens of the *Ghost Portal*. She could see Melissa's concerned face peering in at her. Turning, she saw an endless sprawling fog ebbing away into darkness and, above, glistened what looked like a vast, expansive planet, black and stretching from one end of the horizon to the other. It was like a gargantuan, featureless eye, overlooking everything, though she had no idea of its true nature. She turned back and watched as Melissa positioned the contrap on the ground, leaning it against a wall, and performed chest compressions on Tyler's collapsed body. Melissa drew the lever around the contrap's edge.

"Phasmatis Licentia!" she said.

Suddenly Tyler moved again, was lifted greedily from the portal and spewed into the light beyond. Passing through the contrap's crystal was like drinking ice water, except the drink was not only on the inside of her but also the outside and everywhere in-between. She shivered and realized she was gathering form once more. Blue fire dissipated.

As Melissa worked hard to keep Tyler's body alive, Tyler had a sudden, all-consuming compulsion to dive right back into her failing body. She fought the urge and backed away.

"GO!" shouted Melissa. "Start counting! And for God's sake, don't be late!"

Tyler started counting. Leaving Melissa and her own body behind was the hardest thing she had ever done, but she did it, tearing her eyes from the weakening, moribund shell on the marble floor.

She didn't know where to start. The castle was huge. She knew *that* already, but now, a being with no flesh to hold her back, she found she was swift. Nothing stopped her. She transected walls, rushed through chambers and stairways, all the while counting. She reached forty-five and paused to shout Albert's name. She repeated the call and listened but received no answer. Onwards, tearing through passages and entrances, out of the castle, back in through a high turret. She realized the night air no longer felt cold because its temperature matched hers. She felt like a sliver of dry ice and yet, at the same time, she felt nothing at all. The feeling was indescribable. She searched and counted.

...fifty-eight, fifty-nine, sixty. One minute gone.

She began counting again. Through bed chambers she darted, rushing over the warm bodies of sleeping men and women. No Albert. She had torn through vast swathes of the castle but still she knew she had barely covered any of it. Walls were now blind doors to her. Doors were pointless. Steps were meaningless. Windows served no function. She was quick. That surprised her. She'd seen Albert come and go, disappearing in a trice, reappearing like a shot, and now she understood. She felt free.

Cold. Dead. But *free*.

She tore on, only pausing when she reached a well-lit room where people talked. She saw Himmler amongst them and dashed away. She reached *one hundred* and had thoughts of returning. How long would it take her to get back? What if she lost her way, or couldn't find the ceremonial chamber where her body lay struggling for life? She turned and made a beeline for what she figured was the centre of the castle. She rushed through a cramped chamber containing a single warm body and looped back to investigate. The chamber was dim but enough light spilled from somewhere high above for her to see who was there.

"Tyler?" Lucy gawped at her. "WHAT? They killed you!"

Tyler hovered near Lucy watching her, trying to decipher Lucy's expression.

"Tyler, I'm sorry you're dead. I'm stuck in here. Can you help me get out? Where's Mel? Is she dead too?"

"Wait."

Tyler left the small chamber, shifting easily through a single layer of stone wall into the ceremonial room. She saw Melissa stooped over her body far below and darted back to Lucy.

"Mel's on the other side of this wall, at least one floor down. We need you to dig the mortar out from one of these blocks and remove the stone. Then we'll talk."

Tyler left Lucy looking baffled and darted back into the circular chamber.

"Tyler! Thank God!" she heard Melissa say.

Closing on her body, Tyler felt the familiar tug which quickly became an irresistible draw. She was pulled the rest of the way until blackness hit her.

*

She didn't know how long she had been unconscious when she first understood that she was still alive. She sat up, vaguely aware of Melissa's help, and retched over the exquisite marble flooring. The ringing in her ears was deafening and for several minutes she had a killer headache and her hands and feet tingled madly and were chilled.

"Your time is up, Fräulein. Place the device in the centre of the floor and back away." Himmler's voice echoed about the stone walls. Neither girl complied.

"Very well. That is your choice." The room fell silent.

Tyler shivered in Melissa's arms. Melissa hugged and rubbed her vigorously to warm her.

"Lucy's next door," said Tyler through trembling lips and chattering teeth. It was an effort to talk but she forced herself to continue. "She has her throwing knives. She should be able to scrape away at the mortar and remove a block of stone. Could take her a while though."

"We can wait," said Melissa. "We've nothing else to do. Do you think they'll come for us?"

Tyler shook her head.

"No. They don't want to risk opening a door while we have the contrap. Himmler knows we have his finger bones. He knows he would be risking being drawn into the contrap and it's a risk he doesn't need to take. He'll try to wait us out, I think."

Melissa nodded.

"You need to rest," she said. "You're still cold." She pulled out a snowsuit from a bag and laid it over Tyler like a blanket. "Glad you made it."

"Thanks, Mel."

Tyler slept, exhausted. She awoke, feeling hungry with her head on Melissa's lap. Beneath her the floor was cold but the thick snowsuit had warmed her considerably. A noise disturbed her deep rest and, looking round to see what had made it, she found nothing. She checked her watch: 9.34 p.m.

But what day?

"It's Lucy!" whispered Melissa. "She's broken through!" She pointed to a small hole in the wall where Lucy had excavated the block of stone high up in the wall.

Tyler rose gingerly to her feet.

"Don't make it obvious," warned Melissa. "We're probably being watched."

Tyler nodded.

"How long have I been asleep?"

"Best part of a day, I guess. How are you feeling?"

"Like death."

Tyler tried to glance casually at the small hole in the wall and was rewarded with a glimpse of Lucy's face peering back.

"I'm not sure how this helps us," confessed Melissa quietly.

"Neither am I, unless Lucy is still one of us. If this is a set-up, it's over."

"Yeah," agreed Melissa. "Could be just one more way of trying to get us to give up the contrap."

"Psssssst!" Lucy hissed from the hole. "Can you get the contrap to me?"

"I don't know," whispered Tyler, taking care not to look that way. "How do we know you're on our side? You could be a spy. You could be trying to trick us."

"What?" Lucy responded. "After all this time you still think I'm a spy? You're mad. Both of you! Do you know what it's like, trying to work with people who never trust you? It *really* sucks!"

"You ran down that corridor like you knew exactly where you were going. You disobeyed my command. You disappeared. You're a royal pain in the ass! What part of that should make me trust you?"

"I was trying to find a staircase. I thought that was the idea. I thought I was helping! But that's fine. Keep the contrap. We'll all die and it will be your fault, not mine."

Tyler considered this for a moment.

"They could have planted you in that room, just so you could get the contrap like this."

"I was looking for a staircase, like you, when I triggered some kind of trapdoor. I couldn't get back to you. I've been stuck in here ever since. I'm not a spy. How many more times do I have to tell you?"

Tyler did not respond. It sounded convincing enough.

Perhaps I'm wrong.

"Listen," Lucy continued. "If you can throw me the contrap I might be able to use it to escape. Then I'll have a shot a rescuing you too. But if you don't trust me, you keep it and we're all dead. Your call."

"What do y'think?" Tyler asked Melissa.

"I don't know anymore. She does have a point; we're running out of options. If we take a chance, at least we'll have a chance…"

Tyler took the contrap and boxed it.

"I'll throw it up as close to the hole as I can. You'll have to put your hand through to catch it."

"Right," said Lucy. "I figured that out. Ready when you are."

Tyler tossed the lead box up to the hole. Lucy's hand shot through the hole but she fumbled it and the box came back down into Tyler's waiting palms.

"Well done," she said. "That was *great*."

"Let's just hope they're not watching us," said Melissa.

"Try again!" Lucy urged.

Tyler threw the box and this time Lucy caught hold and took it in through the hole. Tyler and Melissa watched the stone block reappear at the hole as Lucy slid it back into place.

"Now we wait," said Melissa, but as she spoke a door opened across the room and men in Nazi uniform walked in. They leveled guns at Tyler and Melissa, who could do nothing, not even having time to hide behind the solid stone of the numerous pillars. Tyler drew her gun, knowing she was hugely outnumbered.

Nowhere to run!

Melissa reached across and held Tyler's free hand.

Two gunshots boomed, deafening in the domed chamber.

Tyler felt a small missile find its mark above her heart. She fell, incapacitated, to watch a sideways view of her weapon skittering to a stop on the floor and of men coming for her. Her vision failed.

The Glimmer

Mengele's face towered over her. He saw she had opened her eyes and he smiled. Tyler baulked and fought against her restraints unsuccessfully. Strong leather straps pinned her to a cold, steel bed. A sterile, operating table. Her mind was foggy and her head hurt.

She had no idea how long she'd been unconscious, nor did she understand why she was still alive. She thought she'd been shot in the upper chest. She grappled to take a hold on the situation.

Where am I? And why? Where's Melissa?

"Don't worry, my dear," said Mengele with sickening courtesy. "It's normal to experience some disorientation. The drug is still in your bloodstream. You may also feel a little nausea."

You got that right!

Tyler kicked and struggled again. She was alive. Not shot. Not with a bullet, anyway. She looked down and saw the spot of blood on her shirt left by a tranquilizer dart. She tried to call Mengele a sick lunatic, but her mouth emitted only a slurred, indiscernible noise. Her jaw felt like jelly.

"Now, now, my dear, don't struggle. You will only hurt yourself and I shall be forced to give you another shot. It's my own concoction, you know. Unique to my profession." His smile broadened, a smile more nauseating than any drug could ever be. "Now, you will tell me what you have done with the device."

She shook her head.

I wouldn't tell you even if I could.
Where is Lucy? Whose side is she on?

She checked to see if her gun was still strapped to her thigh but, unsurprisingly, it had been taken.

"Still not talking?" asked Mengele. "I have something to fix that." He left her view and she looked around. She was in what looked like an operating theatre. Walls were painted white. The doors were thick, semi-transparent, plastic sheets. To the side of her steel bed stood a medical trolley bearing an array of polished surgical instruments. Panic washed over her and she tried to scream. She saw a figure approaching her room beyond the plastic sheets and flailed desperately against her restraints. She calmed as Albert passed straight through the plastic and came to her side.

"Albert!" she slurred. Albert was in a bad way. He looked as though he'd been beaten. He limped badly and cradled an injured arm.

"Albert? What happened?"

"Oh, nuffin' much, Missy. Don't you worry about me. We needs to get you out of 'ere, before Mengele returns." Albert tried to loosen the buckle of one of the straps but Tyler saw his hands were somehow damaged and he was too weak to move anything very much in the physical world.

"What have they done to you?"

A sound from the next room warned of Mengele's impending return.

"Albert, what've they done with Mel? Where am I?"

"Mel's next door, trussed to a bed, like you. You're still in the castle."

"Go to Mel. See if you can help her. Mengele's coming!"

Albert nodded and limped away. He left the room via the wall as Mengele reentered, bringing a syringe and a vial of liquid with him. He ginned insanely as he approached Tyler.

"Another of my favourites," he told her, shaking the bottle vigorously in his hand. "This should be just what the doctor ordered." He carefully inserted the syringe needle into the bottle's stopper, drew out a measure of the liquid inside and cleared the syringe of air, ejecting a few drops of the drug onto the floor.

"I know the contrap is somewhere in the castle, of course. I have sensed it. I will find it eventually, even if you refuse to tell me what you have done with it."

He placed the syringe on the surgical trolley and grabbed Tyler's arm. She recoiled at his icy touch, but the straps held her fast. Mengele rolled back Tyler's sleeve and pierced her exposed skin as she struggled against him. She watched in horror as he shunted the drug into her body. There came a fleeting flash of red above Mengele's head and he toppled away from her, yanking the syringe from her flesh as he dropped. Melissa stood over Mengele's felled body, staring in bewilderment at the fire extinguisher in her hands. She put it down and began unfastening Tyler's buckles.

"Mel!"

Melissa was almost as groggy as Tyler.

"Hello, Tyler," she managed to say slowly. "Best go before someone finds us."

"Albert?"

"Needs rest. Find us later."

Melissa released the final belt and helped Tyler off the gurney. Tyler's bag was leant against the wall. She grabbed it and put it on her back before following Melissa unsteadily out of the room. Together they staggered through another sterile room, through more plastic doors and into a passage. Tyler paused to search her bag for the tracer monitor. Surprised to find it still there, she took it out and switched it on. She could see from Mengele's amber marker that he was close by, in the room they'd just left. *When* he had arrived at the castle, she did not know. Himmler's green dot was moving, closing on their position.

"He's heading this way!" she told Melissa. Tyler saw a purple ring around the green marker. Melissa noticed it too.

"What's that? It's Lucy!"

"She's with Himmler. Guess that answers the question. Lucy's one of them."

"Wait. She might have been captured. She could still be one of us."

"Whichever it is, we need to get away from them. We don't have the contrap and they've taken my gun and our Tasers. We have nothing but the monitor."

Tyler watched the markers closing. Mengele's was also moving somewhere behind them. They ran as best they could in their half-drugged state and turned right when the passage was truncated by another. They heard voices up ahead, turned back and entered the first door they came to, ran through an empty room and out into another corridor.

"This place is a maze!" said Tyler, eyeing the amber dot as it shifted closer to their own markers.

"It's a labyrinth," stated Melissa. "Designed to leave you disoriented if you don't know the right ways to go."

"It's working! This way, I think." Tyler put an ear to a door but turned away when she heard murmuring coming from the other side.

They entered a wide corridor that curved round to their right, and jogged. The march of footsteps sounded from up ahead so they ducked through a doorway to their left.

Tyler couldn't believe it. They were back in the huge ceremonial chamber.

"You're kidding!"

It was too late to turn back. Peeking back through the door she saw a rank of soldiers tramping towards them along the corridor. She closed the door quickly and watched the tracer markers closing in. Around the circular chamber, doors opened and uniformed men spilled through. They formed a line, parting when Himmler entered. The girls backed into the centre of the circle to stand on the vast, marble swastika. More armed men flooded in and, with them, several ghost soldiers armed with real guns filling gaps in the line. The girls were utterly hemmed in. Tyler heard a door open in the silence as they waited. Two more figures entered to take their place side by side in the ring; Valda Braun and Josef Mengele.

Tyler and Melissa circled, back to back. They both saw Lucy in the line, dressed in full Nazi uniform: peaked cap, riding boots and ammunition pouches on her belt. As well as the P99s strapped to her thighs, she cradled an AK47. She smiled and aimed the machine gun at them.

"Oh look. That scheming witch… She *was* one of them all along," stated Melissa. "Excuse me while I die of shock."

"I don't think we'll have time for that," muttered Tyler, eyeing the surrounding line.

"THIS IS YOUR LAST CHANCE!" Mengele shouted with sudden rage. "TELL ME WHERE IT IS OR YOU WILL DIE!"

Melissa panicked as they circled.

"What do we do? What do we do? What do we do?"

"We do nothing, Mel. There's nothing left *to* do."

"TAKE THEM!" ordered Mengele, and Tyler realized with surprise that he was the one in charge. His followers obeyed, closing the circle. Two soldiers reached Tyler and grabbed her. She watched in vain as they cuffed Melissa, hands behind her back. She felt her own hands cuffed in the same way.

"Search them!" Mengele commanded. Rough hands invaded their clothing and bags.

"It's not here," reported a soldier.

Mengele shot him in the forehead and watched him fall to the ground.

"SEARCH THEM AGAIN," he screamed. The soldiers complied but came up empty handed, fearful of the next bullet.

"Take them to the laboratory!" bellowed Mengele, enraged. "Take them away." He leaned close to Tyler. "My good friend, Heinrich, will escort you to the last room you will ever see."

Himmler led the way, flanked by two SS ghosts who carried only ghost weapons. At the door he halted and turned to point out two soldiers.

"You and you. Come with me. The rest of you search the castle. You know what we're looking for." The two soldiers took the rear as they escorted the girls out of the room, back towards the laboratory, but before they had gone very far, Lucy called out from behind them.

"Mein Reichsführer! A moment!" Lucy ran to catch up with Himmler and saluted him before continuing. "The Master commands me to accompany you, if you please, on the grounds that I have prior knowledge of the captives and may, therefore, be of use to you."

Himmler tilted his head at Lucy, weighing her up. He smiled and gave a curt nod.

"Prior knowledge? Indeed, you should come with me. You will make a pleasant companion. You may walk at my side."

"Thank you, mein Reichsführer." Lucy fell in step with Himmler and they moved on.

"What a slime bag," seethed Melissa.

Lucy turned and jabbed her in the face with the butt of her machine gun. Blood coursed down Melissa's face as Lucy stabbed at her with the gun's nuzzle to make her walk. Lucy returned to Himmler's side. Tyler glared at the back of Lucy's head, willing it to explode. She wondered why she was keeping the contrap to herself, but then it dawned on her. Lucy was merely waiting for the right moment to present it to Mengele. He would likely make her his queen for bringing it to him.

Lucy, Queen of the Damned.

It all made perfect sense.

"You evil, back-stabbing, gutless snake," she hissed. Lucy turned again. She raised her gun to strike.

"Wait!" said Tyler, her breathing rate suddenly rising. She faltered, dropped to her knees. "Wait, I'll tell you." She was swooning, now. The drugs were still taking their toll, but she had gained Himmler's attention. He came closer to listen, raising a hand to postpone Lucy's blow.

"You will tell us where the device is?" he asked.

Tyler's panic attack was slowly engulfing her. Breathe escalating, she slipped to the floor where she lay panting, eyes rolling back.

"I – will – tell – you…" she forced herself to say and then it was all she could do to whisper faintly. "Lucy… Lucy – has – the – device…"

Himmler bent low, coming face to face with Tyler, straining to hear. She needed to lurch forwards only a few inches to clamp his nose in her jaws. She bit as hard as she could, tasting blood as Himmler's screams resonated about the passageway. She held him until the cold barrel of a gun pressed into her temple. Himmler stomped and shouted before back-handing Tyler across the face. She spat dark, oily blood at him defiantly, abandoning her faked swoon.

"Ew!" said Melissa, watching the strange blood seep from Himmler's nose. It was inhuman, an intense shade of blue.

The guards and Lucy pointed their guns at Tyler and Melissa. Himmler drew his pistol and put it to Tyler's head.

"I'm sure that one of you alone can tell us about the device just as well as two."

Tyler braced herself for a bullet to the brain.

At least this way it will be quick.

She'd had enough anyway. She welcomed it.

"Wait, mein Reichsführer," Lucy interjected, edging forward before Himmler could pull the trigger. "Wait. I would like to kill her for you."

Himmler frowned but, intrigued, held fire.

"Why would you wish to do this?"

Lucy glanced at the floor.

"I am young and have had no chance to prove my loyalty. I would do this in your honour and so that my name might be remembered to our Master."

Himmler absorbed this statement and laughed. He took a handkerchief to staunch his bleeding nose.

"Very well. Very well." He offered her his handgun. "You may kill her. What do I care."

"Thank you, Reichsführer." Lucy took the gun and put the barrel to Tyler's head. She stared Tyler in the eyes and Tyler saw something there in that gaze: a frightening glimmer, a certain spirit, a brooding deadly power.

Lucy gave a half-smile.

The Window

Lucy pivoted and shot the closest guard in the chest. He dropped as the second received a bullet to the neck.

"What is this?" demanded Himmler.

Lucy cast the pistol away and drew her Taser to hit Himmler with an electric current powerful enough to fell him in agony. She opened an ammunition pouch at her belt and took out the lead box. The two SS ghosts saw she had the contrap and fled down the corridor. Himmler was recovering and trying to rise.

"Look out!" shouted Melissa.

Lucy shot him with a fresh Taser cartridge. He dropped back to the floor as electricity tensed every muscle in his body. With the contrap in one hand and wielding the Taser in the other, Lucy thumbed the contrap's lever clockwise and positioned the crystal directly over Himmler's stricken body.

"Phasmatis Licentia!" she said.

Himmler's ghost shrieked objection as he was ripped from the mortal body of the child. A shimmering essence gathered and streamed into the *Ghost Portal* with screams echoing. A few agonizing moments later, Himmler was gone and where he'd been, cowering on the floor, was left a boy, unconscious and ill-looking among Himmler's shed clothes. Lucy coolly ejected the Taser cartridge, holstered the gun and plucked the Taser darts from the boy's chest. She glanced up and down the corridor. No one coming just yet. She found a large ring of keys on the belt of one of the dead guards and released Tyler and Melissa from their cuffs.

"Do you believe me now?"

Melissa stared at her with a mixture of wonder, mistrust and disbelief.

"Then what did you hit me for?"

Lucy smiled, having anticipated this question.

"I had to make it look real. I had to get Himmler's gun."

"You didn't have to hit me so flipping hard!"

"That's a matter of opinion. But maybe you'll trust me next time."

"We have to move," said Tyler.

"But… But…" Melissa was speechless.

"Do you think we should try for Mengele now?" asked Lucy. "It's like he's become their new führer."

Tyler bent over the boy, unsure if he was breathing. She answered without looking up.

"No. He's protected from the contrap somehow. I don't want to risk it until we know why. We need to get going. The SS ghosts will fetch the others." She felt for the boy's pulse at his neck. "Do you think he's dead?" she asked.

"Freddy?" She slapped his face gently, trying to rouse him. "Freddy Carter? Can you hear me?"

Freddy stirred.

Lucy found a water bottle on a fallen guard's belt, unscrewed the top and emptied its contents over Freddy's face.

Melissa sniffed.

"Um, I don't think that was water," she said as realization hit. "That was vodka!"

"Nobody light a match," said Tyler.

Melissa gave Lucy a dark look.

"I didn't know!" said Lucy.

Tyler wiped Freddy's face down with her sleeve. He opened his eyes. His nose leaked blood from Tyler's bite, but the fresh issue was now red. She felt bad and helped him to his feet, shouldering his weight.

"Freddy, can you stand?" she asked.

Freddy nodded and gazed blearily around.

"Where am I?"

Freddy Carter, thirteen years old and tall for his age, looked uncommonly thin. He had an unruly mop of blond hair and a face that appeared cheeky even when he wasn't grinning with mischief, which wasn't very often. Melissa liked him immediately, even before he could walk straight. She gave him a snowsuit to wear because he was shivering, naked and embarrassed. She put an arm around him to lend support and as Tyler did likewise on his other side, they hobbled down the corridor.

"Hey, what's the rush?" asked Freddy. "Will somebody tell me what's going on? And where's the train?"

"What train?" asked Melissa.

"The one that just hit me."

"There're a few things you need to know, Freddy…" By the time they had finished telling Freddy, he was silent with shock and they were nearing a hall chamber with a broad stairway leading upwards.

"Beware the stairs," said Tyler.

A siren sounded throughout the labyrinthine fortress.

"They know we've escaped," said Melissa.

They headed up the stairs, listening to footsteps behind them grow louder.

"Hurry! They're coming!" cried Lucy. Around a corner they found a locked door barring the way.

"The keys!" said Melissa.

Lucy tried a key from the bunch she'd taken from the dead guard. The fifth key fitted. The lock clicked and she opened the door. They rushed through, closed the door and Lucy locked it, leaving the key in the lock.

"That should slow them down," she said. They repeated the process with the next door. Machine gun fire and the sound of splintering wood echoed. The guards were gunning out the door locks. They hurried down a long dim corridor that only brightened where moonlight pierced an arched window. They raced past but Tyler stopped.

"You go on. I'll catch up."

Returning to the window, she looked out. No! She hadn't imagined it. The window opened onto a deep courtyard. Looking up, she saw the narrowest of gaps between the rooftops where moonlight entered. Beneath, in the yard, a strange army marched to the call of a drill captain. Hundreds of ghost soldiers filed in rank after rank.

"Come on, Tyler!" shouted Lucy. Tyler dragged herself away from the window and ran, vaguely aware of doorways and corridors, of cries in the depths of the castle, footfalls echoing in angry pursuit. She couldn't shake the image from her mind: the ghost army, preparing.

Preparing for what? War? How is an army of ghosts going to help in a physical war?

She thought of how useful Albert had been to her and understood. She imagined an entire army of Alberts, all at her command. They would be an army of spies and the more powerful among them would be unstoppable assassins.

They stumbled into the spacious entrance hall of the castle with the four doorways.

"This is it!" cried Melissa. "The way out!"

They were soon out in the freezing night, following the track around to the left and down the steep incline to the valley below. They stumbled, slipped and slid, not caring. All that mattered now was escaping. Again they heard voices from the castle and the baying of dogs. Men were giving chase and bringing hounds for the hunt, but the locked doors had bought the girls a good head start and their sliding descent of the snowy slope increased their lead. They paused to draw breath and glance back up at the towering, overhanging castle. Lights were coming their way and they heard the dogs closing.

Zebedee appeared at Tyler's side, unruffled and genteel, as always.

"Zebedee? Is it really you?" The wind stung her eyes and she could scarcely see. He kept pace with her as she ploughed on through deepening snow.

"Miss May, I found your Mr Chapman, after much searching."

Tyler didn't know what surprised her most, his presence or his news.

"You found him?"

"Oh yes, indeed I did."

"Does he know we're here? Is he coming for us?"

Zebedee smiled warmly.

"My dear girl, he's already here!" Zebedee threw an arm wide to indicate the mountainous rise at his back. As he did so a Chinook broke the ridge line and dropped to make its thunderous approach.

The girls cheered to see their rescuers, but their cries were drowned by the monstrous roar of the wind and rotor blades.

"Yes! A fine fellow, Mr Chapman!" said Zebedee, unmoved by the torrent. He carefully lit his pipe and watched with interest.

The girls and Freddy ran for the helicopter as it set down and soldiers streamed out opening fire on the foe careering down from the castle. Tyler was the last of the girls to leave the snow. Chapman himself pulled her aboard.

"I hope you appreciate this, Agent Ghost. I'm putting my career on the line for you," he shouted over the din. "Mission accomplished, I presume."

Tyler nodded.

"Three down. Three to go, Sir."

She watched soldiers retreat under fire to board the Chinook. Its blades pounded snow into a blinding storm all around as the pilot powered-up for liftoff and, moments later, they were aloft and watching their pursuers dwindle into small dots at the valley's tapering head.

Made it!

She noticed Weaver there, too, sheltering his damaged arm, and she understood he must have pulled some serious strings to get on board. He slipped his good arm around Lucy, who cast her Nazi cap out of the open door.

"Not my style," she said. "But I think I'll keep the machine gun."

Hate & Death

Her bedroom was a strange place to be. Here she had slept for most of her life and it had been a retreat, a place of safety and comfort but, right now, it was just plain surreal. Tyler was living another life now, one so utterly disconnected from her prior existence that she struggled to fit the two differing pieces together. They clashed horribly.

She dropped her bags at the foot of her bed and noticed a letter had been left for her to find on her pillow. The spiky handwriting of the address was disturbingly familiar. She placed the letter on her desk. Bates' death threats could wait until later. She had a meeting to attend.

*

They were all waiting for her when she arrived at Adolf's to shove open the glass door and order herself a hot chocolate from the counter. Freddy Carter, looking much improved, sat at one end of a table, next to Melissa. Lucy nestled at Weaver's side. Tyler found a seat feeling like a total gooseberry.

"Any sign of Albert yet?" asked Melissa. Tyler wished Albert was there but the last time she'd seen him was in Mengele's castle laboratory and he'd looked in a bad way. She shook her head.

"Not yet."

The hostess delivered Tyler's drink.

"It's good to see you looking better, Freddy," said Tyler. "How's the nose?"

Freddy grinned.

"It hurts. Thanks. I owe you. My life, I mean. Mel's told me everything."

"Just as well," said Tyler. "But you'll have to sign the Official Secrets Act."

Freddy laughed but soon stopped. "You're serious."

"As the plague."

"Right."

"Great. Well, now that we're a team again, we need to plan ahead," instructed Weaver. "And there are some things I need to say. Yes, you've put three gloves into the contrap, but there are another three out there. Listen, girls, you seriously need to buck your ideas up if you want to stay in this game. You've been acting unprofessionally from the word go. You broke the rules. You disobeyed Chapman and seriously jeopardized the greater mission and national security because of childish bickering..."

"What are you..."

"No. Hear me out. You *must* be a strong unit. Do you understand?"

The girls looked at Weaver askance, but nodded.

"Good. You should know, the Secret Service isn't full of heroes but real people, like us, behaving heroically." Weaver softened into an ironic smile. "You got away with it this time, but smarten up. Okay?"

"Okay."

"So who's next?" asked Lucy.

"We still have to get Adolf Eichman, Reinhard Heydrich, *lord of the reveries*, and then there's Mengele, apparently the new führer," said Melissa.

"We can't go after Mengele. Not yet," said Tyler. "And we don't have tracers on any of the others, so we might not have a choice. We'll go after whoever we find first and I still want to know what's happened to Hitler and what's going on with Mengele."

*

The lamp-lit figure in the street below hadn't moved for twenty minutes. Tyler watched from her bedroom window. She knew exactly who it was out there in the night, looking back at her through the rain. She knew only one living person crazy enough to stay out there in this weather. Tyler closed the curtain.

She slipped a knife through the envelope and unfolded the letter.

Dear Tyler,

So sorry I missed you in Tel Aviv. That was close though, wasn't it? Maybe next time we'll actually meet. I feel it's our destiny...

I must admit I was displeased when I realised you'd already left your hotel room. I'm sorry for the mess I left behind. I hope you didn't find it too upsetting, but after all my hard work to find you, well, never mind...

See you soon.

Hate & death,

Silvia.

PS. Violet says 'Catch you later, Deary!'

Tyler bagged the envelope and the letter, ready to forward to Chapman tomorrow. If his forensics team could render some small clue that might help catch Silvia Bates, then all well and good. In the meantime Tyler wasn't holding her breath. And anyway, she knew exactly where Bates was at this very minute.

Tyler called Chapman.

"She's here right now. Bates is in the street outside my house."

"Are you alone?"

"Yes."

"Lock all the doors and windows. Don't let her see you're there if that's possible..."

Too late.

"...I'm sending someone right over. Don't go anywhere." Chapman ended the call.

330

Tyler slipped her list from the back pocket of her jeans and penned a line through *Heinrich Himmler*. She wrote a single word next to Freddy Carter's name.

SAFE

She refolded the list and checked her watch: 10.05 p.m.

She wished her parents were home but knew they would not return for at least an hour. Through the gap in her curtains she saw the street below now empty, Bates had gone. She was relieved. All the same she felt the need for company, even company on the end of the phone. She called Melissa but, thirty seconds later, Melissa still hadn't picked up and the tone ended with an answer message.

A sudden noise downstairs startled Tyler. She pocketed her mobile and grabbed her new Taser, collecting enough cartridges to fell an ox. She edged out of her bedroom and peered down the unlit landing. Nothing moving. Nothing out of the ordinary.

Except her heart rate.

Shadows played her imagination unhelpfully and she told herself to *get real*. Bates wasn't upstairs. If she was in the house at all she'd surely only had time to get through a ground level door.

Tyler racked her mind. Did she remember seeing a window open in the lounge? Had her parents left without locking the back door? The narrow kitchen window over the sink was, no doubt, open an inch. Mum had a habit of leaving it that way to help air the steam-up. A *bad* habit, in Tyler's opinion.

That noise again. A soft, small sound. Someone moving? Something stirring?

The stairs were tricky to descend with any degree of concealment or stealth. They creaked as she moved and the railings obscured her view of what awaited below. Tyler didn't like the stairs.

She reached the front door and tried the handle. Firmly locked.

Good.

Again, the noise. Closer now. Somewhere in the lounge perhaps?

She crept to the lounge door. Her parents had left for the theatre before twilight and Tyler had mostly been in her room since then. The lights were off and the curtains wide open, allowing a view of the rainy night beyond a single window to one side and large bay windows at the far end of the room.

Rain made soft sounds on glass.

She considered switching the light on but decided this would illuminate her to any malicious watchers and reflect on the glass, blinding her to the outside world. She lingered in the doorway, systematically checking each pane of glass. Nothing broken, no movement outside, except the wind in the trees and the dapple of rain. She edged into the room and crossed to the small window. A noise behind her broke the near silence. She turned and leveled her Taser at a grey figure hunched in the shadows across the room.

Other books in the series

The Haunting of Tyler May
(book one)

Follow the Tyler May series

www.tylermay.co.uk

Acknowledgements

My thanks goes to David Hughes (3 Para) for consultation on parachuting and parachute training.

Also, to Ian Walter of Grundlsee, for supplying research photography of the Roth Villa and Grundlsee.

'The Thieves of Antiquity' was edited by Edward Field.

4981877R00192

Printed in Great Britain
by Amazon.co.uk, Ltd.,
Marston Gate.